NO C...

Certainly there was no question of Georgiana winning the heart of her guardian, the Earl of Aldringham.

First of all, she did not want to. Georgiana considered men a bother and marriage a form of madness.

And even if the handsome, dashing Earl tempted her, what could she offer him that such stunning seductresses as the ravishing Letitia Carrington and the superbly sensual Lady Althea Wyndham did not already avidly grant him? How could she dream of besting either of these bewitching beauties at the game of which they were past mistresses and she was but a bewildered novice?

Unless, of course, Georgiana coupled some most unusual cards she had to play with some most remarkable beginner's luck . . .

EVELYN RICHARDSON decided, even before studying eighteenth-century literature in graduate school, that she would have preferred to have lived between 1775 and 1830. Now living in Boston, she enjoys access to the primary sources that allow her to explore details of the period and immerse herself in the same journals that her heroines enjoyed. She is currently working on her fourth Regency novel.

SIGNET REGENCY ROMANCE
COMING IN DECEMBER 1991

Mary Balogh
Christmas Beau

Margaret Westhaven
The Lady In Question

Dawn Lindsey
The Barbarous Scot

The Nabob's Ward

by
Evelyn Richardson

A SIGNET BOOK

For absent friends—Forbes and Ozzie

SIGNET
Published by the Penguin Group
Penguin Books USA Inc., 375 Hudson Street,
New York, New York, 10014, U.S.A.
Penguin Books Ltd, 27 Wrights Lane, London W8 5TZ, England
Penguin Books Australia Ltd, Ringwood, Victoria, Australia
Penguin Books Canada Ltd, 10 Alcorn Avenue, Toronto, Ontario, Canada M4V 3B2
Penguin Books (N.Z.) Ltd, 182-190 Wairau Road,
Auckland 10, New Zealand

Penguin Books Ltd, Registered Offices:
Harmondsworth, Middlesex, England

First published by Signet, an imprint of New American Library,
a division of Penguin Books USA Inc.

First Printing, November, 1991

10 9 8 7 6 5 4 3 2 1

1

He awoke to a pounding head and a throat that was as dry and dusty as the parade ground in front of him. With a groan, the Honorable Brian Brandon raised his head from the pillar that had been his pillow—and a damned uncomfortable one at that. Cautiously he opened one eye, bracing himself for the shock of the brilliant, relentless glare of the hot Indian sun, only to find his gaze returned by a fairy. His fogged mind reeled. But surely it was a fairy, for the appearance of a small being whose halo of blond curls shimmered in the sunlight could not be attributed to natural causes.

"Are you very, very sick?" the being inquired.

Not a fairy, he decided. The accent was unmistakably English. Accustomed as he was to encountering fellow countrymen in all corners of the globe the Honorable Brian was not so blinded by loyalty to his native land as to believe it extended its considerable influence to the supernatural realms. Besides, as he opened the other eye he could see that this particular being, attired in a white lawn dress with a blue sash and lacy pantaloons, was carrying a pad and pencils, accouterments that were far too mundane for any ethereal creatures.

"Are you sick?" This time there was the slightest undertone of impatience.

"Not at all," he responded courteously.

"No, I suppose not," the being replied. "But you do look foxed," it remarked candidly.

He sat up with a start, for it occurred to him to wonder how such a young female—he had at last identified his interlocutor as a girl of eight or nine and placed her in the general order of things—could know of such a condition. Why, most of the correctly behaved wives and daughters of his brother

5

officers would not admit to knowledge of such a state, much less discuss it. "I was a trifle disguised, but now I am quite recovered."

"That's good." He sounded relieved. "Because otherwise I would have had to call my ayah and I've only just escaped."

The corners of his eyes crinkled in amusement. "And where were you escaping to, my little sprite?"

She frowned. "I am not a sprite. I am Georgie. And I shan't tell you."

He chuckled. "Georgie who?"

A mutinous expression descended on her childish features and she shook her head.

He was even more amused. "Why won't you tell me?"

"Because you're a grown-up and you'll tell and then I shall be made to go inside and do my needlework all over again. Besides, Papa always says that when one is caught in a compromising situation, the less information one gives, the better." Georgie's frown became thunderous.

Brian burst out laughing. It was a novel experience for him, despair of his parents and the rest of the authorities in his life—tutors, headmasters, commanding officers—to be relegated to the ranks of responsible adults who squelched adventurous spirits. "And what makes you think I'm a grown-up?" he wondered.

She had been on the verge of departure, but this question brought her up short. "Well of *course* you are. You're tall and you're wearing a uniform, though I must say it's awfully dusty," she began scornfully, annoyed at being detained for such a stupid question.

He quirked a teasing eyebrow at her, relieved to find that it was only the most superficial of physical characteristics that led her to such an unflattering opinion of him.

A look of doubt crept into the large green eyes regarding him. "Well, aren't you?" she demanded.

"I don't think so," he responded seriously. "You're not a grown-up, after all, but besides being small, what makes you different from grown-ups?"

"Well . . ." She tilted her head to one side, scraping circles in the dust with one tiny slipper as she considered this

problem. "I don't like to do excessively boring things like
. . . like sewing," she answered triumphantly.

He grinned. "Neither do I. In fact, I expect I should enjoy
doing exactly what you were on your way to do."

"Climbing trees and writing stories?" she asked incredulously. A look of dismay came over her face as she realized
what she had done and she clapped a hand over her mouth.

He laughed, his dark eyes alight with amusement. "Never
fear, sprite. I shan't ruin your fun. Actually, I should like
to join you. At one time I was reckoned the best tree climber
in school." Which, he thought to himself, was the only useful
thing he had learned from formal education. Since his
educational career had been notably erratic, owing to frequent
dismissals for one infraction or another, ranging from the
introduction of several lively rabbits into a boring Latin
recitation to being caught with his tutor's wife at Magdalen
in a most compromising situation, this lack of respect for
his schooling was not entirely fair. "May I come with you?"
he reiterated, strolling over to the well to splash some water
over his aching head and smarting eyes. Tepid though it was,
the water restored him and he straightened up feeling much
more the thing.

Georgie still remained doubtful. He seemed to be a right
one, but appearances could be deceiving and he *did* look
suspiciously like an adult. She stood some minutes deep in
thought.

"I could carry your writing things and then you would
find it a good deal easier to climb. With me to lift you up,
you could probably climb much higher than otherwise."
Brian did not know quite why he was so anxious for her to
allow him to join her, but somehow the idea of escaping his
regimented world, where one was forced to defer to pompous
fools, to the dappled sunlit realm high above the dusty ground
seemed infinitely appealing.

This last offer seemed to convince her. "Oh, famous!
Come along, then, but we must be careful not to be seen."
Glancing cautiously in all directions Georgie led him away
from the parade ground to the back of the barracks by the
river, a trickle of water so small it hardly deserved the name.

Following it and moving carefully so as not to attract the attention of the women beating laundry on the rocks, she eventually brought him to an enormous banyan tree whose giant roots made thousands of hiding places and offered easy access to the lower branches.

Handing her writing supplies to him, she clambered up, leaping nimbly from one perch to another. Watching her blond hair as it caught an occasional shaft of filtered sunlight, Brian thought how truly she did resemble some woodland sprite seeking refuge in the ancient tree.

She beckoned to him impatiently. "Come see."

Grasping the paper and pencils, he followed suit and soon was at the level where she stood pointing to something a little beyond his line of vision.

"What is it?" he asked, pulling himself up to her branch with a mighty heave.

"Look, the village. Doesn't it look pretty from here?" she asked.

And indeed, as it shimmered in the heat, thin plumes of smoke rising from cooking fires, the sun glinting on a brass pot here and there while children played in the dust, it did look like an enchanted village.

"Very pretty, and much nicer from up here than it actually is," he remarked.

"Oh, have you been there? I should so love to go, but I'm not allowed beyond the compound without my ayah, and she won't take me. When I ask her why, she just shakes her head and says, 'Missy must not go there. It is no place for missy.' I don't think that's any sort of an answer, do you? But then, that's the sort of answer grown-ups always give when they don't want to be bothered." Georgie tilted her head and fixed her companion with a speculative stare. "But you could take me there, couldn't you?" There was no mistaking the provocative note in her voice.

He chuckled and shook his head. "So young and already making men dance to your tune. Yes, sprite, I could take you there, but I know that village and, like your ayah, I too have my doubts."

She frowned. "I am *not* a sprite, and I am not young. Why

I'm almost nine years old. Besides, I don't want to act silly like other ladies do.''

"I beg your pardon. You are quite in the right of it. I feel very certain that if you continue to be as independent as you are now you will never act like other 'silly ladies,' " he apologized. He was silent for a moment, gazing at the village, which had, oddly enough, been the cause of this entire adventure. Certainly his unfortunate involvement in its affairs had brought about the excesses of the previous night.

For some time he had been aware of the long face and unhappy silence of his usually garrulous batman, Ramaswami, who, after some sympathetic questioning, had admitted to being worried about his younger sister.

"Ranee is very beautiful, but we are very poor. My mother is a widow and we do not have much to give as a dowry for her. She is very gentle and good and takes care of my mother, who is very aged and must walk with a stick. Ranee knew she would never find a husband, but she and my mother were happy until Chandoo Lal offered to marry her without a dowry. He is very rich and will take care of my mother better than I, but he has many wives and I think he is a bad man so I am very sad that my kind and loving sister is to marry him. But that is the way of things. What else can I do?''

Always sympathetic to those who found themselves in opposition to authority, Brian immediately resolved to do something and directly approached the wife of the local resident to see if she could use a maid. Lady Southwold, like her colorful husband, the Earl of Roxmire (or as he was better known to the troops who adored him for his courage and egalitarian spirit, ''Mad Jack''), was truly interested in the people of her adopted country and eagerly promoted their welfare. She listened sympathetically and promised to find a place for the girl in her household, though she really had no need of extra servants. Brian had gone away happy that at least there was some unselfishness in a world that too often he had found to be self-interested and self-serving. He was gratified to discover that Mad Jack's beautiful wife was as kind and concerned as her husband, and happy to think that this bluff and hearty peer, who had quit his seat of power and privilege at home to seek action and adventure in India, had a helplmeet worthy of him.

Brian had thought nothing more of the matter until several days later he was peremptorily summoned to the quarters of his commanding officer, Colonel Denby, a man he loathed as fiercely as he admired Mad Jack.

"It has come to my attention, Brandon," the colonel began in his shrill officious voice, "that you are once again meddling in affairs that are none of your concern."

Brian felt anger rising up in him as he always did when forced to deal with his pompous superior, but, telling himself that for once in his life he would not lose his temper, he kept a tight rein on it. "Oh?" he inquired as mildly as he could.

"Chandoo Lal has come to me claiming that you have been instrumental in stealing something that rightfully belongs to him. I will not have it, Brandon. You know that we are here to show these rascally natives how honorable men conduct themselves, not to stoop to their level."

"Sir." It was with an effort that he controlled himself. "We are discussing a human being, not an object! We are talking about an innocent and virtuous young girl being tied to that scoundrel. No one who knew the case could stand by and let another human being be sold into misery like that. Why it's, it's . . ."

"Nevertheless, you have intruded and taken what he considers to be his, and caused us no end of embarrassment." The high-pitched voice now rose to a squeak, and the colonel, an alarming shade of red, stopped to wipe his brow. "You are forever getting yourself into these predicaments, Bradon, and this time I won't stand up for you!"

As if you ever have, you odious pig, Brian muttered to himself.

"Chandoo has graciously offered a solution to the entire affair. He agrees to forget her if you will buy her from him."

"But I don't want her. I merely wish to offer her her freedom." Brian was so furious now he could barely keep from shouting.

"Come now, Brandon, be reasonable. A few rupees and

the girl is yours and Chandoo is satisfied.'' A sly smile crossed the colonel's fleshy lips. ''You should be delighted. I've seen the girl. She's quite lovely and would be *very* grateful. She'll make quite an armful. Why, damn me if I . . .''

Brian's eyes narrowed and his lips tightened; it took all the remaining shreds of his self-control not to strangle the man, but he spoke with dangerous calm. ''As you may recall, I am a soldier, not a merchant.''

The leering expression disappeared from Denby's face, to be replaced by a choleric flush as the full import of the furious rejoinder sank in. ''You may be a soldier, Brandon, but it won't be in this army!'' he shouted.

''Good!'' Brian had flung out of the room so blinded by rage that he hardly knew where he was going except that he had to escape from the petty, self-serving people who were so dedicated to preserving their own comfort that they insulated themselves from awkward situations by adopting a rigid code of conduct which enabled them to proceed blindly without having to think or feel.

Not having any immediate plans beyond quitting the regiment and pursuing a more congenial form of existence, he, along with some other choice spirits in his company, had sought oblivion in quantities of port, followed by even larger quantities of brandy. They had broken up the raucous party a little before sunrise, when, too exhausted to seek out his bed, Brian had collapsed on the veranda and given himself up to the numbing effects of the alcohol.

Now here he was, sitting in a tree, still groggy from the previous evening's dissipation, admiring the very place that had been the cause of his aching body and uncertain future, discussing women with an eight-year-old.

2

"Oh, do let me see!" An eager voice brought him abruptly back to reality. With a start he looked down at the fair head bent over the pad in his hands and realized that, absorbed in his hazy recollections of events of the previous day, he had been idly sketching the scene below.

"You're very good, aren't you?" Georgie inquired, looking up at him with new respect.

"I don't know, I wasn't thinking, I . . . well, I suppose so, but I've ruined your paper." He grinned ruefully.

"That's all right. I couldn't think of any particularly good stories today anyway." She was quiet for a moment. "You must know some awfully good stories yourself. Papa is always having adventures. I expect you do too. I wish I could have adventures too." She sounded wistful.

He considered carefully. "Much better to be a tree-climbing sprite. Adventures may sound exciting afterward, but they are usually very uncomfortable at the time."

"Oh."

She looked so disappointed that he hastened to add, "But they do make life interesting."

She leaned back against the tree trunk clasping her arms around her knees. "Tell me some of your adventures," she commanded.

Thus challenged, Brian cast his mind over the most colorful events of the past twelve months and launched into a tale of his encounter with a band of murderous thugs.

Georgie's eyes grew round with wonder as he told how a group of them had joined a caravan of merchants traveling to Calcutta. As darkness had fallen and the company had gradually settled down to sleep, they had also wrapped themselves up and laid down to rest, keeping their eyes open and their sabers close at hand. It had not been long before dark shapes had materialized and could be seen seeking out their companions. Brian had leapt up and run one through just as he prepared to wrap his cord around the fat neck of a Bengali trader. Pandemonium had reigned briefly, but it was soon over and they were being overwhelmed with the thanks of grateful merchants.

Recounting the incident struck a chord in his memory of another encounter with another traveler, this one an itinerant Englishman who occasionally left a thriving trade on the banks of the Hoogly to journey around the countryside seeking a greater knowledge of the religion, the language, and the culture of his adopted land. He had greatly impressed the young officer with his eager curiosity, his readiness to explore and accept different customs and beliefs, and his great desire truly to understand the civilization that surrounded him.

"Ned Wolvercote!" he exclaimed triumphantly, startling Georgie out of her visions of wicked-looking natives sneaking stealthily up on innocent travelers.

"What?"

"Nothing. I've just decided what I shall do next when I leave this confounded place," her companion replied.

Her face fell. "Don't you like it here? I do. Mama has read me stories about girls in England, and their lives sound ever so dull and proper."

"Yes. It is certainly less dull than England, but the people here can be just as stiff and unpleasantly proper as they are there. My colonel is just as much a dead bore, prosing on about duty and decorum as much as my tutor or the masters at university."

She tilted her head. "Which colonel is that?"

He told her.

"Oh, him." She dismissed him scornfully. "Papa says he's an officious prig with less intelligence and courage than the horse he struts around on."

Brian let out a crack of laughter. "That's the colonel. I couldn't have described him better myself. I should like to meet your papa, sprite. He and I would deal extremely well together." He raised a reassuring hand at the wary look that crept into her eyes, while at the same time trying unsuccessfully to picture the few commanding officers, officials of the East India Company, and their wives in an effort to trace a resemblance in her to any of them. "Have no fear, I shan't pry and I certainly shan't give you away. But come, tell me something about the stories you write." He patted the branch next to him, inviting her to sit down.

She hesitated and then began shyly, "Well, they're not really stories exactly . . . not like the kinds in my lessons or the books from England. They're just the stories my ayah tells me about Nala and Damayanti, or sometimes I just try to describe the village and the festivals. I don't know why, I just like to." She sounded a trifle defiant, as though this activity had been criticized before. Georgie was silent a moment before continuing. "Mama says that ladies don't write. They sew and they paint pretty pictures. They play the pianoforte and they do things that will find them a husband. I don't want a husband. I would so much rather have a brother or a dog."

He laughed until tears streamed down his face.

"I don't see why you're laughing," she began indignantly.

"Forgive me, sprite," he gasped. "It's just that I was wondering what the attractions are of a brother and a dog . . . as opposed to those of a husband, for example."

Georgie regarded him gravely, silently. This sudden levity sounded suspiciously grown-up and condescending.

Brian saw that he had truly offended her. "I apologize for laughing. I wasn't laughing at you, just at the way the rest of the world would react to your preference for a dog over a husband. Forgive me?"

He honestly did sound sorry, Georgie decided. She hesitated.

"I shan't tell anyone, and I promise not to laugh again," he encouraged.

She was reassured. "Well, did you have a brother and a dog when you were growing up?"

He nodded.

"And what did you do with them?"

He thought back to cricket practice and exploratory expeditions to the Hanger Wood, boating on the pond in the summer and skating in the winter. "We played, mostly, I guess."

"You see, that's just what I want . . . someone to play with," Georgie exclaimed triumphantly.

"You're in the right of it, sprite," he agreed solemnly. "It does make one wonder about the married state."

"Miss Georgie, Miss Georgie. Please come down. I know you are up there. Your mama will be most upset." The anxious voice of Georgie's ayah floated up to them.

Conscience-stricken, Georgie clapped a hand over her mouth. "Oh! I do hope she didn't hear me. I didn't mean to cause trouble. It's just that I like to be by myself without anyone watching over me or telling me what to do."

As do the rest of us, sprite, he thought sorrowfully, as do the rest of us.

"I must be going." She gathered up her things.

"Here, let me help you." He began preparing to descend.

"No, I can get down by myself, thank you, and I don't want you getting into any more trouble," she replied.

Brian was amused. "What makes you think I am in trouble, sprite?"

She didn't answer for some time, merely looking at him, tilting her head speculatively. "Well, aren't you?" she asked at last.

He smiled. "You are wise beyond your years, sprite. Yes, I am in trouble. I've been in trouble all my life, but now I think it is time I start doing something about it."

"Will I see you again?" She sounded hopeful.

"I don't think so. I don't expect anyone wants me around here anymore." He couldn't keep the sadness from his voice. It was not precisely sadness, he decided. It was regret, regret that once again he didn't belong, once again his actions had been misinterpreted and misunderstood.

"Oh." She sounded sad too. "I'm sorry. I should like to see you again. May I keep the picture?"

He smiled. "Yes, by all means, keep the picture."

"Thank you." She regarded him gravely for a moment before holding out her hand. "Good-bye."

He took it. "Good-bye, sprite. I hope you find a brother and a dog."

She smiled. "I hope you find some friends and some good adventures." And then she disappeared to be visible a few minutes later as a fair-haired being running toward the compound calling, "I'm coming. I'm coming."

A shaft of sunlight caught the golden curls just before she entered the dark shadow of the veranda and he felt once again that she did seem like a visitor from another world who had brought him a precious moment of peace and camaraderie.

He sat there for some time gazing into leafy space as he tried to collect his thoughts. Yes, he would sell out and seek out Ned Wolvercote. Though their encounter had been brief, Brian had been drawn to the man. He had sensed an integrity in him that was all too rare in society. Here was a man who did not live by the petty rules which seemed to govern the existences of so many others, but one who encountered life with an openness that allowed him to observe and adopt the best of what civilization, any civilization, had to offer. The last time Brian had seen the merchant, he had been squatting by a fire in a small village discussing reincarnation with a holy man who lived there.

A Brandon in trade. He grinned. Things had come to a pretty pass! Of course, his father had always predicted that he would come to a bad end, and sooner rather than later, considering the frequency with which he found himself in difficult situations. But even acquaintance with Brian's wildest exploits, which, happily, he did not have, would never have prepared him for such an unsavory turn of events.

The more Brian thought about it, the more the idea appealed to him—no commanding officers demanding subservience to their petty tyrannies and regulations, no one whose opinion or expectations he had to cater to, while ingenuity and resourcefulness, courage, and his taste for adventure would reap their own rewards. After all, look at Clive, he reflected. Not only had he done things his way, he had become wealthy beyond his wildest dreams, and a man to be reckoned with. But first he must find Wolvercote, not necessarily an easy task, here-and-thereian that the man was.

That decided, he climbed down and, fortified with the promise of new prospects, headed back to the barracks to announce his decision and pack his belongings. He wished he could convince his batman to join him, but given the precariousness of Ramaswami's mother's and sister's situation, Brian did not expect it. Perhaps he could convince Lady Southwold to take the mother as well as the daughter into her household.

By the time he neared his quarters, his natural optimism had reasserted itself to such a degree that he was whistling. As he passed the well he recalled the start of his day and smiled. Sprite, he thought. I wonder what will become of her. I suppose that in time they will turn her into a proper young lady, but I do hope not.

3

She was in his thoughts again as Brian, now Lord Brandon, Earl of Aldringham, sat in very different circumstances in the somber mahogany-paneled library of one of Grosvenor Square's most imposing mansions reading a creased and stained letter that had taken months to reach him. It was from a dying Ned Wolvercote begging him to manage the affairs of a beloved niece recently dispatched to England to avoid the latest trouble with the Marathas, but who had been a dear and constant companion since her parents' death had placed her in his care eight years ago.

"She is a good little soul," the straggling script informed him, "and has been educated to avoid the foibles of the ordinary English female. Indeed, her grasp of Latin and geometry far exceeds mine, and her tutor, the Reverend William Bayley, assures me that she has a more vigorous mind than most of the young men he has had the privilege to instruct. India is no place for a young woman, but I have been loath to send her home, as her company has been so delightful to a lonely old man who is inclined to avoid that of his fellow countrymen who too often disgust him with their petty concerns and venal ways. She has assumed so many responsibilities and become such an important part of my menage that it is impossible to think how we ever managed without her.

"Unwilling as I am to have her acquire the airs and graces of the *ton*, I feel I must provide for her future by sending her home to London, where she can meet her peers and be given some choice as to her future. I leave the handling of such social details to my other sister, Lady Debenham, who, though entirely frivolous, is possessed of a kind heart and the approbation of polite society. Her financial affairs are another matter entirely. Though Lady Debenham was left by her late husband in comfortable circumstances, and she appears to be well enough looked after by a man of business, Aurelia is in no way fitted to advise someone possessed of a large fortune in her own right and sole heir to my not inconsiderable estate. Georgiana is entirely conversant with such things and has been diligently looking after my affairs for some time, but I know what society is. Without the guardianship of someone wise in the ways of the world and blessed with a rank and fortune that must establish his own disinterest, she would be subject to the most unwelcome attentions.

"Therefore, I pray you, Brandon, if you ever cherished my friendship as I did yours, to act as her guardian in these matters. I fear that this putrid fever which I have contracted will keep me from being able to care for her much longer even at this great distance, and I fear that by the time you receive this, I may very well be gone.

"I do apologize, old fellow, for leaving you without much recourse, or at least the opportunity to damn me heartily for foisting responsibility on someone who does his utmost to avoid such social obligations, but I find myself at a *point non plus*. I shall instruct my solicitor in London to contact you with the particulars and, should you find it impossible to assume such a guardianship, you may turn it over to him. But though he is an honest and hard-working fellow, he lacks your grasp of financial affairs and your air of authority, which must command the attention and respect of both the *ton* and my niece, who is a decidedly indepedent young woman.

"I bid you adieu and hope that the memories of previous days will allow you to forgive me for putting myself forever in your debt. I am, etc., Wolvercote."

The letter, dated more than six months ago, was enclosed in a missive from the offices of Mr. Edward Chalmers informing him of the unfortunate demise of Edward Wolvercote and begging the favor of a meeting with its recipient to discuss the terms of the guardianship at his earliest convenience.

Brian sighed as he laid both letters down. Poor Ned. He

had been the best of friends, a man you could count on to stand by you through the worst of it all, as indeed he had. When Brian had arrived at Ned's small compound on the Hoogly, the trader had not only remembered him but also welcomed him with enthusiasm. The kindred spirit that each had sensed in the other soon proved to be stronger than either had foreseen. The earl smiled as he recalled all the nights they had sat, the smoke from their cheroots growing thick around their heads as they argued about everything from reincarnation and Sanskrit to the proper role of the East India Company or the advisability of employing banyans to act as intermediaries for naive Englishmen who wished to engage in commerce with wily Indian merchants.

Not only had Ned helped a young man who had never made a commercial transaction in his life understand and appreciate the importance of divining what particular goods English markets demanded, locating these materials and bargaining for the most advantageous price, he had filled the roles of father, brother, and uncle in sharing his experiences and views of the world while at the same time appreciating and encouraging the beliefs and values of the younger man. To someone who had all his life been dismissed as a worthless troublemaker by those who never took the time or the effort to discover the bright inquiring mind and sensitive generous spirit behind the renegade or to realize that these excesses resulted from a frustration with the stultifying atmosphere and circumscribed role of a wealthy young nobleman, this understanding and approbation were as nurturing as water to parched fields. For the first time in his eventful existence, Brian had a friend who not only comprehended his inchoate impulses but also fostered them and helped him to focus his abundant energies instead of dissipating them in orgies of rebellion or self-indulgence.

Glancing around the imposing room, its new master had to chuckle, thinking back on the wild and reckless youth who had first invaded the peace and quiet of Ned Wolvercote's residence, and comparing him to the relatively respectable, responsible citizen he seemed to have become.

Had the same thing happened to another rebellious spirit?

he wondered. Reading about the young girl consigned to Ned's care brought back memories of that other girl long ago who had shared a special moment with him and whose kindred spirit had somehow reached out to his. Sprite. He smiled reminiscently, picturing her as she had stood defiantly, tilting a small determined jaw up at him, daring him to be an interfering grown-up. Had the grown-ups in her world had their way and molded the independence of a headstrong girl into the conformable personality of a demure young lady who would now be more desirous of pleasing men rather than challenging them?

Ned's niece was a lucky young woman, he decided. He had never seen her, having left Ned's tutelage to try his fortunes in Benares before she had appeared on the scene, but, having himself blossomed in the relaxed atmosphere of Ned's eccentric household, where all were welcome as long as they had something of interest to contribute and where discussions were allowed to continue only if they were stimulating, Brian felt certain that she must have had a most educational and uninhibited upbringing. How would a young woman who had been companion to a man often known to request the silence of a dinner guest simply because his conversation had dwindled into the banal fare in a society that subsisted on little else? Anyone accustomed to participating in Ned's dialogues on religion, philosophy, and the miserable state of the East India Company would be hopelessly lost when faced with dinner partners who could neither offer nor comprehend anything deeper than the latest *on-dits*.

He frowned. Memories of crowded bazaars and the exhilaration of bargaining with crafty Indian merchants made the earl long for the freedom he had left behind and resent yet another unsought responsibility that had fallen to his lot.

It had taken some time after leaving his apprenticeship with Ned before Brian had established himself as an astute and adventurous trader who understood and appreciated Indian customs better than most. For the first time in his life he had been free to follow his own interests and ideals. Answering to no one, he had relaxed and enjoyed living his life the way he wished, pursuing whatever caught his fancy without having to defend his actions to anyone—parents, tutors, or commanding officers. He had settled into life in Benares comfortably, maintaining amicable distant relations with the other British and equally amicable but distant relations with the Indians. It had been an idyllic existence and he had just begun to decide that there was some place he could fit in after all when word had reached him of the coaching accident that had caused the tragic deaths of his father and brother.

In an instant, the carelessness of an approaching mail coach had metamorphosed him from the Honorable Brian Brandon to the Earl of Aldringham. Even in India the immediate transformation in his social status had been as remarkable as it was annoying. The wives and daughters of his British acquaintances who had hitherto avoided or ignored him as a hopeless bachelor who combined barbaric disregard for the niceties of English society with a rather unsavory enthusiasm for things Indian now sought him out at every conceivable opportunity. Devising the slimmest of pretexts— a desire to view his celebrated collection of ivory miniatures, or the solicitation of his expert advice as to which of the silk merchants could be most relied upon—they came to his house in droves.

Before the new earl had been forced to the point of physical violence to protect his independence and solitude, he had received three urgent letters—one from his sister Elizabeth, one from his mother, and one from Farnham, his father's man of business—all begging him to return to England immediately to take up his duties as head of the family. The tenor of all three was a grim prediction of things to come. The countess informed him that his sister, without the sober influence of her father, was rapidly becoming unmanageable, while Lizzy complained that now that Papa and John were gone and Mama had no one else's life to interfere in she had become a regular tartar. Both of them made slighting references to Farnham's total disregard for their circumstances and the stubbornness of his refusals to deal with anyone but the head of the family. Though couched in far more respectful and circumspect terms, Mr. Farnham's letter hinted at importunate requests from these ladies, whose lack of understanding in financial and other matters was rapidly causing their affairs to fall into such disarray that he doubted his ability to straighten them out if things were allowed to continue.

Reluctantly, but with characteristic dispatch, the new Earl of Aldringham had settled his own affairs and sailed for home dreading the welcome awaiting him. However, his many misgivings at returning to the circumscribed existence of his youth as well as the tedium of the long voyage had been much allayed by the companionship of a colonel's lady returning home to care for her ailing parents. As amorous as she was vivacious, Letitia Carrington, with her mass of auburn hair and alluring figure had first attracted his attention on the dock in Calcutta, and it was not long before the colonel's wife had made it abundantly clear that she found her fellow passenger equally intriguing.

While a bold demeanor and a reckless air had never failed to capture the favors of a wide variety of females from society's less exalted ranks, it was the new earl's first experience of the seductive power of a title and fortune. However cynical his reflections on this sorry state of affairs, he found himself thoroughly enjoying the charms that succumbed as readily to these as to an athletic physique and a handsome profile. Well aware that much of the lady's ardor was inspired by the social cachet that could be conferred on her by a liaison with a wealthy admirer of impeccable lineage, he found her skill in the art of dalliance more than equal to her ability to seize the chance to promote herself in the *ton*. Brian gave himself up unreservedly to all the delights she had to offer with the abandon of a man about to assume the weighty cares and responsibilities of some of the vastest estates in all of England.

The respite of the voyage had been all too brief, and his conversion from irresponsible adventurer to, if not entirely respectable, certainly a much courted member of society had been as swift as it was complete. The mistrust of the fashionable world with its petty concerns harbored by a rebellious young man quickly hardened into cynicism when the new earl saw the alacrity with which he was welcomed by a *ton* who had once been quick to express its displeasure with his youthful escapades. However, age and experience had mellowed him to some degree. Whereas once he would have flung off in disgust at the deference he now commanded as the Earl of Aldringham, Brian was now amused by the transparent attempts to curry favor and, far from spurning society's attentions, he decided to enjoy them as well as the licence conferred upon those of rank and fortune.

In no time at all the new Earl of Aldringham was one of the *ton*'s leading lights. If his seductive ways caused mothers of marriageable daughters to avoid his company, they certainly recommended him to some of society's more dashing matrons. And his inexhaustible repertoire of adventurous exploits, a decided flair for games of chance, brilliant horsemanship, a deadly accuracy with pistols, and a punishing left made him the sought-after companion of Corinthians and clubmen alike.

4

"Georgiana, Georgiana!" Georgiana Southwold sighed and closed the latest edition of the *Edinburgh Review*. She had been trying rather unsuccessfully to read the latest installment of Mr. Scott's *Ivanhoe,* but her mind would not attend and she had fallen into a reverie gazing out the morning-room window, where she saw not the budding trees and flowers of Berkeley Square, but bright green rice paddies and palm trees shimmering in the brilliant Indian sun. How she missed it all, and the happy days of freedom that had been her life with Uncle Ned! At the thought of him, the tears would come to her eyes and a lump to her throat. She had argued with him for the only time in her life when he had first revealed to her his plan to send her to London. "But, Uncle Ned, I am happy here with you. I don't wish to be like those silly English ladies we see when we go into Calcutta. They have nothing to say to any purpose, and their entire existence centers around attracting the attention of some man long enough to make him a husband. I would so much rather stay here with you and take care of things," she had protested.

Observing the determined tilt of her head, Ned Wolvercote had sighed, "I know, Georgie, and I would much rather have you, but I wouldn't be doing my duty to your papa and mama if I were to keep you here. This remote backwater does very well for such eccentric fellows as I, but it is no place for a single woman, whoever she is, and however independent she may be." He cast her a swift apologetic smile before continuing. "I shan't live forever, you know. What will become of you when I am gone?"

"I shall take care of the business just as you have," she maintained stoutly.

He gazed at her fondly. "And you would, too, probably better than I, but I would never forgive myself if I didn't give you the chance to take your proper place in society."

Georgie's dark brows drew together, the green eyes almost emerald in their intensity. "I don't *want* a place in society. I just want to remain as I am now with you, choosing to be with people because they interest me and make me think, not because they are fashionable or well-connected."

Ned was troubled. "It is very well for me to live alone, but even I am considered an odd sort and, as you very well know, people are forever trying to reform me. I fear, my dear, that if something happens to me you won't be allowed to live as you please, no matter how much you may wish to."

"But," Georgie began.

"Now, Georgie, you know as well as I that the Marathas are causing trouble again and a solitary Englishman, however friendly he may be with the inhabitants of this land, however sensitive he may be to their culture, is still a foreigner and therefore disliked. It would be folly not to be aware of the danger. Besides, you know how strongly I feel about an individual's right to decide his own life and thus the necessity of exploring all opportunities open to him."

She nodded slowly.

"If you stay here, you are exposed to only one type of existence. How can you know what is most suited to you? You might very well discover that the delights of London— plays, and operas, museums, exhibitions at the Royal Academy, the chance to meet the writers, politicians, and thinkers of the age—offer you more to interest and stimulate than our small circle of friends here."

The obstinate expression had disappeared from Georgie's face to be replaced by a more troubled look.

Ned laid a hand on her shoulder. "I tell you what, you go to England for two years, and if at the end of that time you feel the way you do now, why then you may do whatever pleases you." He held out his other hand. "Are we agreed upon it, then?"

Georgie returned his clasp. "Agreed. Thank you, Uncle Ned. I shall try to enjoy it, but I don't expect to." She paused before adding softly, "And I shall miss you dreadfully."

"As I shall miss you." Ned sighed again. "I always was a solitary sort, but you have brought me great joy and companionship from the moment you appeared and informed me that you would not, under any circumstances, do needle-work."

Georgie chuckled. "And you quite turned the tables on me by asking why anyone in her right mind should want to do such a silly thing. I was all prepared to be defiant. It was somewhat disconcerting to have the opportunity taken away from me at the outset."

He laughed. "I knew better than to tell any child of Mad Jack what to do."

So they had arranged for her to travel with a clergyman returning to England to accept the parish offered him by an old acquaintance from university. The Reverend Grant and his wife had been all that was kind, providing enough companionship and diversion during the long voyage to keep Georgie from being too homesick.

It had taken time, however, to adjust to life in the household in Berkeley Square. Lady Debenham, childless herself, was delighted at the prospect of chaperoning such an eligible young lady, and was all enthusiasm for the project even before Georgiana had arrived. This enthusiasm increased when she observed her niece's classical features and elegant figure. To be sure, brunettes were all the rage, and Georgie's nose was straight rather than retroussé. Her chin hinted at an uncomfortable independence of spirit, the green eyes saw altogether too much and too often there was a sparkle of humor in their depths which appeared suspicious-ly critical to some of the more pretentious members of the *ton*. But the girl was remarkably well-looking and would appear to even more advantage when she had been properly dressed. Besides, with the prospect of inheriting two large fortunes from her mother and her uncle when she was twenty-one, she was bound to be much sought after.

The only reservations that Lady Debenham had concerned her niece's mind. It was far too active. She had not been a little shocked and distressed to discover that Georgie's first action upon arriving had been to order the *Edinburgh Review*, *Blackwood's Edinburgh Magazine,* and the *Times*. She had exclaimed in horror when she saw them lying on Georgie's dressing table. And when she discovered her niece actually reading one, she had nearly fainted in her distress. "My dear, those are all very well to have lying around one's library, but a lady of fashion would never read one!"

"Why ever not?" Georgie had looked up in surprise. "Indeed, they are very well written and contain articles of import on a wide variety of topics. I find them most informative. Why this on the 'Injurious Consequences of Restrictions on Foreign Commerce' is—"

"Georgiana." Her aunt fixed her with an urgent, pleading look. "Promise me you will *never* admit to such a thing in public." The determined lifting of her niece's chin and the lowering of the delicately arched brows made her hasten to add, "I realize that Uncle Ned would have condoned your reading such things, but it won't do, my child. Why, if it were to be known that you were 'blue,' even with your expectations, you would find that people avoided you."

The mutinous look disappeared. "Very well, Aunt Aurelia," Georgie sighed. "I shall admit to perusing nothing more serious than *La Belle Assemblée* or Ackermann's *Repository.*"

She had kept her promise, confining herself to the most trivial of topics in her conversation, but it had cost her a great deal. Georgie sorely missed the stimulating discussions at Ned Wolvercote's dinner table and longed for someone, just one person, who could speak to her of something besides the weather or the latest scandal.

However, on this particular morning she was having difficulty keeping her mind on her reading. It promised to be a beautiful day. The fresh scent of spring was in the air and she wanted nothing so much as to be able to gallop across fields and hedgerows. At the best, the most she could hope for was a sedate turn around the park in Lady Debenham's barouche, stopping every few minutes to exchange greetings with her aunt's numerous acquaintances. Georgie sighed and was just beginning to think back longingly to the long rides she and Uncle Ned had shared when her aunt bustled into the room waving two stained and crumpled letters.

"Wilson has just brought these. One is addressed to you, Georgiana, and it looks as though it took this age to get here." She peered more closely at the address on one of them. "Why, it's Ned's handwriting. I would know his uneven scrawl anywhere." She put it in Georgie's outstretched hand and began to read the one addressed to her, but a small sound of distress quickly made her look up.

The happy smile that had lit up her niece's face at the prospect of news from India had disappeared and Georgie's eyes had clouded with tears, her dark brows drawn together in a worried frown. "It's Uncle Ned. He says he has caught a fever. He . . . he doesn't say much about it, but I know the signs. He must be very ill, because he instructs me that I am to live with you but to consider an old friend of his, the Earl of Aldringham, as my financial guardian . . . But this letter was written months ago!"

Her aunt laid a comforting hand on her shoulder. "I am afraid that you are correct in thinking the fever to be very bad, for his letter to me has been finished by a solicitor from Calcutta informing me that my brother's last wish was that you should remain with me. I am sorry, my dear." Lady Debenham might not have been a woman of great mental powers or serious concerns, but behind the frivolous exterior lay a warm heart and a genuine fondness for the niece whose green eyes sparkled with unshed tears. "Come now, child, don't repine. Ned lived the life he wished to, and you brought him more happiness than he would have expected. I am just thankful that you were here with me when this happened. I know," she raised her head as Georgie began to protest, "I know you would have wished to be with him to take care of him, but I believe these tropical fevers are very quick," she remarked, forgetting entirely that her niece was well aware of this, having witnessed at the tender age of twelve two parents alive and well enjoying themselves one night and dead the next. "There is nothing you could have done, and you might have caught it yourself. Now, as he leaves everything to you, you can carry on as he would have wished. Thank heaven these letters were so delayed. At least you don't have to go into deepest mourning. That would have been quite disastrous for someone in her first Season. But to whom does he entrust your affairs? Is it someone in London?''

Georgie glanced at the letter, now even more blotched than before by a tear or two that would fall despite her valiant efforts to hide her distress. ''It's an Earl of Aldringham. Uncle Ned says he knew him when—''

She was interrupted by a shriek from her aunt. ''The Earl of Aldringham! Good heavens! Ned was a dear, but sometimes he was all about in the head.'' She paused as a thought struck her. ''Or perhaps he was delirious. Yes, he must have been delirious. We shall give this to Chalmers. He managed Ned's affairs here as well as mine, and he will surely see that my brother's state of mind quite affects these instructions and make sure they are altered.''

''But if the Earl of Aldringham is a friend of Uncle Ned's . . .'' Georgie began doubtfully.

''No, Georgie. It is outside of enough that people like Sally Jersey court that man and that he is accepted by some members of the *ton,* but to have him as your guardian . . .'' She could not think of words adequate to describe such a situation.

Georgie's curiosity was well and truly roused by now. ''Whatever can he have done that is so dreadful?''

''What has he not done! He is a gambler and a libertine. Why it is said he has dropped thousands in a night, not that he isn't rich as the Golden Ball and not that he doesn't always seem to win,'' her aunt continued thoughtfully. ''And he's a sad rake. No woman is safe from him. He never fixes his interest for more than a moment. He will flirt desperately with someone all evening and then not pay her the least mind the next time he sees her. Of course he is handsome and charming enough that women *will* keep throwing themselves at him. And if Althea Wyndham thinks she's going to bring him up to scratch, she's a bigger fool than I thought her.'' Lady Debenham was momentarily sidetracked by these speculations, but not for long. ''However, he's not a fit person for a young lady to know. I can't conceive what Ned can have been thinking of.''

''Nor can I,'' Georgie agreed. Now that she had recovered

from the shock long enough to consider her situation, she was quite certain she didn't need or want anyone in control of her finances, libertine or not. After all, she had been minding all of her Uncle Ned's affairs for the past several years. Now that his death effectively released her from her promise to try the life of a young lady of fashion, she was quickly forming plans to return to India and take up where she had left off—well, not exactly where she had left off. The image of her uncle's intense blue eyes set in a tanned leathery face rose before her and it was with great difficulty that she restrained a sob. The ache for this loss was perhaps even greater than it had been over Mad Jack and her mother. Then she had had her ayah and Uncle Ned; now she had no one. But cheered by thoughts of returning to India, she composed herself and began to devise a scheme to approach this scandalous rake who was in control of her finances.

Georgie felt certain that if she could just meet this Earl of Aldringham, she would be able to convince him to advance her passage back to India. Once there, she was confident that with the help of Uncle Ned's clerk, Siraj, she could continue to run the business and support herself. It would be a lonely existence after all the years of her Uncle Ned's companionship, his enlivening conversation, and his restless explorations of his adopted country, but it would be infinitely preferable to the dull gatherings and the empty social rounds she had attended with Lady Debenham. It was not that Georgie was particularly unhappy—Aunt Aurelia had been kindness itself. She had received her niece with true delight and had thrown herself with great enthusiasm into introducing her to her friends, all of whom, having successfully launched their daughters, had been just as welcoming as Lady Debenham. It was just that, having heard all the *on-dits* for the first time, Georgie did not care to hear them again. The fresh scandals were no different from the old. One gathering was so very much like another that the days were indistinguishable. She had soon found herself heartily bored and, despite all the interest shown in a lovely, wealthy young woman fresh from India, very lonely. Yes, she decided, I shall return to India. And somewhat cheered by this prospect, she began to plot how best to approach her guardian.

5

The opportunity for Georgie to confront the Earl of Aldringham soon presented itself. Several days after the arrival of Ned Wolvercote's letters, Lady Debenham went to make her monthly calls on her husband's frail and aged sister. She had spared Georgie the necessity of pleading a headache saying, "This time you needn't accompany me. She is quite deaf and lives entirely in the past so I am convinced you would think the visit excessively dull. I am sure I find it so myself, but she is so pathetically glad to see me that I feel I must call. I shan't take long, and when I return we can visit Madame Celeste's to order some clothes for you, as I am persuaded that despite our unhappy news you needn't become a recluse. I do not think it would be taken amiss if you were to begin by attending a few select gatherings, and a quiet evening at the opera or perhaps at Almack's with no dancing. Do peruse *La Belle Assemblée* and see what catches your fancy."

No sooner had Lady Debenham's carriage rolled sedately out of Berkeley Square than Georgie rang for her maid. "Alice, I need your help. I must go on an errand to Grosvenor Square, but I can't ask my aunt to accompany me. Will you come?"

Alice appeared doubtful, but it was difficult to resist Georgie's appealing look, especially when her young mistress was more animated than she had seen her since her arrival. "Yeees, miss," she answered cautiously, "but the mistress won't like it above half."

"Then we must be careful to ensure that she doesn't discover it." Georgie's eyes sparkled mischievously. "Besides, I *must* make this call, and if you don't accompany me I shall have to go on my own."

Alice's expression changed from doubt to purest horror. "Oh, no, miss. I couldn't let you do that. It's as much as my place is worth."

"In that case, it's best to guarantee that you keep it by coming with me and lending me some respectability. Run get your bonnet. I shall be ready in a moment."

It was with severe misgivings that Alice complied. She was fond of her young mistress, who, though she had some odd notions about ladies being educated and independent, was as kind and thoughtful as could be. She was always alive to another person's feelings and noticed immediately when someone was tired or out of sorts. True, she wished Lady Georgiana were a little more interested in her toilette. Alice had high aspirations and she would dearly have loved to fashion her mistress's golden curls into a truly stunning coiffure and help her develop an air of fashion that would be a credit to her maid, but she knew others who did cater to such ladies and they were often treated as little better than slaves. It was far better to have someone who said, "You look fagged to death, Alice, go to bed and I shall take care of myself" than to be exhausted from waiting up till all hours for some incomparable who didn't acknowledge one's existence.

At any rate, Alice could not quibble with her mistress's attire as they set out. Georgie had selected an appropriately sober round dress of gray figured silk and a pelisse of gray velvet which emphasized the smoothness of her complexion and brought out emerald tints in her eyes. The white crape fichu and ruff made her appear fragile and feminine, quite disguising the resolute set of her chin.

There was no disguising, however, the determined pace she set as they headed off toward Grosvenor Square. Even Alice, country bred though she was, had difficulty keeping up, and she was panting ever so slightly when they approached the imposing edifice which Lady Debenham had pointed out on their drive the previous day as being the Earl of Aldringham's town house. If it were possible to detect, Alice's worried expression became even more anxious when she recognized their destination. "Oh, miss, we mustn't. You can't call here with just a maid to lend you countenance."

"Oh, pooh. I not only can, but I shall," Georgie responded firmly. "Besides, Papa always said that real courage is needed not to start a mission, but to carry on when one is halfway into it and has had time to think better of it. Nothing in this world is ever accomplished without some risk. Come along." Head held high and shoulders squared, Georgie marched up the steps and rang the bell. It didn't take much time before the door was opened, but it was long enough for Georgie to become aware of the knot in the pit of her stomach and her shaking knees. Buck up, my girl, she admonished herself; after all, it isn't every day one meets a dreadful rake. Fortified by this comforting thought, she was able to present a serenely confident appearance to the stately butler who opened the door. "Lady Georgiana Southwold to see the Earl of Aldringham," she announced, stripping off her gloves and entering as though she were well accustomed to calling on single gentlemen of dubious reputation.

"One moment, please." Not to be outdone by a mere chit of a girl, the venerable Simpson matched coolness for coolness, his face as impassive as though Georgie were one of hundreds of young women who visited his master with only a maid to give them respectability. Not even Lady Wyndham, bold as she was, had the temerity to call on the earl, he reflected as he made his way to the library.

"Yes, Simpson." There was a distinct note of annoyance in the earl's voice. Lord Brandon had just escaped from another of his mother's diatribes on his sister's over-abundance of spirits, her sad lack of conduct, and her extravagance, to seek the peace of his library, where a mountain of bills, reports from stewards of his estates, and letters from his agent in India awaited him and he was in no mood to brook interruption. But he knew that the invaluably discreet and sympathetic Simpson would not have disturbed him unless it was absolutely necessary.

"I am most sorry to intrude, my lord," Simpson apologized, "but it's a young lady."

"A young lady? But I don't know any young ladies. Or,

at least, no young ladies are allowed to know me.'' Brian grinned. ''Young women, perhaps, but certainly not young ladies.''

''Oh, it is definitely a young lady, sir. She calls herself Lady Georgiana Southwold.''

The grin was replaced by a frown of annoyance. ''Bother! I suppose I shall have to see her, but really it is the greatest nuisance imaginable.'' The earl sighed. ''Very well, Simpson, show her in.''

Thus it was that when she was ushered in some moments later, Georgie saw the new Earl of Aldringham at his most forbidding. As he came around the corner of his desk, it struck her that there was something vaguely familiar about the tall frame and the loose-limbed grace with which he moved. When her eyes had adjusted to the dim light of the library and could see the high cheekbones, dark eyes, and fine jaw, the impression was even stronger.

Looking curiously at the girl before him—Simpson had been mistaken, it wasn't a young lady, but a mere school-girl—the earl was also experiencing the same strange feeling of recognition, when a shaft of sunlight peeped through the clouds and illuminated the visitor's golden curls. ''Sprite!'' he exclaimed.

Georgie's puzzled look vanished. ''The Naughty Soldier!''

One dark brow rose quizzically. ''Naughty Soldier?''

''Well, you *were* quite disguised, you know, and your uniform was awfully rumpled so I guessed you must have done something bad. And when I never saw you again, I was certain of it.''

''You were quite correct in your assumptions. I left the regiment the next day, and after some . . . some, er . . . perambulations, I sought out your Uncle Ned.'' Brian was amused. It had been twelve years, but she was no more impressed by him now than she had been then.

''Oh, you must be the 'Brian' Uncle Ned spoke of so often,'' Georgie began eagerly.

''Did he mention me?'' The earl was oddly touched. But then, remembering Ned made him recall the reasons behind this encounter and the responsibilities it entailed, and he frowned. "But you shouldn't be here, you know. Young ladies, especially those in their first Season, shouldn't visit gentlemen, much less single gentlemen, much less unescorted."

The minute he uttered them, Brian could see that his words had been a mistake. The confiding look disappeared, to be replaced by a militant sparkle in the green eyes, the raising of a determined chin, and a frosty tone as she replied, "I am not unescorted. Alice came with me. But as I didn't want the entire world privy to my dealings with you, I didn't bring her along with me. Now, do you want to know why I am here or not?"

"Oh, most definitely," he responded, his brown eyes gleaming with amusement. Sprite might have grown up, but she had lost none of her independent spirit.

Georgie took a deep breath and plunged in. "I promised Uncle Ned that I would visit England for two years and have a Season or two with Aunt Aurelia. We both knew it was a hum because I'm not that sort of person, but Uncle Ned felt very strongly that people should have choices in life, so he was giving me a chance to see what it was like to be a fashionable young lady. Well, I have seen it and I think it's excessively boring. And now that he's gone, it doesn't matter if I have a Season or not, as I really only came here for his sake. He kept worrying that he wasn't giving me a proper upbringing, even though he taught me everything—far more than any girls learn and more than most boys. Now that I don't have him worrying about me . . ." Georgie paused for a moment as the sense of her loss overwhelmed her; then, shaking her head and taking a deep gulp of air, she took up where she had left off. "Now that he's not here, I can return to India and continue with my life. That's what I came to tell you. So, you see, you don't have to be my guardian after all."

The twinkle had left his eyes, but a hint of laughter remained in his voice. "And what would a green girl like you do with a fortune in India?" he wondered, quirking an inquiring eyebrow at her.

Georgie bristled at the amused condescension in his tone. "I should do just as well as any earl. No, I should manage better. For I certainly know as much about affairs as any earl who has so many minions to take care of his that he can disport himself all over town.''

"Now, listen here, my girl. If you think I enjoyed Ned's plan for you and my part in it any more than you did, you are fair and far out. The last thing I need is the overseeing of another obstinate female. But I owe Ned Wolvercote a great deal, and if that means making certain his niece doesn't make a cake of herself, I shall. Despite what you seem to think, I know enough about affairs in India to know that it's no place for a young innocent, and if you think I am going to let you carry out your bird-witted scheme, you are greatly mistaken.''

"They are *not* bird-witted schemes, my lord. They are no more or less than what I have already been doing for the past several years." Georgie's eyes were blazing as she continued, "And, having managed Uncle Ned's accounts this age, I don't need an interfering old busybody telling me what to do.''

Over the years the earl had had countless imprecations hurled at his head, but "busybody" had certainly never been one of them—hotheaded, impetuous, worthless, reckless, and mad, perhaps, but no one had ever relegated him to the ranks of the type of person who had made his life a misery for years. "Busybody!" he shouted. "Let me tell you, my girl, I neither know nor care what else you do, but while I have the control of your finances, a control, I might add, that I neither sought nor wanted, I shall not allow them to be wasted. And I'll thank you not to plague me with your hare-brained ideas. I pledged myself to carry out Ned's wishes and take care of your affairs, but I did *not* agree to allowing some silly little baggage to come here dictating my business to me.''

"Well, of all the unjust things!" Georgie gasped. "Here you are complaining of your monumental responsibilities, and when I offer to relieve you of some of them, you fly into a rage. My Aunt Aurelia was entirely mistaken. You are not a rake and a libertine after all. You are as straitlaced and hidebound as the rest of the town tabbies!" And with that parting shot she turned on her heel and marched out, leaving the earl to stare at the closing door in thunderstruck indignation.

Brian was not allowed to remain in this state for long. His sister, Lizzy, who had sought him out to beg his escort for a ride in the park, had been astonished when Simpson had forestalled her with the news that a young lady was closeted with her brother. She had been highly intrigued and, with a great deal of pleading and some guile, had at last wormed the name out of the butler. "Lady Georgiana Southwold?" Lizzy's ordinarily vivacious face wore a blank look. "But he doesn't know . . . Oh, that must be the niece of his friend from India that he was asked to look after. He wasn't best pleased about it either. Poor Brian," she exclaimed, amply rewarding Simpson for his indiscretion by further revealing the identity of the mysterious visitor.

Lizzy had hung around the library door hoping to hear something of what was going on within. As the voices became louder and higher, she crept closer, agog with curiosity about the girl who seemed to be making her brother take as good as he gave. No one had ever stood up to Brian in a temper, not even her father, who, when it had come to a shouting match, had hidden the fact that he was losing the argument with "I have spoken. You may take it, or you are no son of mine!" and walking out. Unfortunately for him, her brother had taken him at his word, called his bluff by leaving, and the old man had never quite understood what had gone wrong. This time, however, the other raised voice was distinctly feminine and it seemed to be having the last word. Angry footsteps approached the door and Lizzy was just barely able to step behind the marble bust of an early forebear before Georgie came striding out, head held high, a fierce expression on her face, and cheeks aflame.

Though entirely aware of his visitor's identity, Lizzy could not refrain from taxing her brother with it in hopes of discovering more about the highly interesting turn of events. "Goodness gracious, who was that?"

For a moment Brian hadn't seen her. He was still seething with a variety of emotions—anger at himself for losing his temper, frustration at having been put in the uncomfortable and totally unaccustomed position of being an ogre of propriety, injured pride at having been shown up by a slip of a girl not much older than his sister, and fury at once again having enraged someone he had sworn himself to help despite the inconvenience—but his sister's question snapped him to attention. "That," he began grimly, his brow no less thunderous than it had been when Georgie left, "that is the most obstinate, shameless hoyden it has ever been my displeasure to encounter. Of all the arrogance! To come dictating to me what I shall do, when she should . . . What do you want, Lizzy?" With a great effort he wiped the previous scene from his mind and concentrated on his sister.

"I . . . I just came to ask if you were free for a ride in the park," she began hesitantly. Irrepressible and insouciant, beloved by a household that, though it disparaged the follies of her youthful exuberance, reveled in her vitality, eighteen-year-old Lizzy was sure of her welcome wherever she went, especially where her adored Brian was concerned, but even she was somewhat intimidated by the severity of his expression. As he remarked the uncharacteristically timid expression in her large brown eyes, his face softened. The sharp angles from his high cheekbones to his tightened lips smoothed out, the distant, haughty look in his eyes warmed, and he smiled apologetically. "I'm sorry, Lizzy, I was thinking of something else. Now, what were you saying?"

"I was hoping that you wanted to ride in the park. It's such a lovely day, and I'm longing to be outside, but you know Fenton. He is such a very dull dog, he won't let me do anything but walk Titania in the most sedate manner." She dimpled up at him enchantingly and, as always, he was unable to resist her.

"Very well, then, I shall ask Fenton to saddle the horses while you put on your habit." He grinned. "Be off, you minx. In her anxiety about giving you a come-out, Mother fails to realize that the sooner you have come out, the sooner some poor fool will make a cake of himself over you, and then you and your cozening ways will no longer be our responsibility."

Lizzy tried to pout, but a teasing smile kept breaking through. "And am I so much worse than you were, brother dear?" With that parting shot she ran to get changed.

6

It was a beautiful day and the park was jammed with elegant equipages. As the earl and his sister maneuvered by these and slowed to let a group of eager guardsmen pass, Brian complained, "You could as well have come with Fenton, considering the snail's pace we're forced to maintain."

"Yes, but I wouldn't have attracted any notice with Fenton. Whenever I ride with you, everybody recognizes you and, knowing how unaccustomed you are to going slowly, they make way for you." The truth of this statement was borne out by a group of young bucks that scattered to let them pass.

Indeed, seated on a magnificent bay, with his impressive figure and the easy grace with which he molded himself to his mount, the Earl of Aldringham, towering above his fellow riders, was the object of a great many admiring glances. More than one woman, obscuring the boldness of her stare with a well-placed parasol or the brim of a bonnet, sighed over the broad shoulders that rippled under the beautifully cut coat or admired the strength in the calves that gripped Caesar's flanks. The severity of his attire, the proud profile with its square jawline, angular cheekbones, and a face tanned by years in the Indian sun, made the rest of the gaily appareled bucks seem like nothing more than overdressed schoolboys.

Lizzy watched all this with some amusement, delighted that at last the world was taking notice of her favorite. Her amusement was short-lived, however, when an elegant barouche pulled up and a husky voice exclaimed, "Why, Lord Brandon, how charming to see you. What a magnificent animal! Did you just purchase him? I do not recall seeing you mounted on him before."

"Why, thank you, Lady Wyndham," the earl responded, bending over the hand extended to him. Relishing the satiny smoothness of her ungloved hand, the slight pressure which hinted at further intimacy, and drinking in her heady scent, he reflected wryly that Althea managed to turn even the most perfunctory of gestures into one of seduction. Still, she did it with such skill and style that it amused him intensely to go along with it. Looking deep into her languorous brown eyes, whose heavy lids were lowered invitingly, Brian suddenly realized that she was fully aware of the nature of his thoughts, and grinned appreciatively.

"Do call on me," the beauty continued. "I have just purchased quantities of silk for hangings and I need the advice of a connoisseur of such things." She smiled in a way that left no one, not even the sheltered Lizzy, mistaken as to the true nature of her invitation.

For her part, Lizzy was becoming more and more annoyed. I might as well not even exist, she fumed. She had finally become accustomed to having women look at her brother in "that way," but there was something about Lady Wyndham she couldn't like. Maybe it was the way she had treated the earl's younger sister on their previous brief encounters. If Althea paid attention to her at all, it was as a mere schoolgirl and of no account. Or perhaps it was the hungry look that came into her eyes when they alighted on Brian—for all the world as though he is some diamond necklace she covets, Lizzy thought. Or was it the confident manner in which Lizzy had seen her lay her hand on the earl's arm, as if staking a claim to her territory? Growing angrier by the minute, Lizzy tried to puzzle it out. At last she decided that what she disliked most was the uncomfortable feeling she had that Lady Wyndham was out to entrap her brother, not because the lady in question cared about him in the least, but simply because she wanted him. Lizzy was too much of a green girl to have been privy to the gossip surrounding the seductive widow, but she was acute enough to recognize that Lady Wyndham was not considered to be quite the thing by the highest sticklers of the *ton*.

The earl's sister was entirely correct in her suspicions.

Unlike many of her peers, the young Althea D'Urville had welcomed an arranged marriage to an aged but wealthy peer as a means of escaping the restricted life of an unmarried young lady. No sooner had the vows been exchanged than she had taken advantage of her newfound freedom to embark on a series of torrid *affaires de coeur* which had bordered on the improper. She had managed to be discreet enough to avoid overt scandal, but rumors were rampant. After Lord Wyndham's convenient demise, she had decided to marry to please herself and satisfy her considerable appetites, but no willing groom had been forthcoming. Those who had been more than happy to indulge themselves in a passionate liaison looked for something more restrained and proper in a wife. So while men eagerly flocked to share her sexual favors, they were equally unwilling to share their names, their titles, and their reputations. In the main, Althea had not been greatly bothered by this state of affairs. Her husband had left her a wealthy woman, and if some of society's more scrupulous hostesses looked at her askance, their husbands did not, and she contented herself with attending the less select events of the *ton* while enjoying the company of many of its male members in more intimate surroundings.

All this had changed, however, when she had encountered the new Earl of Aldringham. From the moment she had first caught sight of him at Lady Westchester's ball, Althea had determined to make him hers. The tall, well-knit figure and swarthy face with dark eyes that dispassionately assessed the entire glittering assemblage, finding it dull and insipid, had captured her attention immediately and sent flutters of anticipation through her. The more she watched, the more she was intrigued, as he moved through the crowded ballroom with a grace and aloofness of a panther. Usually extraordinarily adept in the arts of dalliance and seduction, Althea had been so desperate to meet him that she had been reduced to practicing the most commonplace of stratagems—she had bumped into him. She was acutely aware that he didn't for one minute believe her blushing disclaimers, dissemble though she would, but she didn't care. As the earl's amused gaze had traveled slowly from the aigrette glistening in her dusky hair to her satin slippers, dwelling appreciatively on the creamy expanse of bosom, Althea had become unaccountably breathless with desire. She had never wanted a man so much in her life, and the fact that he sensed this immediately only served to titillate her further.

In the space of a waltz she had enticed him into leaving the ball and accompanying her home. They had barely climbed into her carriage before they were locked in an embrace so passionate that it had taken her some minutes to rearrange her clothing when they arrived at her house in Mount Street. Lady Wyndham's butler, wise in the ways of his mistress, had retired immediately after opening the door to her, but he did not even have time to close the door to the drawing room before she had entwined herself with the earl and was hungrily exploring his muscular physique, running caressing hands across the broad shoulders and down the sinewy back to the narrow waist, kissing him lingeringly on the mouth and tracing the line of his jaw with her lips.

Hours later he had left the house, welcoming the cool dawn air that soothed his reeling senses and refreshed a body that ached from the violence of their lovemaking. Even Brian, who had enjoyed women from Benares to Madras and in some of the most select boudoirs of London, was taken aback at Althea's fervent sensuality. He was highly intrigued and at the same time somewhat wary of a woman with such appetites. Still, adventurer that he was, he allowed the intrigue to win out and decided to escort her to the theater the next evening.

As her lover had stumbled home in the early-morning light, Althea had stretched luxuriously on her satin pillows and smiled a deep satisfied smile. More thoroughly satiated than she could ever remember having been, she was congratulating herself on having at last found a lover to match her in skill and appetite, and if her first impression were correct, one who was equally unconcerned with the rigid and superficial of the *ton*. The dazzling bouquet of hothouse flowers which arrived later that morning, bringing with it an invitation to the theater that night, confirmed this impression and Lady Wyndham immediately fixed on becoming the

Countess of Aldringham before the year was out. Embarking on her plan out of lust and a desire for allowances made for the wives of those with an elevated rank and enormous fortune, she soon became obsessed with the object of her machinations and not a day went by but she contrived to encounter him.

It was this determined and single-minded pursuit which had alienated her quarry's sister. At first Lizzy had been delighted at her brother's success in the petticoat line. Lady Wyndham was both beautiful and sophisticated, but she was so intent on claiming the earl's attention that she remained oblivious of everything else, most notably a sister whose gathering frown would have warned anyone not wrapped up in her brother that she was not best pleased by the beauty's continuing to ignore her completely. She might at least have acknowledged me before making such a cake of herself over Brian, Lizzy muttered under her breath. Finally, able to stand it no longer, she gave a quick jerk on the reins, making Titania emit a startled snort and pull at the bit as she sidled restively. This maneuver made Caesar remember that he too had come to the park for exercise, and he began to make it known that he wished to be moving.

Ever an alert and sympathetic rider, the earl tore his admiring gaze from the voluptuous curves straining against the tightly fitting carriage dress. "Forgive me, Caesar. We must be off, Althea, but I shall be delighted to call upon you." Brian bent over the hand he had somehow retained and smiled lazily into her dark eyes, amused by the naked hunger he saw there. The smile remained as they edged back into the flow of horses to continue their ride while his mind dwelt appreciatively on the latest evening he had spent with Althea. She never tired of lovemaking, it seemed, and she continued to remain a stimulating partner who summoned all her considerable charms and skills to ensure that it was always fresh, always exciting.

Brian had never encountered such a practiced lover. He frowned slightly—she was almost too practiced. It was not that he minded her experience, nor did he particularly care that he might be one among many. After all, she as a most sensual, intoxicating woman, and very beautiful. But the very amount of thought she obviously put into such skilled dalliance belied any emotional involvement. It was almost as though the Earl of Aldringham were incidental to the experience and not the principal reason for it.

The earl would have been the first to laugh at anyone who insisted that one had to care deeply about a woman to enjoy making love to her, but he did wonder somewhat wistfully if the passion might not be more intense if there were more than the sheer abundance of physical attraction behind it. He sighed and shook his head, grinning ruefully at himself. You're always hoping for the impossible, Brian, my lad, he admonished himself. You are attracted to someone because she is a woman of the world, and then you wish her to act like some romantic miss, all dewy-eyed sensibility. No, that was not quite it either. But something was missing and he felt the lack of it—just couldn't put a finger on precisely what it was.

These slightly gloomy reflections were not allowed to run their course, however, as Lizzy and her brother had not ridden ten paces before the earl had heard himself hailed again.

"My lord, how enchanting it is to see you. I vow, this is my lucky day, for I had just been thinking about you and wondering how you were getting on now that you are fixed in town. And this must be your charming sister, Elizabeth— so lovely, my dear." The vivacious redhead who had accosted them smiled intimately at Lizzy.

If Lizzy had been miffed at Lady Wyndham's refusal to acknowledge her existence, she was not at all certain she liked the encroaching manners of this obvious admirer of her brother's any better.

Even the earl seemed to find her effusiveness a little coming as he stiffly made the introduction she had forced upon him. "Er, ah, Elizabeth, this is Mrs. Carrington, the colonel's wife who booked passage on the same ship from India that I took."

The coolness of his tone and the rigidity of his spine were certain indicators to his sister that this was an acquaintance that Lord Brandon did not wish to pursue. She looked at him in some curiosity, for he was normally open and friendly, especially where a pretty woman was concerned, and he frequently voiced his disgust at his fellow peers for being too puffed up with their own consequence. Yet here he was behaving as high in the instep as the worst offenders, and to someone who obviously expected a warmer welcome.

Blithely unaware of any undercurrents, the colonel's wife prattled on. "Oh, yes, Brian, that is to say, the Earl of Aldringham, was the most diverting companion you can imagine. Why, he kept us entranced by the hour with the most amazing stories. One could hardly credit their being true. He is deliciously amusing, and so clever. I am sure we never had a dull moment. How very lucky you are to have such a charming gentleman for a brother. And do you make your come-out this Season?"

Lizzy acknowledged that she did, and then felt like the greenest of green girls for not being able to think of a thing to say beyond that.

She needn't have minded, for her interlocutor barely drew breath before continuing, "How delightful! I enjoyed my come-out immensely, though I admit to being the teeniest bit nervous. However, I was bespoke almost immediately." Here, she did her best to blush modestly—not a very natural expression for Letitia Carrington. "Of course, the sister of the Earl of Aldringham and someone as pretty as you is certain to take the *ton* by storm. I am sure you have all the support you need from your dear mama, but I shall be most happy to act as chaperon if she should find herself fatigued, or if you should wish for a companion who is more youthful."

Though the colonel's wife addressed Lizzy, the meaningful smile was all for the benefit of her brother, who, awake to her game, was cynically amused at the emphasis she placed on the last word. He had been wondering how much she had witnessed of the encounter with Althea as she had followed so closely on that other lady's departure. On horseback herself, Letitia would have been able to maneuver more quickly than Althea's cumbersome barouche. Now, hearing the stress she laid on that last adjective, he was sure she had seen the entire interchange and was ever so subtly entering

into competition. For whatever she may have lacked in
fortune or rank, Letitia Carrington made up for in youth and
vivacity. Practically a child when married to the colonel, she
was no more than a few years older than Lizzy, though vastly
more experienced.

Inexperienced though she might be, and as little as she
knew of the world yet, Lizzy was nobody's fool, and she
had taken instant exception to both of these women with their
predatory attitudes toward her brother. Brian's sister was not
as familiar with the motives of women like Lady Wyndham,
but she had attended enough country assemblies to know a
toad-eater when she saw one, and she was as certain as her
brother that the colonel's wife intended to make the most
of her shipboard acquaintance with the earl to secure herself
a place in the *ton*.

Lizzy remained thoughtful during the rest of their ride.
The more she considered it, the more curious she was about
her brother's visitor. Watching the ever so lightly complacent
smile with which Lord Brandon acknowledged the greetings
of various beauties taking the air in the park, she began to
think it might be a very good thing for the Earl of Aldringham
to see more of his ward. If further encounters proved to be
as explosive as the first, they would at least have a salutary
effect on his pride, which was being done no good by all
the attention he was attracting.

7

Once she had an idea in her head, Lizzy was not the sort of person to sit quietly by. It took some doing, but by smiling sweetly at Farnham the next time he delivered papers for her brother to sign and inquiring solicitously after his wife and children, she was able to lead him ever so gently into a discussion of the burdens of heads of families, and from there it was easy to make him divulge the direction of her brother's latest encumbrance. So oblivious was the earl's agent to the stratagem being worked on him that Farnham even remarked to his employer that his sister had become a most charming young lady.

If he had been less involved in perusing the documents submitted him, Lord Brandon would have informed his man of affairs that Lizzy's charm usually increased in proportion to the favor she was about to ask, but this time his preoccupation kept him from noticing anything amiss.

No sooner had the earl's sister discovered where she could call upon Lady Georgiana Southwold than Lizzy began to scheme to get out of the house without attracting any notice. Unlike Georgie, she was at last reduced to pleading a headache, which would have instantly aroused her brother's suspicions had he been there, but he had gone off for a bout of exercise at Gentleman Jackson's. His mother, who might ordinarily have remarked on such a weakness in one whose excess of spirits she frequently bemoaned, was too intent on her visit to Lady Bromley to discuss her own latest megrims to wonder at it.

To own the truth, Lizzy was a trifle disappointed at how ridiculously easy it had been to outwit the household and convince her maid to accompany her to Berkeley Square. As they marched up to the doors of Lady Debenham's town house, she was assailed briefly with doubts. What if her brother's ward were not at home, or what if her aunt were with her, and what if she would not acknowledge a caller whose acquaintance she had not yet made?

She needn't have worried. Lady Debenham, who seldom rose before noon and then took an inordinate amount of time to complete her toilette, was still with her dresser and Georgie was alone in the morning room when Wilson came to announce the visitor. As to her fear that perhaps Georgie would not be at home to someone she had never met before, that too was groundless. Even if the sister proved to be as irritating as the brother, Georgie's natural curiosity compelled her to reply, "Do show her in, Wilson, and bring us some tea if you please," when her visitor was announced. Directly she had requested this, she began to have second thoughts. Surely someone as autocratic as the earl would not send his sister as emisarry? But what if he had? How was she to react? Trying to divine the precise significance behind it all, she had only a minute to collect her thoughts before Lady Elizabeth Brandon appeared on the threshold.

Entering the morning room rather less confidently than she had set out from Grosvenor Square, Lizzy was impressed. Georgie had been taking advantage of her aunt's accustomed early-morning absence to peruse the *Edinburgh Review* and the *Times* in peace, jotting down thoughts in her journal as she did so. Thus the earl's sister was privileged to discover her brother's ward relaxed and in her natural element, and she liked what she saw—a graceful young woman in a round dress of jaconet muslin whose delicate shade of gray showed off the richness of her complexion. The blond curls were slightly disheveled and there was a pink spot on her cheek where she had rested it on her hand. The straight nose, the direct appraising look in the green eyes framed with dark lashes, and the confident set of her head spoke of someone at ease with herself while curious about the rest of the world. The welcoming smile was open and friendly, if a trifle reserved, and the beautifully shaped hands were most definitely ink-stained. Seeing that, Lizzy smiled. Here was a person who was more interested in meeting her caller and learning the nature of her visit than she was in presenting herself in the most advantageous light.

Most of the women with whom Lizzy was acquainted, if they had been reading at all, which was highly unlikely, would have shoved the books and papers from view, rubbed the ink off their hands, and smoothed their coiffures before languidly disposing themselves on chairs likely to show them in the most flattering light.

Georgie, too, was encouraged by her visitor's appearance. Though Lizzy was not strictly beautiful, her animated face with its laughing brown eyes, pert nose, generous mouth, and irrepressible dimples was a countenance that won her friends on sight. No one, on seeing Lady Elizabeth Brandon, could not be drawn to her.

"How kind of you to call. Do sit down. I have asked Wilson to bring us some tea directly," Georgie began, indicating a clear space on the fragile-looking sofa and disposing herself in her original seat, which was the only one in Lady Debenham's house comfortable enough to occupy for long periods of time. Her ladyship, as much a slave to fashion in her furniture as her dress, had thrown out the more welcoming *bergères* and well-padded sofas of previous eras to adopt the most severely classical furnishings, which, for all their grace, did not offer a great deal in the way of support or cushioning.

Having made her visitor welcome, Georgie, ordinarily forthright to a fault, was at a loss how to continue, when she was saved by her equally forthright caller, who had no compunction about dispensing with the niceties to plunge directly into the purpose of her visit. "I daresay you are wondering why I am calling on you," Lizzy began. Then, not giving her hostess a moment to reply, she continued, "Well, you see, I was standing outside the door, not eavesdropping, you understand, just waiting for a chance to speak with Brian. I could not help hearing the raised voices, so naturally I crept a little closer." Her half-guilty, half-confiding smile was so infectious that Georgie could not help smiling in return. "It sounded to me as though you were getting the better of my brother, and I was just wondering what sort of woman would dare stand up to him—most of them fall all over themselves in the most foolish way to win his regard—when the door opened and I saw you come out. I was already intrigued by someone who not only would take him on in an argument but also seemed to have had the last word as well, and after catching a glimpse of you, I decided I should like to know you.'' Lizzy paused before unburdening herself in a rush, ''Most of the young women Mama chooses as friends for me are excessively timid and dull. You don't look at all like that. Are you?''

''Nnnno,'' Georgie responded hesitantly, unsure of how to take this dubious compliment to her character.

''Good! I didn't think so.'' Lizzy nodded with satisfaction. ''Do you make your come-out this Season?''

''I promised Uncle Ned that I would try it, but after his death I had been hoping that I might return to India. Now I suppose I must adhere to my promise,'' Georgie conceded reluctantly.

The earl's sister was nobody's fool and she could easily guess the reason for the change in plans and the resentful tone in her new friend's voice. ''It's Brian, isn't it?'' she demanded bluntly.

Georgie nodded silently.

''He's the best of brothers and I love him dearly, but sometimes he thinks he is the only one with the wit to have a valid opinion.'' The kindling look in Georgie's eyes attested to the accuracy of this. ''Well, I find the best way to counter that is to go along with him and then prove him wrong. He may be a trifle overbearing at times—how could he help it with everyone hanging on his every word—but he is fair, and if he's in the wrong he will own up to it. Poor dear! He doesn't like responsibility above half. Why, the reason he went to India was to stop everyone's telling him what to do, and now he's not only lost his chance for adventure and freedom, but he has to take care of everyone as well. I must admit I shouldn't like to be the one forced to look after Mama and me. Mama does nothing but lie around all day and complain so much that I think I shall go mad if I don't escape and do something, which usually means I fall into some muddle or other,'' she admitted candidly.

Georgie nodded sympathetically. ''Uncle Ned always used

to take me with him when he visited traders in their villages, and we had such wonderful times exploring together. Now all I do is sit in one drawing room or another, it doesn't really matter which, because the conversation is all the same—insipid and dull. Aunt Aurelia is the dearest aunt in the world and she has been kindness itself, but she could happily spend her whole life visiting the dressmaker, making her toilette and showing it off, and remarking on her friends' similar efforts." Georgie sighed.

"Precisely! Only with Mama it is not fashion, but her health which is the sole interest in her life," Lizzy sympathized. "And for my part, I prefer someone who is devoted to dress to someone wedded to nervous complaints." She stopped, struck by a sudden happy thought. "What if you were to persuade your aunt that it would be most advantageous if you were to be seen in the company of your guardian's sister? After all, Brian is most sought after by the *ton*. And I could point out to Mama the wisdom of allowing me to go about with you and your aunt so she would be free to indulge her shattered nerves to the top of her bent." Lizzy beamed triumphantly at her own cleverness.

Georgie looked doubtful. "It all sounds rather contrived to me," she confessed.

"But it would be above all things delightful to have a confidante to share it with while one is being auctioned off on the Marriage Mart, would it not?" Lizzy grinned impishly.

"I suppose so, but I never intended to be married, you know. I merely promised Uncle Ned that I would try life in the *ton* before I returned to India."

"Famous! I don't wish to be married as yet either, but I assure you that I intend to enjoy myself before I am packed off to the country as the devoted spouse of some pattern card of propriety with a distinguished title and expected to present him with a token of my affection every year."

Lizzy made such a grimace that Georgie could not refrain from laughing. "Surely you would not be consigned to such a fate."

"No. Of course Brian would not be such an ogre, but

Mama would," Lizzy muttered darkly. Then she brightened. "But think what a pair we should make, you so fair and me dark. I daresay we could take the *ton* by storm if we put our minds to it."

"Or wanted to." Georgie still remained unconvinced.

Looking up, Lizzy caught sight of the ormolu clock on the mantel. "Good heavens, the time. I must fly." She rose quickly, snatching up her French bonnet and buttoning up the becoming canary-colored pelisse. "It would never do to have Mama discover my absence." She paused at the door as Georgie rang for Wilson to show her out. "Do please consider it, will you? Promise me you will call on me soon? Except for the times Brian takes me riding, it is so tediously dull at home that I shall very likely go into a decline."

A damsel less likely to suffer a decline than Lady Elizabeth Brandon could hardly be imagined, but Georgie, like so many others, was no proof against the entreaty in the big brown eyes. "Very well, then," she assented smiling. "I promise."

"Famous! I knew you were a right one the moment I saw you," Lizzy exclaimed triumphantly as she followed Wilson into the hall, leaving Georgie wondering just what she had gotten herself into and whether her life was about to become more enlivened or merely more complicated than it already was. She sighed. You'll just have to call on her and decide for yourself, won't you, Georgie, my girl? she admonished herself as she hunted for the page where she had left off when interrupted.

As it turned out, Lizzy needn't have worried that the length of her absence would cause her to be missed. Sneaking into a side door, she heard a great deal of commotion in the front hall and was able to slip undetected upstairs. Quickly disposing her bonnet and pelisse, she slowly descended the stairs, rubbing her forehead and trying to look as pale and drawn with a headache as one who had just topped off a brisk walk with a dash upstairs could possibly make herself look.

A scene of utter confusion met her startled gaze. There were trunks and boxes everywhere, footmen running here and there, and maids scampering up and down. Simpson stood in the middle, trying to bring some semblance of order.

"Bessie, just you grab that bandbox, there. No, Jem, don't pick that trunk up by yourself, lad, you'll do yourself an injury. Tom, here, put that down and help Jem. There's a good man." Meanwhile, her mother leaned against the drawing-room door clutching her vinaigrette.

"Mama, whatever—?" Lizzy began impetuously.

"Hush, child." Her mother nodded toward the drawing room, where Lizzy could see a bevy of servants hovering around. "It's your grandmama," the countess exclaimed lugubriously as she took another desperate whiff of the vinaigrette.

"Grandmama!" Lizzy exclaimed joyfully. All pretense of a headache forgotten, she skipped down the remaining steps and rushed into the drawing room.

Her mother withdrew, sniffing audibly. She had never had any great love for the dowager Countess of Aldringham, who, upon being introduced to her future daughter-in-law, had looked her up and down and remarked badly, "In my day, we looked for someone with a bit more dash to be a countess, not some namby-pamby milk-and-water miss."

Seeing how life would be with such a poor-spirited creature, the dowager had immediately retreated to a small estate in Kent left to her by her late husband. There she lived precisely as she pleased, inviting only the most stimulating members of society and the most interesting of her grandchildren to visit her. To her son's intense annoyance, she had completely ignored his heir, infinitely preferring the adventurous Brian to all her other grandchildren. In fact, she had been the only one in his family, save Lizzy, that he had regretted leaving or that he had corresponded with while abroad. Lizzy, too, with her merry ways, had won her grandmother's heart, and though they saw little enough of each other now, they had remained extraordinarily fond of one another.

Thus it was that the old lady's face lit up at Lizzy's "Grandmama, how wonderful to see you!" and she extended a beringed hand to draw her down to the stool beside her.

"Come, tell me about yourself, child. I hear they're to puff you off this Season."

Lizzy nodded, her eyes sparkling.

"Humph. I thought as much. And that fool Charlotte afraid to tell me for fear I would interfere. Well, for once in her life she was in the right of it. If I didn't step in, she would have you paired off with some wellborn dullard within a week, the nodcock." The dowager dismissed her daughter-in-law with a snort. "Not that I couldn't count on my grandson to save you from such a match, but he's got his plate full as it is, poor boy. But come, tell me how you have been amusing yourself."

So saying, the dowager leaned back, an anticipatory smile on her face as her granddaughter launched into a description of her life in London thus far.

8

It was several days before Georgie could return the promised call, and in the interim she had an unexpected family visitor. She and Lady Debenham were in the morning room poring over *La Belle Assemblée*, which Georgie, at her aunt's urging, had reluctantly agreed to peruse, when Wilson came in. "A visitor to see you, Miss Georgiana," he announced. "He would not give his name, but he looks to be quite the gentleman and says he was a friend of your father's," he continued apologetically.

"A friend of Papa's?" Georgie was mystified, but intrigued. "Please send him in, Wilson."

He returned in an instant followed by a willowy young man nattily attired in buff pantaloons, a jonquil waistcoat, an intricately tied cravat, and an exquisitely cut coat of Bath superfine. His open, amiable countenance looked distinctly worried, but when he saw that Georgie looked more curious than resentful at the unexpected intrusion, he relaxed, exclaiming, "Oh, you do look like your mother! I knew I should like you."

He was saved from offering further explanatory details by Lady Debenham, who tore her eyes from the picture of a young lady in a beautiful ball gown draped on an improbable ivy-covered pillar. "Why, Ceddie, I didn't know you were back in town. How lovely to see you. Georgiana, let me make you known to your cousin Cedric Fotheringay."

Georgie's face lit up, but Ceddie, his anxious frown more pronounced than ever, forestalled her words of welcome. "I feel I should apologize for this abrupt introduction, but I wasn't at all certain you would welcome the man who inherited your family estate."

His patent apprehensiveness was so comical that Georgie

had to laugh. "Don't refine upon it in the least, Cousin. I always knew about the entail and I never bore you the least ill will, particularly since I had always planned—no, preferred—to remain in India with my Uncle Ned. But I am delighted to know that I have more family."

Cedric's relief was as heartfelt as his anxiety had been. "I am delighted to hear that. You can have no notion how blue-devilled I've been, thinking that I had cut you out. It was not so bad when I knew you to be in India with Ned Wolvercote, but when I discovered upon my recent return from the Continent that you were actually here, I became quite uneasy lest you think me lost to all family feeling, especially since I didn't call upon you directly you arrived, but I was in France at the time. At any rate, I have come as quickly as possible to make your acquaintance and to see if I might escort you and your aunt"—he sketched an elegant bow in Lady Debenham's direction—"to the opera next week."

"Oh, how I should love that," Georgie began, then, looking at her aunt, "that is, if it pleases Aunt Aurelia."

"Oh, by all means," the lady replied. "I do not admit to being any great admirer of the opera, with the exception of Catalani, but it is an excellent way for Georgie to become familiar with the *ton*. You are most fortunate, Georgie, in having Ceddie as your cousin, as he is accounted a man of great taste and one who can be relied upon to be up on the latest *on-dits* as well as the latest fashions."

Ceddxit demurred gracefully, but he looked to be highly gratified. "Lady Debenham is too kind. You mustn't listen to such Banbury stories, Cousin. I do look forward to introducing you to the delights of London opera. Mozart is one of my passions and *Don Giovanni* is, in my humble opinion, his best work."

Georgie, never having been privileged to hear it before, was eager to go, and it was soon settled that he would call for them on Tuesday evening and she was left to reflect with satisfaction on the kindness of another recently acquired relative.

"Well, it is most fortunate that we were at home," Lady

Debenham declared as Wilson ushered their guest out. "It is a great piece of good luck that he is your cousin, for you could do no better than to have Ceddie as your guide in all matters of taste. One sees him everywhere, and without being precisely a leader of the *ton,* he is friends with absolutely everyone. Such a dear boy, and always to be counted on when one is matching ribbons or deciding on a bonnet. His aesthetic sensibilities are exquisitely acute, and it doesn't do to appear in something that does not win his full approval. Why, I remember several Seasons ago I wore a bottle-green dress to Lady Spencer's rout. He had seen the material when it was delivered from the dressmaker's and hinted ever so delicately that it might be too strong a shade. I had no more put it on than I could see he was perfectly correct. I looked positively hag-ridden and was forced to endure dozens of solicitous inquiries as to my health. It was a most miserable evening, I assure you, and now I never fail to take his advice."

Georgie found it difficult to envision such a person succeeding to Mad Jack's title, but he had been kindness itself with his invitation. Besides, it would be reassuring to have another friend in London, especially the Earl of Roxmire, as her only other experience with a gentleman of that exalted title had given her no very good opinion of either men of rank or men in general. And that thought reminded her of her promise to call on her other new friend, which she resolved to do the very next day.

Georgie had felt a moment's qualm about asking for the carriage, afraid that her aunt might question her more closely about the invitation to visit Lady Elizabeth Brandon, but Lady Debenham, closeted with her hairdresser, merely waved her hand. "By all means, my dear, take it. I shan't be using it until I go to Madame Celeste's this afternoon."

In no short time, she was again walking up the steps to the imposing mansion in Grosvenor Square. Having witnessed Georgie's precipitate departure after her first visit, Simpson adopted the blandest of demeanors so as not to disconcert her by alluding in any way or by any expression to her previous call. However, his mind was agog with curiosity, especially as it was Miss Elizabeth she was calling on. Under no illusions about his young mistress, he chuckled to himself. That little slyboots must have sought her out after her meeting with the earl. The butler looked forward with eager anticipation to further developments.

"Oh, I am so glad you have come!" Lizzy exclaimed, jumping up as her visitor entered the room. A wave of her hand indicated the copies of *La Belle Assemblée* scattered over the floor. "As you see, I have been trying to select a gown for Lady Astor's ball. I do think it is the geatest shame that young girls must wear white—so insipid, don't you think? And I look positively washed out in it if I do not have some color to brighten me up."

Georgie had never thought about it in quite that way. Looking upon her entire come-out as something she only did to honor her uncle and please her aunt, she had allowed Lady Debenham to guide her selections, an attitude which had delighted that lady no end, as dressing was her chief joy in life. Georgie admitted this deplorable state of affairs rather shamefacedly.

"Ah, well, you blonds need not worry. You're all the rage now. It's those of us who are dark who must do something to make ourselves noticed."

Privately Georgie thought that there was no danger of the *ton*'s being unaware of someone like Lizzy, but she merely smiled.

"I had hoped to ask my brother to take us for a drive in the park as it's such a fine day, but he is nowhere to be found," Lizzy began. "We shall have to—"

But whatever they would have to do was lost as the door to the morning room opened and a small boy wearing a woebegone expression on his chubby countenance entered, dragging a cricket bat. "Brian was s'posed to play cricket with me, but some lady in a carriage came by and he went off with her. He said he would be back soon, but I can tell from the way she talked to him they'll be gone for just hours and hours," he announced in disconsolate tones. He plumped down on a small stool by the fireplace, the very picture of dejection.

"That's too bad. I'm sorry, dear," his sister commiserated. "But let me introduce you to my visitor. This is Lady Georgiana Southwold, Percy."

Georgie smiled sympathetically. "You may just call me Georgie, as the rest is a bit of a mouthful. I could help you with your cricket if you wish," she offered shyly. "I expect you'd like someone to bowl for you. I used to play with Uncle Ned in India. There were so many times when he could not find anyone that in desperation he taught me. I don't know, because of course I have never played with anyone else, but he accounted me a fair bowler."

Percy, who had looked dumbfounded at such a revelation, now found his tongue. "You do? I mean, you could, you would? That would be famous! Did you ever see elephants and tigers in India, and all the exciting things Brian tells me about?" Suddenly the little boy's day had taken a turn for the better.

Georgie was touched by the admiration in his eyes. It was almost as good as having a brother of her own. "Yes, I did see all those things. As a matter of fact"—she grinned impishly—"I even saw your brother once and he told me some of those very same stories. But perhaps you had better ask him about that. Now, where is the pitch where you were planning to practice?"

"It's not much—just a place I have in the square. Come along, I'll show you." Excited at having a new friend who appeared to be as much a right one as his revered elder brother, Percy headed out the door, completely forgetting the existence of his other sibling.

Lizzy was too amused to take offense. "I shall just get my bonnet and pelisse and join you," she called as the other two headed down the front steps.

Thus it was that a few moments later, back from putting Lady Wyndham's new carriage horses through their paces and offering his opinion on them, Brian, in search of his brother, encountered his sister on the stairs. It had been difficult to tear himself away from the seductive appeal of Althea's dark eyes, inviting red lips, and intimate conversation, but the earl was a man of his word, and he had promised his younger brother he would return. "Off to give more custom to the merchants in Bond Street?" he teased her.

"Oh, Brian, I do other things besides spend my pinch-pursed brother's blunt. No, in fact I am going to watch Georgie bowl to Percy," Lizzy replied, her eyes dancing in anticipation.

"Georgie?"

"You know, Lady Georgiana Southwold?"

"And just how have you made the acquaintance of Lady Georgiana Southwold?" Brian's voice was dangerously quiet, but his sister was undaunted.

"I called on her."

"You what!" he thundered.

"You needn't shout so. I said I called on her. I saw her leaving the other day and I thought she looked like someone I would like to know, so I called on her. And I *did* like her and I invited her to call on me," Lizzy concluded defiantly.

"You thought no such thing, you little minx. You just wanted to learn more about someone who had stood up to me." Annoyance and amusement were at war in the earl's face, but amusement finally won out.

"Well, you might have a point there," she conceded. "But I do like her, Brian. She is not at all like the other niminy-piminy girls I have met so far. You would like her too if you hadn't gotten so angry at her because she wouldn't do what you wanted. But after all, you don't like people telling you how to manage *your* affairs."

"You jade." A reluctant grin tugged at the corners of his mouth as he wondered just how much of the encounter she had overheard. "Very well, then, take me to this cricket game."

Smiling triumphantly to herself, Lizzy led the way to the square, where they arrived just as Georgie let one fly.

"Brian!" Percy was the first to spy his brother. "Georgie is helping me practice my cricket."

"So I see." The earl sauntered over to where Georgie stood rooted to the ground, a distinctly guilty look on her face. "So we meet again. Why is it that every time I see you, you are up to some mischief?"

Georgie's chin came up. "I am not up to some mischief. I am merely helping Percy," she replied with as much dignity as she could muster.

"So I see. And do you hit as well as bowl?" he inquired, stripping off his jacket.

"I am accredited a fair shot," she defended herself. "Why, thank you, Percy." Georgie accepted the bat that Brian's brother had silently handed her and took her position.

The earl let one fly. There was a resounding thwack and the ball sailed into the bushes.

"A capital hit, and with a spin on it too," Percy yelled as he raced to retrieve it.

"Well done, sprite," Brian whispered softly, coming up behind her.

She smiled shyly at him. "Thank you."

The earl cleared his throat. "It occurs to me that though we, er, discussed my financial guardianship, we did not precisely discuss the terms." He raised a hand to forestall the angry frown that was quickly erasing her smile. "Easy, my girl, don't get on your high ropes. I merely meant to say that though I will not countenance allowing you to return to India to spend your fortune, I intend to put it at your disposal as much as possible. I merely wished to inquire whether you wanted to direct your bills to me or to have me give you an allowance every quarter day."

Mollified, Georgie replied, "An allowance, I think, would be best." She hesitated, unsure of how to continue, her pride warring with her sense of fairness. "And, if you please, I am sorry I ripped up at you. After all, it can be no very pleasant thing for you, especially when you have so many other responsibilities."

Brian grinned. "Doing it much too brown, aren't you, sprite? However, I accept such a handsome apology. I realize that until you met these two hellions here you had no notion of how burdensome these responsibilities actually were." His tone was teasing, but there was a serious look in the dark eyes fixed on her face. He had seen how proud and how independent she was and how irksome it was to her to have to ask someone's permission every time she wished to spend money. After all, it was that very sort of situation which he had always found so intolerable. He had also seen how her honesty and fairness forced her to acknowledge that her situation might be as onerous to someone else as it was to her. He had recognized and sympathized with the struggle going on inside her and he honored her for acting as she had. "Furthermore, if you insist on turning up here like a bad penny, we had better become formally introduced before your aunt censures me more than she already does." He cocked an inquisitive eyebrow. "I presume she had no idea that you have ever set foot within the hallowed portals of Aldringham House?" His amusement deepened as Georgie nodded guiltily. "I am indeed fortunate only to have the overseeing of your finances. Your reputation, I thank God, is in someone else's hands. Very well, then, I shall call on you tomorrow to present myself. And no conscious looks, mind you."

"As if I would—" Georgie began indignantly.

"Peace, sprite. I was only funning. If there is anyone who can be counted on to be awake on every suit, it is you. I shall be on my best behavior and shall bring Lizzy to allay your aunt's fears about her niece's having 'a rake and a libertine' as her guardian."

"Thank you. I shall look forward to your visit. And, speaking of my aunt, I had best be going." Georgie's carriage was soon called and she bade adieu and drove home far less lonely than she had been since she left India.

9

He was as good as his word, and the next morning at a respectable hour the Earl of Aldringham and his sister presented themselves in Berkeley Square. Recognizing Lady Debenham for the slave to fashion that she was, the earl had allowed her enough time to rise and complete her toilette sufficiently so that he was able to remark with some semblance of truth that she was in great good looks that morning. If Lady Debenham were made uncomfortable by the attentions of one who was known to be dangerous where women were concerned, she did not appear uneasy in the least. Instead she laughed, disclaimed, accused him of being a sad rake who was offering Spanish coin, and looked excessively pleased at having someone confirm her impression that she had been right after all in thinking that her new Parisian mobcap and morning dress of rose cashmere were most becoming. So flattered was she that after a quick approving glance in the looking glass over the mantel, she said, "But I must make known to you my niece Georgiana. Georgie, my dear, this is the Earl of Aldringham, who, as you know from his letter, was one of Ned's dearest friends in India. I am sure, my lord, that my brother did not write to me but he constantly sang your praises."

"And now who's offering whom Spanish coin?" Brian wondered, winking at Georgie, whose expressive face belied her aunt's extravagant praise.

Realizing from his knowing look that her face must have revealed more than she would care to, Georgie adopted her most proper social expression as she extended her hand. "I am so pleased to make the acquaintance of someone Uncle Ned spoke of so often."

The earl's lips twitched as he bent over her hand. Lady

Georgiana Southwold might consider it excessively boring to be a fashionable young lady, but she could certainly do a fair imitation of one when it suited her. "I have brought my sister, Elizabeth, along with me. I was hoping to invite you for a drive around the park and thought you might find it more comfortable to have her along."

Looking up into his dancing eyes and teasing smile, Georgie stifled a sigh of exasperation. Truly, he was the most provoking creature. Here he had been the one to suggest this farce to forestall the possibility of their appearing to be on terms of easy intercourse should they happen to encounter each other, and now he was doing his best to make her overset her countenance. She turned her back on him to smile warmly at Lizzy. "How delightful. And how *kind* of your brother to think I might be needing a friend. Are you making your come-out this Season?"

Brian's shoulders shook. He was not deceived by the excessive sweetness of her tones. One look at the stiffness of Georgie's spine and he knew she was longing to give him a tremendous set-down. Unable to resist giving her that opportunity, he broke in. "I know you girls are longing to exchange confidences, but perhaps you'd best wait until we get outside, as I don't wish to keep my horses standing any longer than absolutely necessary."

"Yes. I shall just run fetch my pelisse." Thankful to escape before her emotions got the better of her, Georgie darted out of the room, leaving the earl and his sister to take their leave of her aunt.

Though he would have been willing to wager that she was not one to spend time primping in front of the looking glass, even Brian was surprised at the speed with which she rejoined them on the front steps. But the reason for her haste was soon made clear as she rounded on him the minute that Wilson closed the door behind her. "Of all the odious . . ." she began angrily as he helped her into the curricle.

He raised an appeasing hand. "Now, sprite, don't fly into the boughs. Forgive me, but the temptation was too great. Yesterday you were so put out that I dared to imply that you might give yourself away that I couldn't resist giving you a challenge. I must say, you did splendidly. Not even Mrs. Drummond Burrell could have been more icily correct than you were.''

"And with good reason," Georgie retorted. But she was no proof against his apologetic smile. It had been so long since she had laughed. It had been so long since she had shared anything with anyone, and here he was appealing to her to join in the humor and fellowship of the situation. Here he was making her a partner in crime, as it were. Her lip quivered. "Well, you were outrageous, you know."

"There has never been a time when Brian hasn't been outrageous," his sister volunteered from the other side of the carriage. "Mama is forever saying that he should have been born with a bottle of vinaigrette in one hand because he's been a trial to her nerves since the moment he drew breath."

"How very taxing it must be to live with him. I used to long for a brother, but if this is what they turn out to be, I count myself lucky not to have one," Georgie remarked with a challenging gleam in her eyes.

The earl chuckled appreciatively. "Best not to annoy the driver too much, sprite, lest he communicate that to the horses and they become unmanageable."

"Pooh." Georgie watched him admiringly as he easily negotiated the narrow space between a barouche and the park gate. "What fustian, when anyone can see you drive to an inch. It must be lovely to be a man and allowed to drive one's own curricle and pair," she sighed wistfully.

Looking at her pensive profile, Brian thought how confining she must find the fashionable existence of the *ton* after her life in India. Certainly, living as removed from the major British settlements as she had, she would have been allowed a measure of freedom unusual even for most boys. He was familiar enough with Ned Wolvercote's unconventional and adventurous ways to think that she must be finding London very dull indeed, and he resolved to do what he could to make her stay more enjoyable.

"Brian is a member of the Four Horse Club," Lizzy volunteered proudly, "and there is hardly anyone who can match his time to Brighton. He has promised to teach me to drive his curricle when we go to Aldringham for the summer."

"Perhaps I was beforehand in condemning them—brothers do seem to have their uses." Georgie couldn't help sounding envious as she thought of Lizzy, who had one old enough to drive her around in an equipage that attracted envious stares and one young enough to seek her out when he had a problem or wanted companionship.

At this moment Lizzy was concentrating on her older brother and, remembering her plan to introduce him to a female who would provide sufficient contrast to his two rapacious admirers, turned to Georgie. "When I called upon you the other day, you were surrounded by books, papers, and journals of all types. Were you reading all those?"

"Well, I . . ." Georgie looked somewhat uncomfortable. "I do like to know what is going on in the world. I mean, you see, I still feel more at home with news from India and elsewhere than I do with the latest *on-dit,* and, not knowing anyone who has just returned, I find that is the only way to keep up."

Lizzy, to whom periodical literature was *La Belle Assemblée,* or, at most, Ackermann's *Repository,* had never before considered that a woman might read such things. "Are they interesting?" she asked curiously.

"I think so. Why, when you came in I was reading a most illuminating treatise on the relation of the Greek and Latin languages to Sanskrit and tracing some of their deities back to India. Uncle Ned would so have enjoyed reading it because he was forever saying that we had much to learn from the Indians and that it was a mistake to try to impose our forms of religion and government on them."

"Most Englishmen would not thank you to hear such sentiments," the earl remarked acidly.

"Yes, I know, because everyone would prefer to think of man as being capable of improving himself and of England as the nation where he has done that to the highest degree. Most of the English people I encountered in the large English settlements we visited seemed to believe wholeheartedly in this and therefore had little interest in learning about the land where they were living. But that is a dreadful mistake because one can learn so many unusual and intriguing things, and certainly the more one learns of the people, the better able one is to understand them in order to trade with them and help them govern.''

"Oh, so you believe along with Elphinstone that we had better make certain that India welcomes English law and order?'' The earl was intrigued. For too long he had been dealing with the likes of Farmer Tweedie, who complained that his neighbor Stubbs was not keeping their common fences repaired, or the flattering letters from obsequious and indigent clergymen who coveted the rich livings within his gift. He made decisions quickly and fairly, dispensing justice where it was called for, but they all had seemed like so many mongrels snapping at his heels and vying for attention. He had longed for the days when he had traveled over India learning from all he encountered, trading his knowledge and his perceptions of the world for theirs and having his vision enlarged and the respect he commanded increased because of the understanding he exhibited for their languages and their beliefs.

"Yes, I do. Of course, there have been some times when we have been able, by virtue of being foreigners, to put a halt to endless battles among rival native princes, but just because we have done that does not mean that we have the right to impose our system of laws upon them.''

"Quite so. And the more one makes use of existing officials, village headmen and the like, the less one has to devote to administering.''

The carriage slowed. The earl had become so involved in the discussion that he dropped his hands while he fixed his eyes on Georgie. The reins had slackened and the horses were turning around looking at him curiously, unused to such unresponsive behavior from someone who could ordinarily be counted on to be aware of the least flick of an ear. Recalled to his surroundings by the halting of the curricle, he smiled ruefully. "It's a rare person who can make me forget my cattle. I should like to see the treatise on Sanskrit, as I'd wondered about the similarities myself.''

"Oh, do you know it? Would you teach me?" Georgie could not keep the eagerness out of her voice.

Looking down into the animated face whose green eyes were alight at the prospect of learning, he reflected cynically that it was a rare person who wished for something from him besides money and advancement. He laughed. "Very well, sprite, if you are certain you wish to waste your Season on such a musty subject."

"I should like it of all things!" She paused. "I suppose I should not talk of such things. Aunt Aurelia is forever telling me that I should not admit to reading *Blackwood's* in polite society, but then"—she looked troubled for a moment, then smiled impishly and concluded triumphantly—"but then, I am not at all sure that Aunt Aurelia considers you polite society."

"Repellent brat. Your Aunt Aurelia has good reason to be severe if she has someone as irrepressible as you in her care." He grinned good-naturedly.

"That is very well for you, Brian," Lizzy sniffed. "Everyone knows your reputation is beyond mending, but I do not believe that mine is."

"Oh, I do beg your pardon." Georgie looked the picture of guilty contrition.

Lizzy laughed. "I was merely funning, Georgie. If I can still lay claim to being a member of polite society, I am sure it will not be for long. I always end up in a scrape of some sort and Mama says the only uncertainty lies in whether I'll ruin myself at the outset or wait until later. We Brandons are always on the brink of disaster, so I wouldn't refine upon it too much."

By this time they had made a circuit of the park, and the sky, which had been a brilliant blue at the beginning of the day, was darkening at an alarming rate and the wind began to pick up. "We had best be getting you home. I may have allayed your aunt's fears by bringing Lizzy with me, but it would never do for her niece to spend too much time with 'a rake and a libertine.' "

They arrived at Berkeley Square just as the first drops were beginning to fall, and Georgie bade them the briefest of goodbyes and thank-yous before scrambling down. Pausing inside to collect herself, take off her bonnet, and unbutton her pelisse, she realized that she had not enjoyed herself so much since she had left India. For the first time she had not been greeted by a blank or disapproving stare when she began to discuss something other than the weather or the latest fashion, and it had been a wonderful feeling. She had forgotten what it felt like to share her ideas and interests unreservedly with someone, and it was wonderful to be able to do so. Then, giving herself a shake, she admonished herself, "You had better take care, Georgie Southwold. You saw how he took Aunt Aurelia's measure and had her eating out of his hand. Rakes and libertines are quite good at that sort of thing, you know. He's doing the same with you so you will forget all about the fact that you have to apply to him every time you wish to perform any financial transaction." She tossed her head. "Well, I won't be taken in," she vowed to herself.

10

But she had reckoned without the Earl of Aldringham. Having made a resolution to ensure that his ward's sojourn in the capital was as pleasant as possible, he immediately set out to do something about it. Brian had a fair notion that what Georgie had found hardest to bear after her life with Uncle Ned was not so much the frivolous and insipid nature of the most common amusements of the *ton*, but the confined life that a young lady in her first Season was forced to live. He had seen the longing in her eyes when they alighted on particularly fine specimens of horseflesh during their ride in the park. Certainly it would never occur to Lady Debenham that her niece might wish to ride, and if, perchance, such a notion did strike her, she would in all likelihood send her groom looking for a mount suitable for a lady. The earl had taken Georgie's measure and he knew she would scorn such an animal.

The next day found him at Tattersall's carefully examining their prime bits of blood. It was not an easy task because he was looking for a mount that was not only a sweet goer but would provide some companionship for what he suspected was a very lonely existence. At last he settled upon a chestnut mare who was as spirited and graceful as Georgie herself and, well pleased with his choice, he instructed his groom to take it back to Grosvenor Square while he went around to Berkeley Square to arrange for stabling.

The earl had toyed with the idea of calling on her with it in Berkeley Square, but had decided against it. First of all, he wasn't at all certain that someone as proud and independent as Georgie would accept such a gift, and he had decided that the best way to ensure that she did was to employ a little coercion by presenting it to her in the presence of

Lizzy and Percy. Second, her aunt might object to her receiving a present from a rake and a libertine, even though he was her guardian. However, if she were presented with a *fait accompli*, she was not the sort of person to make her niece return it.

So it was that Georgie received a note later in the day informing her that "The Earl of Aldringham presents his compliments to Lady Georgiana Southwold and begs her to call on him in a matter of great importance at her earliest convenience." Certainly there was nothing to offend in the invitation. Lord Brandon had tried his best not to make it sound peremptory, but Georgie, looking at the bold black script, resented the implicit command and was seriously considering ignoring the summons, but curiosity won the day. Having decided to respond, she then debated over how long to postpone her visit. At last, realizing that someone as acute as the earl would expect some show of independence through a delaying action, she determined that it would be most discomfiting if she were to return with the messenger. Ordering him to wait, she rang for Alice and wrote a quick note for her aunt.

Georgie had gauged the earl's thinking exactly. He had been fairly certain that she would make him cool his heels for a day, and had, therefore, just been preparing to go out when Simpson came to inform him that Lady Georgiana was waiting for him in the drawing room.

"Is she, now?" There was an appreciative gleam in the earl's eyes as he donned his jacket and sent the butler in search of his brother and sister.

Georgie was inspecting a family portrait over the fireplace, wondering if Lord Brandon had truly ever looked that quiet and well-behaved, when he strode into the drawing room.

"Thank you for responding so quickly to my note." Try though he would, he could not keep some note of surprise from his voice.

"I was under the impression that it was your intention for me to be prompt, since you did state that it was a matter of some importance," she responded frostily.

He grinned. Resentment was writ large in every line of

her posture, and he could well imagine the battle that had gone on within her over it. "I apologize if it sounded as though I were ordering you—"

"Well, it did," she replied boldly.

The grin became wider. "I truly did mean that you could come at your convenience."

The incredulous look that met this remark almost overset him, but fortunately he was saved by the entrance of Lizzy and Percy. "You wanted to see us?" The blatant curiosity in Lizzy's face was enough to warn Georgie that something unusual was afoot here.

"Why, yes. I wanted your opinions. I purchased something today for Georgie that any guardian worth his salt should make sure his ward is provided with, but I wanted to make sure that I had chosen well." Three pairs of eyes, two unabashedly curious and one wary, regarded him. "Well, come judge for yourselves." Brian led the way to the mews, where Fenton was putting the mare through her paces.

Percy was the first to comment. His passion was horses and he liked to think that someday he just might rival his brother as a noted whip. "A prime bit of blood, I'd say." He sauntered over to examine the mare's hooves, look in her mouth, and stroke her velvety nose.

"Oh, what a beautiful horse!" Lizzy exclaimed enviously.

Georgie, for once in her life, was speechless. She stood rooted to the spot, looking from the earl to the mare and back again, wondering what to say. She was not even precisely certain how she felt. On one hand she had been longing to be able to ride, and though she could not imagine how he had guessed, was immensely touched that he had recognized this wish and fulfilled it. On the other hand, she hated to owe anyone anything, especially the person to whom she wanted to prove her independence above all things. And last, but not least, she was most curious, and not a little suspicious, as to Lord Brandon's motives in giving her such a present. "It . . . it is very kind of you, but, but . . . my aunt, Lady Debenham, what will she say?"

Perfectly understanding the conflicting emotions raging within her, particularly her desire not to be beholden to anyone, Brian grinned. "I have taken care of that and have arranged for stabling, so you cannot find any objections on that score."

Responding to a significant look from the earl, Fenton had brought the horse over to her side. Sensing Georgie's unease, the mare snuffled and nuzzled her nose against her hand. Looking into the liquid brown eyes that appeared as though they comprehended a good deal of what was going on inside her, Georgie was lost. She fondled the mare's ears, rubbed her nose, and ran her hand along the graceful neck. Encouraged by this response, the mare sniffed her pockets and hands in search of some possible hidden treat.

"Here . . ." The earl reached for Georgie's hand, opened it, and placed several lumps of sugar in her palm.

Georgie was overcome. "Thank you," she whispered, smiling up at him, her eyes bright with unshed tears. "How did you know?" she asked shyly.

"I saw you examining every mount in the park the other day. Anyone who spends more time looking at horses than at the riders deserves a horse. Besides, I expect you are a bruising rider and I should love to see the right person put this mare through her paces."

His voice was teasing, but there was such a wealth of understanding in his dark eyes that Georgie stood transfixed. Not since she had waved good-bye to Uncle Ned from the deck of the ship in Calcutta had anyone understood the sort of person she truly was and responded to that instead of trying to shape that person to fit into a certain role in society. They stood thus for a moment, each enjoying the sense of an invisible bond that existed between them, until a wet tongue on her wrist reminded Georgie that she was holding something that someone else badly wanted. "Oh, you! You are very naughty to interrupt like that. I can see that I shall have to teach you manners. It will be a pleasure teaching someone else how to behave for a change." She smiled ruefully as the mare licked up the last bits of sugar.

"We shall have to go immediately to purchase you a riding habit. I say we go to Madame Celeste directly to have you fitted," Lizzy interrupted briskly.

"Oh, but my aunt," Georgie protested.

"She won't notice your absence for a little while longer. We shall send a note saying that you have gone to the dressmaker. If she receives it, she will be so pleased at your direction she will not likely think to wonder at it. I shall come with you to keep you from choosing anything too serviceable or severe."

"Thank you, but I can manage . . ." Georgie hurriedly assured her.

"Now, Georgie, all anyone has to do is look at you to see that though you may be elegant enough, you have no sense of style. I say that if one can cut a dash, why shouldn't one? Come along. We shall take Brian with us, because if anyone is an expert on feminine fashion, it is he." Lizzy was not to be dissuaded by a few paltry objections.

"But what about me?" Percy wailed. "I think we should all ride in the park first to try out Georgie's new horse."

"She can't do that without the proper attire, you bacon brain," his sister snorted in disgust.

"Oh." Percy looked crestfallen. He had been enjoying his part in this group of grown-ups and he didn't like to see it come to an end. "Mayn't I come while she chooses her riding habit?" he wondered.

"A little boy in a dressmaker's? You must be all about in the head!" His sister could hardly believe her ears.

He hunched a defensive shoulder. "Well, Brian's going."

"Yes, but he's a man and he knows about such things."

Here Georgie decided it was high time to intervene. "Well, it's *my* habit and I should like *everyone* to come along and help me select it." If this reply left Lizzy openmouthed, it was highly gratifying to her younger brother and something more to her older one.

The earl was still for a moment, bemused by the variety of emotions washing over him. He had never encountered a woman before who acted purely out of kindness, and he was touched and charmed by it. His mother was inclined to be self-centered and complaining. His sister was lively and could be a merry companion, but often she was unheeding of others. His grandmother, though witty and intelligent, was also acerbic and would have died rather than betray any softer emotions. His various mistresses had been sensual, always seeking to gratify his physical desires, but otherwise they thought only of themselves. Yet here was someone willing to have a small boy tag along on an errand where he would be more hindrance than help, merely to make him feel included. In fact, the earl suspected that the entire errand was more to gratify his sister and him than because Georgie wished to spend time selecting a habit. It was an enlightening moment for the earl and it made him appreciate just how unusual a person Lady Georgiana Southwold was. These thoughts were interrupted by Percy, who called impatiently, "Come along, Brian." He came to with a start as he realized that the others were already leaving.

It was a motley little group that strolled down Bond Street, and not a few fashionable passersby took a second look at a shopping expedition that contained two young women barely out of the schoolroom, an obvious man of fashion, and a small boy, but the group remained blithely unaware of the attention they were attracting, occupied as they were by more serious concerns.

"What will you name your horse?" Percy had asked.

Georgie thought for a moment. "I shall call her Lakshmi."

"Very good, sprite." The earl was pleased by the choice, feeling somehow that it was selected to honor their first meeting.

"Lakshmi?" Percy was bewildered.

"Lakshmi is the Hindu goddess of fortune. She is also very good and very beautiful, and often the carvings in the temples show her with four arms."

"Four arms?" The little boy was intrigued. "Why ever would someone have four arms?"

"To own the truth, I don't really know. Perhaps your brother does."

But at this moment his brother's attention was elsewhere. They had arrived in front of Madame Celeste's elegant establishment just as she was ushering out an honored customer.

"Why, my lord, what a surprise to see you here." Althea

Wyndham's throaty voice broke into the discussion of Hindu goddesses. "Come. Escort me to my carriage. I have been meaning to ask you about selecting a new barouche now that I have fixed upon some horses . . ." Smiling enticingly, the beauty took his arm and led him out to the street, where her groom was holding open the door of her carriage for her.

"That's the lady that took Brian away when he was s'posed to practice cricket with me," Percy muttered darkly. "There's something havey-cavey about her, if you ask me, and I don't like her."

"Nor do I, dear, but let's not talk about it here. Come into the shop," his sister answered briskly.

Georgie, glancing back over her shoulder, slowly followed the other two into Madame's exquisite salon. "She's very beautiful, though," Georgie remarked, impressed by the alluring and fashionable woman with the glossy dark hair, ripe figure, and inviting red lips.

"That's as may be. Beauty like that may make her Brian's mistress, but it won't catch him in the parson's mousetrap," Lizzy snapped. "Now, come along, Georgie, we're here to select you a riding habit, not discuss the attractions of someone who is *de trop* and excessively boring besides."

Georgie nodded obediently as she acknowledged Madame's enthusiastic welcome, but her thoughts were elsewhere as she allowed Lizzy to explain the purpose of their visit and suggest the fabrics and colors most likely to be becoming to her friend. She wondered at Lizzy's show of temper. It was not like her sunny-natured friend to be so short. True, she had not known Lizzy long, but she had seen enough of her to feel that there was something more than "boredom" in her attitude toward Lady Althea Wyndham. Georgie shook her head. It really was none of her affair, but she couldn't help being the tiniest bit curious as to the true reasons behind Lizzy's dislike.

11

Georgie was given more opportunity to reflect on this state of affairs, and sooner than she would have expected, as she and her aunt, escorted by her cousin Cedric, settled into their box at the opera that evening, for who should be in the box opposite them but Lady Wyndham, resplendent in an emerald parure that called attention to daring décolletage. Trying not to appear as though she were staring, Georgie examined the beauty over the top of her ivory fan. If Georgie had cared to aspire to such things, she would have liked to look like Althea Wyndham, who, secure in the knowledge of her beauty and her seductive allure, radiated this confidence with a magnetism that drew men's eyes both in the pit and in the boxes. It was not just the gracefully rounded shoulders, the creamy expanse of bosom whose charms were more revealed than hidden by a corsage cut so low as to barely exist, or full red lips that captivated attention. There were, after all, many other equally beautiful women in the audience. It was her absolute belief in her power to attract, her assumption that she aroused desire in every man who saw her that permeated her being and made every look, every gesture, tantalizing and irresistible. It would never have occurred to anyone observing this complete assurance to think otherwise, and therein lay her power. It was that confidence that drew Georgie's attention and admiration, and just for once she wondered what it would be like to have people look at you as if nothing else existed, as if nothing else mattered in the world.

As she watched the throng around Althea, she noticed one tall form in the background standing somewhat detached from the eager swains crowding around her chair. It was the earl. And Georgie noted that while there was an appreciative smile on his lips, he did not appear to be as besotted as the rest. There was something in the proud tilt of his head and the set of his broad shoulders that distinguished him from everyone else. For some obscure reason Georgie was glad that he was not as slavish in his attention as the other gallants surrounding the beauty.

Lost in these thoughts, Georgie forgot to dissemble, and her fan slipped into her lap. The intensity of her gaze must have been almost tangible, for the next instant the earl glanced up and saw her. A look of amusement crept over his face. He quirked an eyebrow and winked. The sheer boldness of this gesture tickled her sense of humor and she choked back a laugh. Brian smiled at her only partially successful attempts to keep a straight face, reflecting as he did so that she looked like an adorable little girl caught in some scrape.

Their brief interchange was interrupted by Althea, who, with an accomplished flirt's sixth sense toward the attention of her admirers, felt rather than saw that the earl's was wandering. With a dazzling smile she turned around and extended a swanlike arm. "Do come here where I can see you. Otherwise I shall think I am not being sufficiently entertaining." She drew him down on the chair next to her. It was an effectively seductive gesture, as the movement allowed an even better view of her enticingly rounded bosom and sent up a wave of heady perfume, but somehow the practiced skill of it robbed it of some of the allure. The earl, though he was never immune to her charms, could not keep some detached part of his brain from noticing this and reflecting on it. He wished it were otherwise, because he would have preferred to be as intoxicated by her as were the rest of those in her retinue, but he had spent too many evenings with similarly seductive women not to recognize the deliberate nature of her every movement.

Perhaps it was Althea's very self-consciousness that made him again look across to Georgie's box, for there at least was one woman who employed no arts to attract, rather the opposite. He smiled to himself as he observed her, so oblivious of the social scene enacted all around her that she was leaning on the edge of the box with unfashionable abandon, her chin in her hands, her whole attention fixed on the stage below. She was so entranced with the music that she was unaware of his scrutiny, or of anything else for that matter, and her enjoyment of it was all so palpable that he had to chuckle. Every other woman in the theater, the youngest, most unsophisticated of them included, though she acknowledged the action onstage, was far more interested in the attention she was attracting from the audience. There was something innocent and very endearing in Georgie's total absorption in the opera, and her guardian was overcome by the oddest rush of tenderness toward her as he sat watching the variety of emotions playing over her face and the light from the chandeliers glancing off the bright golden curls.

For her part, Georgie was entranced. She had been sorry when Lady Wyndham recalled the earl's attention because she had been enjoying the brief moment of camaraderie between them. It had been so long since she had shared anything with anyone. Always before she had been able to count on Uncle Ned in humorous situations. When her sense of the absurd had overcome her, she would look up to see an appreciative twinkle in his own eyes and they would laugh together. She had missed this intensely when she left India. Somehow no one else ever seemed to see or enjoy the ridiculous. Alive to every nuance of the fashionable scene as she was, Lady Debenham never saw anything the least bit laughable in it. And everyone else in the *ton* seemed to treat it with equal seriousness. It had been heartening to see Brian's amused detachment, and when he had looked up and seen her, and had acknowledged their mutual reactions to the scene, she had experienced a rush of warmth and friendship that she had thought was gone forever. Georgie had felt a small pang of disappointment when the beauty had recalled his attention, but that was soon forgotten in her enjoyment of the opera.

Fortunately for him, the earl had seen *Don Giovanni* several times before, because he certainly was not allowed to pay a great deal of attention to it this time. Althea was in a talkative mood and she entertained him with a fund of scandalous stories. She did have a certain wit and could be very entertaining, though always at someone else's expense, while the gestures that accompanied these *on-dits* were as provocative as the stories themselves. Her eyes flashed, her red lips pouted, her beautiful shoulders shrugged, or the tip of her tongue ran delicately over her lips. It was not too long before her companion had almost entirely forgotten his surroundings and could think of nothing so much as the end of the performance. At the entr'acte she laid a hand on his arm, whispering huskily, "My head aches quite dreadfully. Please take me home."

"But of course. Your wish is my command." The earl, fully aware that it was quite another ache which prompted her departure, leapt up to comply, escorting her solicitously to the entrance, where he found a place for her to sit while he sent a boy in search of her carriage. Once in that vehicle, however, her languorous air and his solicitousness vanished instantly as they were drawn into a passionate embrace. It seemed no time at all before they were in Mount Street stumbling up the stairs to her perfumed boudoir.

"Are you always this insatiable?" the earl wondered aloud as he expertly undid the fastenings of her gown and pushed it to the floor.

She gazed up at him through half-closed lids, her eyes dark with desire, her breath coming in gasps. "Only where you are concerned. The others—I won't pretend there haven't been others—have been mere boys compared to you." She ran her hands over his muscular body. "They are amusing for an evening." She shrugged and her chemise slipped to join her dress on the floor. "But you, you are sensuality itself. Come." Althea fell back on silken pillows, pulling him on top of her.

Brian gave himself up to her ardor, overwhelmed by the intensity of her hunger for him. Always before he had initiated the lovemaking and led his partner to the heights of passion and satiation, but this time he followed her lead. It was a novel sensation and one he was not altogether certain he liked.

He was considering this more fully later as he staggered home in the early-morning light. The cool air was soothing on his face, still flushed from the night's amorous activities. After the close perfumed atmosphere of Althea's boudoir, the light breeze was wonderfully refreshing, and he inhaled deeply. A remarkable woman, Althea. He grinned reminiscently.

The earl had always considered himself more experienced than the next man, what with his liaisons with Indian as well as English women and his knowledge of some of the Eastern refinements in lovemaking, but Althea had introduced him to some things even he didn't know, and he'd enjoyed them thoroughly. But now that he was at leisure to think about it, he wondered. He was not jealous, nor was he shocked. He knew, had always known, the sort of woman she was. In point of fact, he had welcomed a woman who was so unabashedly sensual, who did not demand any false professions of love and undying devotion from him. Furthermore, her widowhood made her a safer partner than married women whose husbands might prove to be inconvenient or unmarried ones with designs on his title and his fortune.

Why, then, was he not exuberant this morning? Why was there a stale taste in his mouth? Perhaps it was her very hunger that made him uneasy. She seemed to desire him so much physically that she did not appear to acknowledge or care about what else he was. Brian, you are a fool, he admonished himself. One of the most beautiful women in all of London throws herself at your head, and you have to ask questions. Smiling ruefully and shaking her head, he climbed the steps to Brandon House. He nodded to the footman who opened the door, and headed to the breakfast parlor. It was early yet, but the idea of a cup of strong coffee was infinitely appealing.

Much to his astonishment, he discovered that the room was already occupied. His grandmother sat in regal solitude, sipping chocolate and reading the *Times*. "Grandmama, whatever are you doing here?"

The dowager hastily removed her spectacles and laid down her paper. "I might ask the same question of you," she responded, looking up at him with quizzical amusement. "I suspect, however, that your reasons and mine are vastly different, for I certainly have not been carousing." She sighed. "More's the pity."

He grinned. "Had I known you wished to carouse, I would certainly have invited you to carouse with me. But surprisingly enough, I wasn't carousing. I went to the opera."

She was not to be fooled. "You can't tell me, Brian Brandon, that attending any event, even one as tame as the opera, with Althea Wyndham is not carousing."

"What do you know about Althea?" Even the earl, accustomed as he was to his grandmother's acute intelligence and her impeccable sources of information, was taken aback.

"I know that she's your latest inamorata and I also know that she has decided she is going to be the next Countess of Aldringham."

Brian's dark brows drew together. He allowed his grandmother more license than he allowed most, but this was intruding too much into his affairs.

"Don't poker up at me, lad. I know you won't stand for other people interfering in your life, but I wager from the look on your face that you never thought someone like her would be trying to lure you into the parson's mousetrap."

The glowering look disappeared. "I don't know where you get your information, Grandmama"—he held up an admonitory hand—"and furthermore, I don't wish to know, but if the first half is so accurate, there must be some grain of truth to the second."

She smiled complacently and nodded. "You won't thank me to tell you this, but she ain't the woman for you."

"And do you have in mind the type of woman who would suit me?" His voice was dangerously quiet.

The dowager knew herself to be treading on hazardous ground, but she was too concerned for her grandson's happiness to back out now, all for the want of a little backbone. There was no doubt that Lady Wyndham was beautiful, sophisticated, passionate, and as intelligent as most of the women of the *ton*, and the fact that she was very much her own mistress would appeal to Brian, who had always loathed those women who clung as his mother did, but she lacked the kindness, the sensibility, and the intellect to appreciate her grandson's true nature. "She's a beauty, I'll grant you that, and enough to set most men's pulses racing, but you need someone who is more than that."

"More than Althea, Grandmama? I'm not sure that even I—" he began.

"I don't mean *that* way, silly boy." She rapped his knuckles with the newspaper. "You need someone who will challenge your mind and your spirit of adventure, but someone who is kind and loving as well."

The earl remained unconvinced.

"Well, do you love her?"

"Love Althea? Good heavens, no!" The earl was thunderstruck.

"Well, there you are, then. No point in getting leg-shackled unless you're head over heels. Life is too short to spend it with someone you ain't in love with."

"But, Grandmama, I'm not thinking of getting married," he protested.

"Maybe *you* ain't," she responded darkly, "but what do you have to say in the matter?"

At this juncture Simpson appeared bearing a steaming pot of coffee and the dowager retreated behind the paper while Brian applied himself to eggs and a rasher of bacon that a footman had placed in front of him.

12

Georgie was also getting off to an early start that morning. Despite Alice's frequent admonitions that "Ladies lie in bed till all hours, 'specially when they have been at the opera or such like the night before, and they wait till their maids bring them their morning chocolate with the mail," Georgie continued to rise at at unfashionably early hour, proceeding to the morning room, where Wilson would bring her coffee. There, instead of poring over the gilt-edged invitations that came by the score to Lady Debenham's establishment, she would peruse the *Times* and then pick up *Blackwood's* or the *Edinburgh Review*. The lightest reading in which she indulged was Ackermann's *Repository,* and even there, much to the dismay of her aunt, who insisted that its only value lay in its fashion plates and its "General Observations on Fashion and Dress," Georgie skipped over those and turned straight to the "Intelligence, Literary and Scientific." This morning she had just finished reading a review of Sir Thomas Lawrence's portraits and was proceeding to a discussion of Mr. Haydon's picture being exhibited at the Egyptian Hall when the dappled sunlight filtering through the trees became too much for her resolution to spend the morning indoors catching up on her reading. "Botheration!" she exclaimed to no one in particular as she consigned poor Ackermann to a pile of unread reviews.

She rose and rang for Wilson to request that Lakshmi be brought round and that the groom Digby be prepared to accompany her to the park. Georgie sighed. She would have preferred to ride alone with her thoughts in the freshness of the morning, but little as she cared for all the strictures of the *ton*, she knew without being told that a groom was essential if one had no more suitable escort. And there were those sticklers who might even remark on a young lady's taking a morning ride with only a groom as a companion, but such people were unlikely to be abroad at such an early hour. Truth to tell, she had not been allowed to ride alone even in India, but that had been more as a protection to her than for her reputation.

There were certain advantages to civilization, however. Even Georgie, who had little use for the finer points of fashion, though she always looked well groomed, had to admit that the new riding habit was vastly becoming. It was a delicate lavender, which showed off the brilliance of her complexion. The lace around the high collar emphasized her delicate features, while the small round hat and the braid up the front lent her a jaunty air.

Lakshmi's ears pricked up when she saw her mistress and she snorted eagerly, snuffling at her side in search of the lumps of sugar Georgie always carried for her. "You are truly dreadful, Lakshmi, and I am afraid your ways are as cozening as those of the worst coquette in the *beau monde,*" Georgie scolded. The mare's only response was to butt her head against her mistress's shoulder. "Very well, then." Georgie produced the desired lump of sugar and patted her nose. "See that in return you behave on our way to the park instead of taking exception to every cart horse you encounter."

As Digby tossed Georgie into the saddle, she once again blessed the earl for having provided her with such a wonderful way to forget about the confines of her new life. As they made their way through the streets, she reflected on the many and varied sides she had seen in her guardian. There was the peremptory head of an ancient aristocratic household who resented anyone's questioning his autocratic way of running things, but who could at the same time be an affectionate brother. There was the reckless adventurer whom she'd glimpsed in India, and the amused man of the world she'd seen at the opera. And finally, there was someone who took the time to observe the type of person she was and who was thoughtful enough to hit upon a way to make her happy. Truly, he was something of a puzzle and she was never exactly certain which of his many roles he would be assuming whenever she encountered him.

It looked as though she were going to have to figure that out in short order, as it appeared that the earl was heading directly toward her. There was no mistaking the broad shoulders and the erect carriage, as well as the magnificent mount he sat so easily, even if he weren't accompanied by a small figure on a pony whose posture so very closely mirrored that of his elder brother.

It was Percy who first recognized her. "I say, it's Georgie and Lakshmi!" he exclaimed, urging his pony toward her. "Well, have you tried out her paces, is she well behaved, is she a sweet goer?" The questions poured from him.

Georgie laughed. "Yes to all of that, but I confess to wishing to know how she would do if I could truly give her her head. Trotting sedately through the park is all very well, but I am itching for a gallop across the countryside and a few fences and hedges to jump."

"I know," the little boy sighed. "Lizzy was cock-a-hoop at coming to London, but if you ask me, I find it sadly flat."

Georgie smiled sympathetically. "So do I."

"You do? I thought ladies liked to shop and go to balls and things."

"Not this lady," his brother remarked as he approached at a more sedate pace. "Good morning, Georgie. You're up betimes for someone who was at the opera last evening."

"I might say the same for you, for I am tolerably certain that you were out far later than I," she retorted.

He raised his eyebrows. "Touché, sprite. I would have stayed abed this morning except for this young cub here. He is adamant about daily matutinal exercise and it seems no one will do for a companion except me."

Percy was still digesting Georgie's confession to being bored in London. "If you don't like going to parties, what do you wish to do?" he wondered. A lady who was not interested in fashion or social events and who didn't constantly complain of her nerves was new to his experience and he could not imagine what such a person would do.

"I should say that I probably wish to do many of the same

things you do—ride, and explore—but chiefly I should like
to return to India." This last was added with a darkling look
at Percy's brother.

"I say, I should like to go to India too. I would hunt tigers
and ride elephants and . . . But ladies can't do those things."

"They most certainly can and do," Georgie rejoined with
some spirit, "but I want to return to India because I wish
to try to grow tea."

"Tea?" the borthers echoed with one voice.

Georgie's chin rose. "Yes, tea," she replied with a
challenging look at the earl.

If Percy's interest was beginning to wane once the topics
of elephants and tigers were dropped, his elder brother's was
fairly caught. "Why tea?" he inquired, looking at her
curiously.

"From what I can determine, the climate in the hills is
no different from that in China. Certainly there is much
demand for it here, and it could be sold more cheaply if it
were shipped direct to England from English-owned lands
rather than paying for so many transactions along the way
as is done now. Besides which, coming from a country where
we are already established, the trade is much more likely
to be reliable and therefore more profitable."

Brian was highly intrigued. "You have it all worked out,
I perceive."

"Yes, I do," Georgie responded firmly. "And if I am
unable to carry out my scheme immediately, why, I shall
wait a few years and by then I shall know that much more
about tea cultivation."

"By the time you are twenty-five, you should be quite an
expert." There was a challenging gleam in the earl's eye.

Georgie took instant umbrage, but managed to keep herself
tolerably well in hand. "If that is how long I must wait, then
I shall, for I don't mean to be put off."

"Peace, sprite. I was only teasing. In fact, it sounds like
a very good scheme. Shall I see what I can discover about
the feasibility of such a thing? I am tolerably well acquainted
with Lord Petersham. While it is true that he is mostly a
connoisseur, he does at least have a vast store of knowledge

and has come into contact with many experts in the pursuit of his passion.''

Georgie was somewhat taken aback by this abrupt change of face. "Why . . . why, thank you. You are most kind.''

"It's not kindness, sprite. Good ideas ought to be encouraged.''

"No matter where they originate?'' she demanded in a rallying tone.

He gave a shout of laughter. "You are incorrigible, are you not?''

She tilted her head to smile at him. "So I have been told.''

"And undoubtedly many times over.'' He grinned at her.

"Yes,'' she sighed, "Aunt Aurelia is forever telling me I show a sad lack of sensibility.''

"But aside from laughing at me, you behaved entirely properly at the opera last evening. Did you enjoy it?''

"Oh, yes, ever so much. The music was enchanting and the performers beyond anything I have ever seen,'' she replied, her face alight with enthusiasm.

Here Percy, who had remained respectfully silent for far longer than was usual for him, interrupted. "Oh, opera, I don't know how you can stomach such dull stuff—all those screeching females.'' He spoke in the world-weary tones of one who has endured countless such evenings, when in fact he had heard only operatic airs sung at a musicale his mother had held at Aldringham. "If you want to see a real spectacle, you should visit Astley's.''

"Astley's?'' Georgie was mystified.

"You have never heard of Astley's Royal Amphitheater?'' Percy could not fathom such ignorance.

Georgie shook her head.

"They have the most wonderful equestrians, who can perform all sort of feats, and the horses are magnificent. They can do tricks as well. Right now they are enacting Xaia of China with the ascent of the Calmuc cavalry, the rescue of the prince by his horse, as well as the splendid horsemanship of Mr. Brown. Brian has promised to take me and I can hardly wait to go.''

Georgie was impressed. "Gracious, I can't conceive of such a thing. It must truly be a sight to behold."

"Would you care to join us?" If asked, the earl would not have been able to say what had prompted him to issue such an invitation. Any young lady of his acquaintance would have been highly insulted at the implication that she had not outgrown such childish amusements ages ago.

But Georgie was not any young lady. "Oh, I should love to!" A more thoughtful look crossed her face and she hesitated. "Only . . . only I shouldn't like to intrude in a special party that you and Percy have got up."

"Oh, no," Percy assured her. "The more, the merrier, and Lizzy has already scorned it as a 'nursery-party excursion.' Besides, I believe the horses are magnificent. There are also tumblers, rope dancers, and a pantomine. We are certain to have a bang-up time."

The earl added his voice to that of his brother. "We should feel quite selfish indulging in such an orgy of amusement by ourselves. Percy will have a companion to share his thrill at seeing it all for the first time, and I shall have someone to talk to when he becomes so excited he can't speak a word. Do say you'll come."

Presented with such a genuine desire for her company, as well as the prospect of a more lively evening's entertainment than she ordinarily endured, Georgie could not resist. The idea of having two people who wanted her along for herself and who wished to share something with her made her feel very special and she groped for the words that would convey her gratitude. The best she could muster was, "Thank you ever so much," but the look on her face spoke volumes.

Though at the outset he had not been entirely aware of his reasons for wishing her to join them, Brian discovered that the more he thought about it, the more he was hoping she would say yes. There had been an eagerness in her curiosity about Astley's that he had sensed almost unconsciously, but suddenly he had envisioned her as she must always have been, ready for anything but too shy and too independent to demand attention or ask for any special favors, and he found himself wanting to gratify her every whim and make her eyes shine all the time the way they were now as she listened to Percy's further descriptions of the delights in store for her.

Georgie was not particularly looking forward to the entertainment projected for that evening. It was to be her first experience at Almack's and, from her aunt's glowing references to the place as the temple at which polite society worshiped, she was not at all certain how she would be able to support an evening whose only activities were dancing and the ruthless observation of other people. Familiar enough with the *ton* to realize how fortunate she was to have an aunt on intimate terms with Mrs. Drummond Burrell and Princess Esterhazy, Georgie was fully aware how enviable a position she was in and that most young women spent a goodly part of their Seasons trying desperately to obtain the vouchers for which she cared so little. Some of these unwelcome thoughts must have showed on her face, for her riding companion leaned over to ask, "Why so serious all of a sudden?"

Georgie sighed. "I was thinking about this evening. My aunt and I are to attend Almack's, and I would far rather stay at home. Aunt Aurelia is all that is kind, and she knows everyone who is anyone in the Upper Ten Thousand, but somehow she doesn't include among her acquaintances anyone that is very interesting to talk to, and I fear that, as I don't know the latest *on-dits* or what is the latest rage, I am an equally dull companion for them."

He smiled. "You can always take advantage of its main function, which is to serve as the marriage market for the *ton,* and look for a husband. The conversation and dancing are purely secondary, you know."

The mutinous expression he had seen several times before spread over Georgie's face. "I have no more wish to be married than you do," she responded stiffly.

"And what makes you think I don't wish to be married?" The earl was amused.

"Well, just look at you. Anyone can see that you like beautiful ladies too much to be married."

Brian burst out laughing. "You are nothing if not

outspoken, sprite. And what makes you think that 'liking beautiful ladies' precludes marriage? I, for one, intend to marry someone that I fall in love with, and there is no way to discover someone to fall in love with unless one looks, you know. You should do the same. You might enjoy it. Falling in love can be one of life's most delightful experiences, I assure you." His amusement deepened as he saw the look of distaste on her face occasioned by his last remark.

"You aren't talking about love, but about lust. I don't know anything about lust, but I do know about love, and that isn't love," Georgie declared stoutly.

"Oho, and what do you know about love, little one? That is a strange stricture coming from one who would rather have a brother or a dog than a husband and who has other plans for her future," he teased.

"I loved my parents and I loved Uncle Ned, and I don't think that love for one's husband should be so very different. It's being comfortable with someone. It's having someone to talk to who shares one's interests. It's having a friend. It's . . ." Georgie paused for breath.

The earl regarded her closely. The amused look had disappeared and his expression became unfathomable. "That's asking a great deal, sprite. I doubt if it is possible to find such a thing." The teasing note had entirely left his voice, to be replaced by one that was serious to the point of sounding wistful.

"Why ever shouldn't it be possible?" Georgie wanted to know. "Of course I was very young when they died, but Papa and Mama were like that."

The earl was silent, remembering the dashing Mad Jack and his beautiful wife. There had been something special about their relationship. "Yeees," he answered slowly, "they were. But your parents, sprite, were two very unusual people. Most people count themselves fortunate if they are leg-shackled to someone they respect, which is rare enough, and love is beside the point. But look around you—do you see any love in any of the couples you know?"

Georgie hesitated. Her acquaintance with the fashionable

world was not great, but she was forced to admit that of all the husbands and wives she knew, the greater portion were indifferent, if not downright hostile, to each other. "I fail to see why people get married, then," she maintained vigorously. "I should much prefer being alone to spending my life with someone with whom I had as little in common as most husbands and wives seem to."

"You are forgetting that very few women, or even men, are as independent as you. Society is made uneasy by those who avoid the parson's mousetrap. And most people are so desperately afraid of being alone or causing comment that they will do anything, short of murder, to avoid it." A harsh, cynical note had crept into the earl's voice, which was reflected by the mocking bitter smile in his eyes.

Georgie regarded him curiously. She had never seen quite that expression before, and she wondered about it. Sometime, long ago, he must have been hurt very badly, she thought. All of a sudden—it was the oddest sensation—she found herself longing to comfort him. She, who knew so little of the social world, found herself wanting to reassure him that there were people, few and far between though they might be, who adhered to their own values and not society's, who cared about others for who they were and not what they were, people who could be trusted and believed in.

The intensity of her gaze brought him up with a start. There was something sympathetic and, strangely enough, pitying in it, as though, young as she was, she understood all the disappointments he had suffered, all the people he had put faith in, only to find that petty social concerns instead of their hearts governed their lives. "Don't refine upon it too much, sprite. Those who marry because of society's dictates are usually satisfied with their lots. And"—he grinned—"the search for a life companion can be most enjoyable, whether or not you find one, believe me." He held up a hand. "I know, I know, it may be lust and not love, but lust can be extraordinarily pleasant, you know."

"I would *not* know," was the frosty rejoinder.

"What, have you never secretly longed to kiss some dashing young buck, never even nursed an unrequited passion

for a handsome soldier in a scarlet coat? I thought these were
a requisite part of all young ladies' existences."

"I am not all young ladies. Nor, I am happy to say, have
I ever been so idiotic," Georgie defended himself.

"If I weren't aware of it before, it is being rapidly borne
in on me that you are not," he agreed. "Come now, don't
poker up. It doesn't become you," he admonished.

Here he was interrupted again by Percy, who, having
ridden ahead and then returned to them for a third time,
exclaimed in exasperation, "Do come along, Brian. You're
riding like a regular slowtop."

"Very well, cawker, we shall go at a slapping pace as is
allowed in this respectable location. Come along, Georgie.
I want to make certain Lakshmi is all that the man who sold
her to me claimed her to be." Brian dug his heels into Caesar
and trotted on down the path.

The rest of the conversation turned to the less dangerous
topic of horseflesh, and the three rode companionably to the
gate, where they separated. But Georgie was not allowed
to escape unscathed. Grasping Lakshmi's bridle, the earl
leaned over. "Do not be so quick to dismiss this love or lust
or whatever you call it, as foolish, sprite. It can be very
pleasant, enlightening even, and it is no bad thing to have
one's sensibilities heightened. You'll see."

With that, he beckoned to Percy and they cantered off,
leaving Georgie prey to a variety of emotions, chief among
which was exasperation at this certainty not only that such
feelings were to be welcomed but also that she, Georgie
Southwold, would succumb to them. Giving a snort of
indignation, she dug her heels into Lakshmi's flank and
trotted toward home at a brisk pace, resolving even more
strongly that she would not give in to such foolishness.

13

Her determination to avoid this idiocy, especially at that noted scene of marital intrigue, Almack's, was such that even Cedric, who accompanied the ladies in their assault on the venerable institution, remarked on it. "Come now, Georgie, no need to look so Friday-faced. Of course the refreshments are meager and quite dreadful, the patronesses odiously starched up, the young ladies awkward and shy and the young bucks overeager, but it is the premier haunt of the *ton* and you can learn how to go on there better than anywhere else. Besides, having secured a voucher from Mrs. Drummond Burrell and as an heiress to ten thousand a year, you need do nothing more than appear and you will be proclaimed a resounding success. And the sooner you are safely through your first Season, the sooner you can leave off dressing in insipid white muslin and wear something more suited to you. Not that you are not all that is elegant, but . . ." He cocked his head and scrutinized her carefully. "Yes, you need something with a touch of color to give you more éclat."

Georgie was not at all certain just how to respond to such a remark, but she was grateful for his escort and she had been touched by the bouquet of pink roses in a filigree holder that he had so obviously selected to match the trimmings on her gown. "Why, thank you, Ceddie, but I hope that this will be my only Season."

"Your only Season?" Her cousin was aghast. "Why, you have only just begun. Surely you can't mean to bury yourself in the country the rest of your life."

"No." Georgie had to smile at the patent horror of his expression. "As soon as I come of age, I plan to return to India."

"India?" If Cedric was horrified at the thought of a rural

existence, this was beyond his comprehension. "My dear girl, what will you do? Surely you'll go quite mad living with all those natives and having no contact with society."

"I shan't, for I shall be fully occupied taking care of Uncle Ned's business and seeing if I can cultivate tea."

"Never say so, Georgie," he moaned. "Not only India, but trade. You mustn't breathe a word of this scheme to a soul. I should have known, though. You really are Mad Jack's daughter."

Georgie could see he was truly upset. "Don't worry, Ceddie. You needn't distress yourself. I shan't tell a soul. And if my schemes succeed, I shall take care not to claim kinship with you," she soothed.

Cedric Fotheringay might be the soul of fashion, but he did have a kind heart and he hastened to reassure her, "I shall always be happy to own you as my cousin, Georgie. I know your family can't help their madness. I just wished for you to be aware that what was eccentric but charming in your father would be fatal to the existence of his young unmarried daughter. Undoubtedly you will go your own way—the Southwolds always do—but I am trying to save you from immediate social disaster."

Here they were interrupted by Georgie's aunt. "Georgie, here is Mrs. Drummond Burrell coming over on purpose to see us. Do try for a little countenance."

Georgie, watching that august lady as she made her imposing progress across the room, nodding ever so slightly here and there to a few favored acquaintances, wondered that people who were blessed with money, titles, and looks could accord so much power to someone who appeared to be outstanding in nothing so much as sheer disdain for her fellow creatures. Some of her thoughts must have been reflected in her face, for the haughty patroness found herself subject to a scrutiny as critical as her own when Georgie was presented to her.

Oddly enough, she did not appear to take it amiss. "Well, Aurelia, I can see you have brought out your niece at last, and she should do well. However, she does not appear to be impressed by what she sees here."

"Oh, no, Georgie is a little shy, but she is delighted with Almack's I assure you," Lady Debenham hastened to explain.

But Almack's most exclusive patroness was not to be put off, and turned to Georgie. "And what do *you* think of all this, child?" she demanded.

Georgie, who at first had possessed the grace to look conscious at Mrs. Drummond Burrell's remarks, now raised her chin. "I think it does very well for those who wish an introduction to the *ton.*" Try as she might, she was unable to keep a slightly defensive note out of her voice.

"But you aspire to higher things, eh?" her interlocuter prodded.

"Let us just say that I aspire to different things, and if that offends people, why then I beg their pardons." The defiant note was stronger now and the glint of battle was in Georgie's eye. She had agreed to try London society for her Uncle Ned's sake, but she had not agreed to having her motives examined and she resented the barefaced interrogation.

"Georgiana, how can you say such things when you know you are—" her aunt broke in, in distress.

"Never mind, Aurelia, the child has the good sense not to be impressed merely because everyone else is. It is refreshing in one so young and inexperienced. If there is anything I cannot abide, it is a toad-eater." And with this final pronouncement she left them to continue her stately promenade.

Georgie barely had time to recover herself before they were interrupted again, this time in a far more welcome fashion. She would have been glad of anyone who could spare her from the exclamations so obviously hovering on her aunt's tongue, but when she saw that it was Lizzy she was truly delighted.

"Georgie, I am so pleased to see you. I meant to speak to you directly you arrived, but Grandmama would not let me approach when she saw Mrs. Drummond Burrell making her way toward you. Are you nearly dead with fright? I should be ready to sink through the floor if I had to talk with her, but you appear to have held up very well. I am so relieved that it is Lady Cowper that is Mama's friend instead of that high stickler.'' Lizzy could have chattered on in this vein indefinitely, but a quizzical look and a cough reminded her of her companion. "Oh, heavens, I do run on, and I am completely forgetting Grandmama." Lizzy was the picture of contrition as she made her second-favorite family member known to her friend.

Studying Lizzy's grandmother, Georgie found it difficult to believe that anyone could be unaware of her for long. Though tiny and frail with age, the dowager Countess of Aldringham was a presence not easily ignored. The snapping dark eyes, which missed nothing, hinted at a spirit to be reckoned with, an intimation borne out by her next words. "I have been wanting to meet the gel who not only broke straws with my grandson but also got the better of him."

Not at all sure whether this was a feat to be proud of, and intensely aware of her aunt's curious gaze, Georgie remained silent, not knowing where to look or how to reply.

"No need to look so conscious, my dear. I like a gel with spirit, and so does my grandson. It's just that he is so accustomed to flouting everyone else's authority, he doesn't know how to take it when it's his authority being flouted. Come, tell me about yourself. I've heard a deal about you from Lizzy and Percy, but I wish to know more about you from yourself. I always did have a partiality for your father—a handsome scamp if there ever was one—and your mother was certainly the most beautiful of the belles that came out that Season. What a dashing couple they made." The dowager smiled encouragingly at her new acquaintance.

"Oh, did you know Papa and Mama? I should so love to hear about them." Georgie's confusion disappeared in her eagerness to hear stories about her parents.

"Oh, yes, I knew Mad Jack, he was always ripe for any mischief. I used to wish my own son had been more like him instead of the confounded slowtop that he turned out to be. Why, I remember the time he and your mother . . ." The dowager smiled reminiscently, but whatever recollections she was about to impart were cut short by the appearance of her grandson.

If the Earl of Aldringham was impressive on a horse, he was even more so in a ballroom, where the severity of his attire made him a commanding presence. A head taller than most of the men around him, with a powerful figure that owed nothing to the tailor's art, he was the cynosure of all eyes as he made his way across the room. The whiteness of his cravat emphasized the swarthiness of his complexion, and the elegant cut of the dark coat stretched across broad shoulders called attention to his proud carriage.

As heads turned, Georgie could not help glancing in that direction and, watchin him out of the corner of her eye, she decided that, unlike other men, the assurance in his bearing came from confidence in himself as a person capable of dealing with any situation, rather than an awareness of his great wealth or the importance of his social position. His complete disregard for those whose fawning expressions acknowledged him as a leader of the *ton* made her suspect that he saw himself simply as Brian Brandon, a man resourceful enough to win a reputation and fortune for himself in a foreign and hostile land rather than the Earl of Aldringham, a person of rank and privilege. These thoughts were soon banished by memories of their most recent conversation, which were uncomfortable enough to bring a darkling look to her face as he approached.

Remarking the rebellious set to her jaw, Brian was able to hazard a fairly accurate guess as to his ward's feelings, and immediately he set about to confound them. Having acknowledged his sister and grandmother and paid his respects to her companions, he turned to Georgie with a most earnest look on his face. "I have been making inquiries of Lord Petersham as to your scheme to grow tea in India, Lady Georgiana, and I find him most intrigued and eager to discuss it with you. I had hoped he might be here so I could introduce you." It amused the earl no end to see the blank look on Georgie's face. He could tell from the set of her shoulders and her rigid posture that she had been prepared to take up their argument where they had left off, and that his omission of any reference to that, as well as the respect he appeared to have accorded her project, effectually took the wind out of her sails, leaving her with no response except a stammered "Thank you."

Having caught her by surprise, Brian took advantage of her confusion by asking her to dance, knowing full well that if she had been totally in possession of herself she would have thought up some excuse not to. As it was, she faltered. "Why, thank you, but Uncle Ned's death, it's been such a short time . . ."

Here her aunt came to the earl's rescue. "Nonsense, my child. It has been an age, and he was not your father, after all. Besides, it happened in India." She spoke as though the distance in miles and cultures could make up for any possible disrespectful haste.

"Do go, Georgie," Ceddie chimed in. "Why, even if your uncle had been dead only a fortnight, the honor of being led onto the floor by such an eligible partner would erase all possible objections in the minds of the highest sticklers."

Outmaneuvered on all sides, Georgie gave in with as good grace as she could muster, only to find her escort smiling down at her with a disturbingly perceptive light in his eyes. "I shan't eat you, you know," he whispered softly as he took her hand.

"Pooh! I am not afraid of that," Georgie began indignantly.

"Then what are you afraid of?" He cocked a quizzical dark brow.

"I am not afraid of anything and I quite fail to see why I should be or why you should think I am," she defended herself.

"Then why that uneasy look, as though I were something nasty you had just discovered under a rock?"

She gave a spurt of laughter. "I didn't look at you that way."

He nodded approvingly. "That's much better, and you certainly did." Then, on a plaintive note he continued, "I am not at all used to being looked at in such a way. If you keep it up, I could very likely go into a decline."

This infelicitous remark brought back their discussion in the park, and the rebellious look returned. "You have hundreds of ladies looking at you in the way you wish to be looked at, my lord. It would be a most salutary experience for you to have someone who didn't do so."

"And how is that, sprite?" There was a dangerous glint in his eyes.

"You know very well how they look at you—the way Lady Jersey looked at you earlier. You are conceited enough as it is, and you don't need me to add to it."

"Why, you jade," he gasped indignantly. "I am *not* conceited."

Georgie was somewhat abashed at the vigor of his protest. "Well . . . maybe not conceited exactly," she admitted. "But you do take feminine admiration as your due, you know."

It was his turn to look sheepish. "Perhaps you are right. Perhaps I am something of a coxcomb, and I should be worried about myself if I thought their attention were directed at me, but I assure you it is not. It is at who I am, a man of rank and fortune . . . and a bachelor besides," he added somewhat grimly.

Privately Georgie, having observed the languishing looks cast in his direction, thought it had less to do with his social position than with his outstanding physical presence, and the half-challenging, half-seductive look in his eyes, but it would never do to admit such a thing, so she adopted a sweetly sympathetic air. "Poor Lamb Brandon, such a trial to be so sought after."

While her tones were those of pure commiseration, her eyes were dancing and he was not fooled for an instant. "I *am* such a coxcomb, then." He chuckled. "But I shan't be for long with you to ride roughshod over me, sprite. Why, even Lizzy isn't as hard on me as you are."

She tilted her head, smiling mischievously at him, and all of a sudden he was struck with the sense of how delightful it was to be teased by a partner instead of seduced by one. The more he considered it, the more the earl realized that he could not recall when he had enjoyed a dance more or felt more comfortable with a woman.

And that brought him up short. That he, Brian Brandon, lover of scores of women from all levels of society and an equal variety of cultures, should, by dint of feeling so at ease with one woman—no, not a woman, a mere chit of a girl—come to recognize that he did not feel that way with the others, was most enlightening. Despite his vast experience, which had taught him just how attractive he was to the opposite sex, he had always at the back of his mind mistrusted this attraction, attributing it in part to his wealth or his rank. Therefore, he had never completely relaxed with any woman. Certainly he had been tantalized, challenged, excited, or intoxicated by them, but always he had been wondering just exactly why they had sought him out—was it for pleasure, vanity, the opportunity to relieve the tedium of their existences? Whatever the reason, it would have been gratified by any reasonably attractive man of his station. Fully aware of the transitory nature of such relations, his flirts had always been careful to flatter him, to cater to his every whim. Now, here was someone who refused to do that, someone who recognized his faults along with the rest and did not scruple to say so.

Oddly enough, it was just this acknowledgment of his imperfections that made him trust Georgie. And the fact that she was able to risk his friendship by pointing them out to him and teasing him proved that she cared more about him for his own sake than she valued his attention to her. That she dared to be critical of him showed a greater concern for the state of his soul than for his position in life, and he liked that. The earl experienced a rush of gratitude mixed with a tenderness for his companion, who could be at one moment independent and awake on all suits and the next as innocent and unsure as the little girl she had been when he first met her. Brian smiled to himself at the memory. Even then, so many years ago, she had been the same mixture of innocence and independence, wary and critical one minute and trusting the next.

Lost in his thoughts, he had been moving mechanically through the figures of the dance and he was unaware of his silence until she brought him up short. ''I have little in the

way of feminine vanity, my lord, but, having been informed
by my cousin how much social cachet has been conferred
on me by being solicited by you for a dance, I must confide
my fears for my reputation. If you continue to stare so fixedly
into space, all and sundry will think you find me a dead bore
with no wit or conversation. And as I am no diamond,
undoubtedly I shall be ruined in the eyes of the *ton*."

"I am sorry, sprite. I was thinking." He smiled contritely.

"So I should hope. And if your mind were on anything
less serious than the state of the nation or the perfectibility
of human nature, I should be grievously offended, so
abstracted as you were," Georgie responded with some
asperity.

He grinned. "Ever the critic, sprite. You would be well
served if I were to tell you that I was thinking of you."

"Of me?" Her astonishment and disbelief were as
complete as they were endearing.

The earl could not name another woman who would not
automatically have assumed him to be thinking of her, or
at least have expected him to maintain it as a polite fiction.
"Yes, of you. I was thinking how little you have changed
since I first met you. How you are as forthright now as you
were then."

Georgie blushed and hung her head.

"Don't look so conscious, sprite. I find it refreshing to
know there is someone who will always say what she is
thinking, to discover someone that the world has not trans-
formed as she grew up. Stay as you are, sprite. You are a
rare creature."

She smiled ruefully. "So I am told, and I am afraid it
causes Aunt Aurelia no end of worry."

"We shall have to reassure her on that score. Despite your
cousin Cedric's claims, your dancing with me is nothing
compared to the favorable impression you made on Grandmama. You have obviously won her approval, and believe
me, more reputations are won or lost in the drawing rooms
of the town tabbies than in the clubs of St. James. If Grandmama were to tell one of her cronies that you are a 'pretty
behaved gel,' your success would be more assured than if

you were declared an Incomparable by all the bucks who frequent White's, Boodle's or Brooks's.''

He led her back to the little coterie where Cedric was regaling a round-eyed Lizzy with tales of the eccentricities of the *ton* while the dowager and Lady Debenham discussed the upcoming events of the Season, arguing as to which were likely to be the most brilliant.

"Ah, there you are, Georgiana. We have been putting our heads together, the countess and I, and since Lizzy's mama is too often unwell to accompany her to these things and she herself is inclined to tire easily, I told her I should be delighted to have Elizabeth accompany us." Lady Debenham looked as proud as though the idea had been all of her own making, but one glance toward Lizzy's mischievous countenance and Georgie knew, as she had suspected all along, the identity of the true originator.

"A capital scheme," the earl broke in, "as then my two most irksome responsibilities will at least be in one place and easier to keep under close scrutiny." He was watching Georgie as he said this, and her swift challenging glance revealed that his remark had hit home. He chuckled.

His sister, however, was a more worthy opponent. "Then we shall have to see to it, brother dear, that we provide you with every opportunity to prove yourself capable of rescuing us from even the most disastrous of situations."

Georgie laughed. Her own independence was too dear for her to view it with any humor, and she greatly admired her friend's impudent insouciance, telling herself that, given the rigors of the Season, she would do well to copy it and cultivate it.

"Relax, sprite, I was only bantering." The earl could see that he had touched a sensitive issue. "And to show you that as guardian I have more to offer you than I take from you, let me remind you of my promise to teach you Sanskrit and invite you to call on us tomorrow. I have collected quite an unusual library of Indian works in both English and Sanskrit at Brandon House, which I believe would interest you."

Lizzy could not help but add her entreaties. "Oh, yes, do come, Georgie. The pictures in them are perfectly exquisite, so that even I like to look at them, though I don't pretend to understand a word in them."

Georgie was mollified. "Why, thank you. I believe I would like that. That is—" she turned to her aunt—"if I may have the carriage."

"Why, of course, dear child." If Lady Debenham had had qualms about the reputation of her niece's guardian, they seemed to have disappeared with the prospect of what such an advantageous connection could do for her young relative. Highly attuned to every nuance of the *ton*, she had been well aware of the envious looks cast at Georgie as the earl had led her onto the dance floor. And she had also observed the heightened interest with which the eligible bachelors and the inveterate matchmakers had watched as the two of them had carried on what appeared to be a most interesting conversation. That, coupled with the unlooked-for but welcome attention of that former leader of fashion, the dowager Countess of Aldringham, made her acquiesce to her niece's request with alacrity.

Meanwhile, another acute observer was taking in the significance of the scene. The sharp eyes of the dowager, more alert than ever where the welfare of her loved ones was concerned, had watched the interchanges between her grandson and his ward with greatest interest. No one, with the possible exception of his irrepressible sister, had ever dared to stand up to Brian Brandon, much less tease him, but judging from the expressions on both of their faces as they had danced the quadrille, Lady Georgiana Southwold had done just that. That her grandson was going to share his precious library with anyone, much less a young woman, was little short of astounding. Truly, this was an acquaintance that bore watching. She hadn't enjoyed herself so much since her husband had died. The inconvenience of the journey had been worth it alone for the sight of her daughter-in-law's discomfiture at her arrival, and she was genuinely interested in her grandchildren, two of whom, if she were not mistaken, were approaching very critical periods in their lives.

14

Well aware that he had far more equipages at his disposal than did Lady Debenham, the earl had sent a footman around with a note instructing Lady Georgiana to be ready to be collected at two o'clock. Independent as always, Georgie was ready to take instant umbrage with such high-handed interference in her affairs, but was soon talked out of her ill humor by her aunt. "For my part, I think it excessively kind in him to realize that a widow such as I does not keep a large stable and is dependent upon her carriage. And I had rather thought of going to see Madame Celeste. There is something in my new cashmere morning dress that I cannot like . . . perhaps a little too much fullness in the sleeves . . ." Lady Debenham gazed absently at the figurines on the mantel as she tried to think just what it was that was amiss with the offending garment.

"Brian always was thoughtful to a fault, as I recall—odd in one who was forever getting into scrapes and was at daggers drawn with every master from the headmaster on down," Cedric remarked, crossing one lemon-pantalooned leg over the other. He had been sauntering along in the vague direction of St. James, with no very clear objective in mind, when he had decided it might be pleasant to stop in and see the ladies in Berkeley Square to discuss the previous evening. He had heard a perfectly delicious *on-dit* that he was simply dying to share with someone about how the new Lady Faversham's father had tried to offer Lady Jersey five thousand pounds to ensure his daughter a voucher for Almack's. Cedric had his doubts about the young viscount's choice of such a vulgar young woman for his wife, but now the reasons for his alliance with a cit's daughter were abundantly clear. For his part, Cedric had had no idea, nor had anyone else, for that matter, that the Favershams were at the *point non plus*.

"Never say so." By this time, Lady Debenham had decided that it was most definitely the sleeves on her dress that were wrong, and she leaned forward eager for news. "I should never have guessed. They were keeping all their carriages and still frequented the best tradesmen. Why—"

Here Georgie, never the one for gossip, especially if there were a topic of greater interest at hand, broke in, "Did you know the Lord Brandon when you were young, then, Cedric?"

"Lord, yes. He was ahead of me at school. Of course, he's years older than I, but one couldn't be in the same county with Brian for long and not know he was there," Cedric replied airily.

"Was he very bad, then?" she asked eagerly.

"Bad? No, not exactly bad. He was just adventurous and ripe for any mischief. Actually, I believe he was quite clever, but he would rather have died than be considered bookish, and he chafed under the petty rules and regimentation. He fell into scrapes out of pure boredom. We younger boys admired him tremendously. There was nothing he wouldn't do, but he was always kind to us and protected us from the bullies who liked to pick on the weaker boys. He wasn't at all like the other boys, who treated us like lackeys. Said he didn't like the way the masters treated him and he wasn't going to do the same to someone else just because he was younger. He was sent down my second year, though—something about rabbits in a Latin recitation or a pig in the headmaster's room—I forgot which, or maybe it was both."

"What happened after that? Did he—?" Georgie's question was cut short by a discreet cough from Wilson.

"Excuse me, Miss Georgie, but the Earl of Aldringham's carriage is here." He was about to add that it was best not to keep such prime bits of blood standing too long, but Georgie had already leapt up and ran to get her pelisse.

She received a warm welcome when Simpson ushered her into the drawing room at Grosvenor Square. There was a chill in the air and a fire had been lit. Lizzy was ensconced in a chair near it, poring through *La Belle Assemblée*, while Percy was lining toy soldiers into battalions along the patterns of the rug. The dowager and her other grandson were deep in discussion of the depressed state of the woolen manufacturing industry and its implications for the rest of the nation. But no one was so engrossed in his or her own particular activity that they didn't all look up, eager for distraction, upon hearing her name pronounced in Simpson's sepulchral tones.

"Georgie!" Lizzy and Percy exclaimed at once, but Lizzy, being the eldest, was the first to speak. "I am that glad you have come. You simply must tell me what you think of this gown. Grandmama says it's far too daring for someone in her first Season, but I assured her at Almack's I saw several girls as young as I wearing such things. There, now, didn't you see Amanda Billingsley-Hurst wearing just such a one?" she inquired, thrusting the fashion plate under Georgie's nose. "Grandmama has been rusticating so long, she's become devilish straitlaced." Lizzy cast a teasing look at the dowager.

"I can't say I remember," Georgie apologized. "But I am not the least judge of fashion, you know. I resent the amount of time I am forced to spend on my own toilette so much that I barely notice anyone else's." Which, she quickly admonished herself, was not entirely true, because she had been well aware of Lady Wyndham's stunning appearance the night at the opera.

"Oh, Amanda Billingsley-Hurst," the dowager snorted. "I should hope, Elizabeth, that no Brandon would look to anyone in that family for fashion. They may go back to the Conqueror, but they're no better than they should be and never have been. They have always been bad *ton.*"

Here Percy took advantage of his grandmama's audible sniff to break in with his own concerns. "How is Lakshmi doing? It seemed to me that when we last rode together she was favoring her left hind leg. And do you remember you promised to go to Astley's with us?"

"Peace, all of you." The earl strode over to lead Georgie to a chair. "You might at least make your visitor welcome before bombarding her with questions.'' He continued in an undertone, ''I took the liberty of sending my carriage, knowing that if she had access to hers, your aunt might fidget less about your being here. I hope you did not take it amiss.'' He cocked an inquiring eyebrow and was amused to see from her conscious look that she had taken it amiss. ''Sprite, just because someone tries to do you a kindness does not mean that a person is encroaching on your freedom, you know,'' he whispered softly.

She was somewhat mollified. True, his gesture had been kindly meant, but he might have consulted her.

Her expressive face was a perfect mirror of these conflicting emotions, which he had interpreted correctly and comprehended so well, far better than she herself, perhaps. Jealous of his own independence and proud of his capacity to look after himself in any situation, the earl knew how difficult it was for someone such as he or Georgie to accept a favor, no matter how kindly meant. ''Truly, I meant no harm, sprite, but I knew if I were to ask you, you would refuse.''

He spoke so quietly that she could barely hear him, but when she looked up it was to encounter such a wealth of understanding in his dark eyes that she was slightly taken aback. She nodded. ''Yes, I should have, but less because I cannot accept a kindness than because I do all I can to discourage high-handed behavior in anyone.'' The twinkle in her eye and the impish grin belied her critical tone.

''Touché. You are in the right of it. The truth of the matter is that I am grown so accustomed to doing things alone, I am unused to consulting others. Then again, I do not suffer fools gladly and have discovered that the most effective way to accomplish anything is to do it without asking anyone. Uncomfortable as it is to have it pointed out to me, I suppose I have become rather despotic over the years. But on to more pleasant things. I invited you to see my library and to take instruction in Sanskrit, and whatever else I may be, I am a man of my word. Having just helped you to a comfortable chair by the fire, let me disturb you and take you to my library.''

''But Georgie just got here,'' Percy wailed. Having learned

from his brother that his newfound friend had lived in a colonial garrison, he had counted on discussing formations and battle plans with her. "I wanted to ask her about the army."

"I am most flattered that you should think of asking me, when I am sure your brother must certainly know more than I," Georgie replied, smiling. "But Brian promised to teach me Sanskrit, and when one receives an offer such as that, one must take full advantage of it."

"You are going to do lessons with Brian?" Percy asked, round-eyed with astonishment. That someone should actually choose such an activity, especially when a far more enticing invitation had been offered, was inconceivable to the little boy.

Georgie laughed. "You must think that I am all about in the head, but I like to learn, and I have always wished to know Sanskrit so I could understand more about Indian culture. After all, if your brother knows Sanskrit, he must have chosen to do lessons as well, because I am certain no one *made* him do it."

This last was uttered with a challenging look at the earl, who winced visibly. "Ah, too well you know my obstinate character. Come along, sprite."

But Percy was not to be put off. Intrigued by this new perspective on lessons, he trailed along behind. "Why do you call her 'sprite?' Her name is Georgie."

"It may be Georgie now, but when I first met her, it was definitely 'sprite,' " his brother replied smiling at Georgie. "You see, with her blond hair and white dress, she looked like a being from a different world in the heat and dust of India. Besides which, she declined to tell me her real name."

"Why was that? Grandmama says that her father was one of the most famous adventurers in India."

"That is most definitely true, but when I met her, Miss Georgiana was running away from her ayah and she did not want her whereabouts known."

"Running away? Were they being dreadfully wicked to you?" Percy turned to Georgie.

"Not in the slightest, but I just wished to have an adventure on my own without anyone else's spoiling it, so I managed to escape, and then I was discovered by your brother, but he, being a regular Trojan, didn't give me up, and joined me in my adventure instead," Georgie replied, quizzing the earl as she did so.

"Oh." Percy digested this slowly. Truly, this had been a most revealing morning.

"Would you care to join us?" his brother invited him.

"Oh, no, thank you. I shouldn't want to be a bother," Percy, whose distaste for books and lessons was almost legendary, quickly replied.

"What a bouncer! Do you take me for a complete flat?" his brother snorted.

"Well"—Percy hunched a defensive shoulder—"it's just that I don't care for books all that much. I . . . I prefer cricket and soldiers."

"Not like books? Why ever not?" Georgie exclaimed.

"They're musty old things. I like things that are fun, like horses and adventures and such."

"Goodness! The best adventures I know of are written in books. And, what's more, when you read about them, you can have all the excitement without being the least bit uncomfortable. Did you never read about King Arthur or Charlemagne?"

Georgie's astonishment was so patent that Percy paused uncertainly. "Well, no . . . I just thought that they were some boring dead fellows from history."

Georgie grinned. "Percy, what on earth do you think that a great deal of history is but various people's battles and adventures?" she wondered.

Effectively silenced, the small boy could do nothing but look at her with an expression that was both sheepish and quizzical, until his older brother, following Georgie's lead, pulled down some beautifully bound books from the shelves. "Here, lad. Have a look at these and you will see that Georgie's in the right of it." With a conspiratorial wink at his ward, he handed Percy a copy of *Morte d'Arthur*, open to an exciting engraving of knights in battle.

Having seen that his brother was safely ensconced in a

large wing chair with the intriguing volume, he turned to
Georgie. "And now for your lessons." He went to the
shelves and retrieved some more books, remarking as he did,
"I think you will be amazed when you look at this *Sanskrit
Grammar* by Wilkins to discover the similarity between it
and Greek and Latin. I know, as your aunt confided her fears
for your future to me, that you read the *Edinburgh Review.*
Do I recall your mentioning the excellent treatise there on
the similarities of these languages and the discussion of the
possibility that many of the Greek myths may have had their
origins in India? It is a most fascinating theory."

"Yes, it is. I am at present reading 'Observations on the
Injurious Consequences of the Restrictions upon Foreign
Commerce,' though I seem to have so little time to read that
my progress is quite slow." Georgie bent her head to peruse
Mr. Wilkins' grammar.

The lesson passed most pleasantly for both of them.
Georgie was surprised to discover in someone she had
previously considered to be rather brash and inclined to be
domineering an excellent and most patient teacher. While
Brian was delighted at the quickness of her mind and her
grasp of languages in general. As he watched her pore
eagerly over texts and observed her enthusiasm for learning,
he reflected on the unusual nature of this. He so rarely
encountered that passion for knowledge in anyone but himself
that he never expected to find it in others, and when he did,
he treasured it enormously and honored that person as an
individual whose acquaintance was worth cultivating.

"Oh, I see! Why, I remember now so many similar words
my ayah used when she was telling me stories. It is coming
much clearer to me now." Georgie looked up, her eyes alight
with excitement and her face flushed with the thrill of
discovery.

The earl thought he had never known her to look more
lovely. Even the smudge on her chin where she had rested
it on a hand dusty from the book served only to emphasize
the glowing complexion and the vitality of her expression.
He had never particularly looked for intelligence in a woman,
or even considered it useful, but now, observing the alertness

in her eyes, and hearing the interest in her voice as she questioned him, the earl realized how enchanting it could be, how attractive it made someone, and he smiled to think what his friends would say if he were to tell them that, at least for the moment, he found a clever woman more alluring than his voluptuous mistress.

A cough interrupted his reverie. "Excuse me, milord, but Lord Waverly is here to see you," Simpson announced.

Georgie looked up. "Good heavens! The time! I was going to be home ages ago."

Even Percy, who had been quietly absorbed in his book, looked up in some surprise. "Lord Waverly? Are you going to Gentleman Jackson's, then?"

"No, cub, Manton's."

"Manton's," Georgie sighed enviously. "How I wish I were a man! I should so love to see if I've lost my skill with a pistol. I must have become sadly rusty, I fear."

"What a bloodthirsty creature you are, to be sure," Brian teased.

"Not at all. Uncle Ned made certain I knew how to defend myself, and I enjoyed our shooting practice. I was accounted quite a respectable shot, I would have you know," she defended herself.

He flung up a protective hand. "I do not doubt it in the least. I, for one, would never dare question your skill at anything."

"Can you really shoot a pistol, Georgie?" Percy was intrigued. If all girls were like his new friend, then they weren't half bad.

"Yes, but as I say, it has been a very long time," she replied apologetically.

"It's time Percy learned. We shall all three of us go down to Aldringham sometime and have a match. I have a very fine pair of dueling pistols I would like you to try."

"Oh, I should like that ever so much," Georgie responded eagerly. "But now I must fly or Aunt will be wondering what has become of me." She bade adieu to Lizzy and her grandmother and arranged to ride in the park with Lizzy before climbing into the carriage that had been brought round for her. Riding home in this luxuriously appointed vehicle, Georgie reflected that perhaps she had been mistaken in her original opinions and that life in London was not so unpleasant after all.

15

It was several days before the weather permitted any hope of riding in the park, and Georgie chafed at the inactivity. She endured several very dull card parties, where, as far as she could ascertain, the chief activities were the loss of pin money and reputations. Never an enthusiastic card player, she discovered herself winning almost every game merely because she paid attention and did not try to outdo her fellow players in the gleeful repeating of scandalous *on-dits*.

Before the advent of the lively Brandons, she had been content to spend her mornings reading, making the obligatory "most assuredly" or "vastly" when her aunt would hold up Ackermann's *Repository* to ask if she didn't think it was the sweetest bonnet of gray *velours simulé* that went with the gray bombazine carriage dress, or didn't she deem the evening dress of white crepe spotted with white satin vastly becoming, but now she began to feel that these quiet mornings were very boring indeed.

On one particularly dull day, which was made even more so by the leaden sky outside and the steady drip of rain, the monotony was relieved by the appearance of Cedric, resplendent in a striped waistcoat under a beautifully cut bottle-green jacket. He had come to invite the ladies to view the exhibition of British artists at the gallery of the British Institution. "I have heard that a number of painters from the Royal Academy are represented and that the original sketch for West's *Death on the Pale Horse* is on display," Ceddie added by way of enticement.

Lady Debenham shuddered. "You and Georgie go. For my part, I find such things excessively dull, though of course I should never admit to such a thing. Why should one look at pictures of dead people or landscapes of places one has never been nor intends to visit? I depend upon you and Georgie to tell me which pictures I ought most to remark on should I be asked." Georgie, on the other hand, was delighted, and ran off to fetch her pelisse.

They spent the rest of the morning wandering through the rooms looking at the offerings of West, Jackson, Wilkie, and Howard. In general, Georgie was well pleased with the exhibit, though the work which was drawing the largest crowd, *Waterloo Evening* by Jones, left her unimpressed. "Well, just look at it," she defended herself when taxed by Ceddie for not admiring it as all the others did. "The proportion is all wrong. He has put the main figures right in the center, without the least regard for accuracy, thus making everyone else look like a midget. And so much attention is focused on them that it looks more like a poorly executed group portrait than an inspiring study of a vast scene. No, Ceddie, despite everyone else's enthusiasm, I cannot like it and I most certainly find it inferior to this." Georgie pointed to the unusual and affecting *Alpine mastiffs re-animating a distressed Traveller.*

"Ssh, Georgie," Ceddie cautioned in an alarmed whisper. "You mustn't say such things."

"Why ever not? I happen to think it's true," she began indignantly.

"You're supposed to exclaim over them. You ain't supposed to criticize them. If you do that, people will think you are clever and label you a bluestocking. Even ten thousand a year won't help you find dancing partners then."

Georgie defended herself. "If one has something to the point to say, one should say it. I see no use in trading inanities. I find that excessively dull, and I fail to see—"

"Georgie, you don't understand." Ceddie was desperate now. "You like to think, but other people don't. And, what's more, they don't appreciate someone who tries to make them do so."

"Oh." Georgie digested this slowly. "But you agreed with me, and you were the one who thought *Hercules killing the man of Calydon with a blow of his fist* unoriginal."

"Yes, but I did my best not to show it and make other people uneasy," he responded seriously.

"But, Ceddie, I can't be a pretty ninnyhammer, and furthermore, I don't wish to be. Besides, there are quantities of them around for everyone to choose from. And, as I don't wish to catch anyone, where's the harm in it? I think I rather like the idea of being on the shelf. It's a great deal more comfortable than trying to bring people up to scratch, you know," Georgie concluded in a confiding voice.

Faced with such a hopeless case, Ceddie was left with nothing to say, and they finished their tour of the exhibit with the most desultory of conversations.

Riding home in his beautifully appointed carriage, Georgie was unusually silent. She was fond of Ceddie, she reflected. He was truly kind and he was doing his best to help her be in style and keep her amused, but there was a certain limpness about him that, after an hour in his company, made her stifle a yawn, and she could not help thinking wistfully of the more invigorating companionship of the earl, Lizzy, and Percy.

Georgie was soon to enjoy this very thing, as the next day proved to be a fine one, and a note from Lizzy begging her to join her in the park was brought up with her morning chocolate. Flinging aside the bedclothes, Georgie grabbed her wrapper and called to Alice to get her riding habit.

The little maid was appalled. "But, Miss Georgie, it isn't yet noon. No one will be in the park."

"That is precisely what I am thinking. Besides, if Lady Elizabeth Brandon can be seen at such a place and at such a time, so can I," she remarked with satisfaction.

Not more than a quarter of an hour later, she and her groom were riding sedately through Berkeley Square toward the park, where they were soon able to pick out Lizzy in a very dashing riding habit and jaunty hat.

"Georgie! How glad I am to see you! I have been shut up with Mama this age, until I thought I should go mad. There was nothing to do but read," she greeted her friend with enthusiasm.

Georgie grinned. "I find it difficult to sympathize with you when I have been enduring card parties with no possibility of distraction even from Percy."

"Oh, Percy." Lizzy dismissed her younger sibling with a nod. "All he wants to do is play at soldiers."

"Infinitely preferable to card parties, I still believe. Come, let us ride. I feel cramped from being confined indoors for so long. That is the hardest thing for me to bear about being in London. One is so rarely outside with the flowers and the trees."

The two girls rode along discussing another upcoming evening at Almack's, Georgie complaining that one attendance at the temple of high society was enough and Lizzy maintaining that she had met hardly anybody yet, so how could she possibly judge? So engrossed were they in their conversation that they barely noticed the barouche until they were upon it.

"Why, hello Lizzy, Georgie." The earl broke off his conversation with Lady Wyndham long enough to hail his sister and her companion.

"Botheration! That woman!" Lizzy muttered under her breath as she reined in Titania.

It was no accident that Althea was in the park at such an unseasonable hour with such an escort. Always a firm believer in gathering all possible intelligence concerning the movements of her cicisbeos, she had instructed her maid to allow herself to be courted by one of the footmen at Brandon House. This connection had revealed the frequency with which the earl rode in the park, often accompanied by his siblings and sometimes by Lady Georgiana Southwold. This same Lady Georgiana, it also appeared, had been a visitor to Brandon House upon several occasions. Confident of her own beauty and charm, Lady Wyndham was not alarmed in the least, but she did object to her lover's spending so much time with such paltry companions when he could have been enjoying it with her. Again using her new barouche and pair as a pretext—she wondered if one of her horses were not going the slightest bit lame, not that she would actually have known or cared—she had arranged for the earl to drive her around the park at the earliest opportunity.

Althea had not counted on meeting up with Lizzy and Georgie, but when this opportunity presented itself, she welcomed the chance to demonstrate the superiority of her powers to amuse their respective brother and guardian.

"Why, Lady Elizabeth," she began in a sweetly condescending tone that made Lizzy long to wring her neck, "you are up betimes for someone not accustomed to the life of the *ton*. I wonder, did you enjoy Almack's? It is all very well for young people, but it does become sadly flat after a while." Althea shrugged her beautiful shoulders with a world-weary sigh, directing an intimate smile at her companion.

A silent observer to all this, Georgie began to understand her friend's dislike for this woman, which she had first divined during their previous encounter at Madame Celeste's.

Turning to Georgie, the beauty continued in the same honeyed voice, "And so this is the little ward from India. And are you enjoying London?"

It was Georgie's turn to bristle, but she swallowed the spurt of anger that welled up inside her in favor of more devious forms of warfare, for warfare it certainly was. Adopting the respectful air and the tones reserved for addressing the most decrepit of elderly persons, she replied, "Very well, thank you, ma'am. It is most kind of you to inquire." She had the satisfaction of seeing that her way of speaking to Althea had hit a sore point. The beauty's lips tightened involuntarily and an angry and unbecoming flush crept over her face. Nor was it lost on the earl, whose eyes twinkled appreciatively as he directed a knowing look at his ward.

The uncomfortable silence that ensued was interrupted by a burst of whinnying and yipping. As they had been talking, Lady Wyndham's nasty little pug, already a sore point between the earl, who detested the overfed creature, and Althea, who insisted he added to the prettiness of the picture she made riding through the park, had leaned over and taken a vicious nip at Titania's flank. The mare, who had been dozing silently during the interchange, awoke with a start and no thought but to put as much distance between herself and the horrid source of such pain.

Lizzy, too, was caught unawares. In her effort to maintain her temper toward Althea while at the same time combating

her stratagem to make her out as a mere schoolgirl, Lizzy's
hands had slackened on Titania's reins. When her horse
reared and plunged off toward parts unknown, she was forced
to grab for her mane and hang on for dear life. Lizzy was
an adequate rider, but not a strong one, and it was doubtful
how long she would be able to maintain her grasp. Knowing
this, her brother cast frantically and helplessly about for some
way to save her. He had just determined that the only thing
to do was leap on one of the carriage horses and cut the
traces, when help appeared from another quarter.

In a second, Georgie had recognized the danger of the
situation, and she reacted instantly. Digging her heels into
Lakshmi, she tore off after her friend at such a blinding rate
of speed that even the earl, who had assured himself of the
mare's capabilities before purchasing her, was surprised.
Though it seemed an age to the onlookers and the victim of
the incident, it was no very long time before they caught up
with Lizzy and her frightened mount. Leaning over, Georgie
grabbed for the trailing reins with one hand, keeping her own
in a firm grip, and pulled with all her might. Time seemed
to stand still while she wrestled with the frantic creature,
but at last it ceased its plunging and shuddered to a quivering
halt. Dropping Lakshmi's reins, Georgie slid off and went
to Titania's head, talking softly and stroking her neck sooth-
ingly. By the time the earl arrived, the horse was in a lather
and breathing heavily, but its eyes had ceased to roll and
it was nuzzling Georgie's neck.

Never in his life had Brian undergone such a quick succes-
sion of such intense emotions. First and foremost had been
his fear for his sister, quickly followed by the frustrating
helplessness of being encumbered with two ornamental but
sedate carriage horses securely attached to a barouche; then
came a sense of relief when Georgie plunged off in pursuit,
and his tension was lessened by the feeling that at least
somebody was doing something. As it became clear that
Georgie had the situation well in hand, anxiety gave way
to admiration for her immediate grasp of the scene, her
instantaneous response, and her superb horsemanship.

Ever since he had seen her, the earl had felt that his ward

must be an excellent horsewoman and had selected the spirited Lakshmi accordingly. He had always been sorry that the dictates of society did not allow her more than a sedate trot, and now he was a privileged observer of her skill. As she headed off across the park, hands firm, eyes alertly ahead, wisps of blond hair escaping her jaunty hat, she attuned herself so expertly to Lakshmi's motion that she and the horse appeared as one creature. It was truly a beautiful sight, and the earl felt an odd lump in his throat. As he watched, impressed by the adroit handling of her horse and Lizzy's, and her own lack of concern for her own safety, he felt proud that he knew someone as capable and resourceful as his ward was proving to be. At the same time, he was chagrined that he, Brian Brandon, known in school, his regiment, and all over India as being as bold and quick-witted as anyone, was forced to let a mere chit of a schoolgirl rescue his beloved sister. Furthermore, he was forced to witness this in the presence of a mistress who was not only the inadvertent instigator of the entire mishap but also an extremely critical spectator.

"How dreadfully embarrassing for you, Brian," she cooed sympathetically when he returned to the carriage after reassuring himself that his sister had suffered no ill effects and was no more than badly shaken.

The earl stared at her blankly. "Embarrassing?"

"To have your ward expose herself in such a way in such a public place. I assure you I shall do all I can to see that the whole affair is put in the best light possible and as little damage done as can be." Lady Wyndham laid her hand on his arm in a gesture that was more possessive than comforting.

"Damage? Althea, Georgie saved my sister from what could have been grave danger. The only possible light such an act could be seen in is admiration and gratitude, and she commands the utmost of both of these from me." The earl spoke in his usual firm tones, only the twitching of a muscle in one tanned cheek betraying his agitation.

"Of course you are all that is grateful." Althea gave him a melting look. "And your feelings do you honor. You are always warm in your appreciation for those for whom you are responsible, but a groom should have saved her and kept Lady Georgiana from behaving like a perfect hoyden. I fear that the rest of society is not as generous as you are. You must let me do what I can to smooth this over for you.''

If Brian had not been so preoccupied, he would have recognized Althea's strategy for what it was—a ploy to bring discredit to his ward while at the same time establishing a firmer, more public connection with him and his family, but he was too concerned for the principals involved to examine his mistress's motives very closely.

A slight cough behind him warned him that they were not alone. ''Excuse me, my lord, but I thought perhaps my groom and I might accompany Lizzy back to Grosvenor Square. There was no harm done, but she is somewhat unnerved and might feel more the thing if there were others beside her own groom with her.'' Georgie spoke lightly, but there was a conscious look about her that suggested that she had been privy to his companion's comments.

Brian descended from the carriage and, grasping Lakshmi's reins, led her a little apart. ''I . . . I don't quite know what to say. I wish that it had been I instead of you who was able to rescue my sister, but . . .'' He stopped, groping for words that would convey his gratitude for Lizzy's safety, the discomfort he felt at his own helplessness, and his indebtedness to a woman younger than himself, and the gratification that filled him when her actions had confirmed what he had sensed ever since he had first encountered her— that she was a rare and courageous spirit who recognized and accepted the challenges and dangers of life in the same way and with the same energy that he did.

Gazing up at him, waiting for him to complete the sentence, Georgie thought that she had never seen him at such a loss before. She wondered at it, and the confusion she read in his eyes.

They remained that way for some time, each aware that the moment was fraught with significance for both of them, each trying to decipher just what that significance was. The earl was the first to look away. There was something in the directness of her gaze, the purity of her clear green eyes, that overwhelmed him. He reached for her gloved hand and raised it to his lips. "Thank you, sprite. Thank you," he whispered fervently. And then he was gone, turning back to the barouche and Althea, who was waiting none too patiently.

Georgie sat for a few minutes, transfixed by a tumult of feelings. She had arrived in time to catch the last of Althea's remarks. When Lizzy's horse had bolted, Georgie had acted instantaneously to help her friend. It had never occurred to her to stop and consider what others might think, and ordinarily she would have scoffed at such a notion, but she now had enough experience in the *ton* to know what damage could be done if such an escapade were to be bruited about in certain quarters by someone like Althea Wyndham.

It was not for herself that Georgie minded. She had never aspired to cut a dash in the *ton* in the first place, and, fully aware of her own propensity for falling into scrapes, she had felt certain that sooner or later she would do something that would cause polite eyebrows to rise and tongues to wag. But Georgie did very much care about Lizzy. She knew that that lively damsel was hoping for a brilliant Season and she did not want to do anything that would lessen her chances of being sought after. Furthermore, though he had initially put her off with his autocratic attitude, the earl had, of late, been most kind, and Georgie was not the sort of person to take such kindness for granted. Raised in an army garrison, she had early on absorbed the soldier's code of honor, and in some strange way she felt indebted to the earl for the extra care and attention he had lavished on her in the selection of such a wonderful mount and companion as Lakshmi, for offering to teach her Sanskrit, and for taking her interests seriously enough to broach them with Lord Petersham. In a way she had been glad of the opportunity she had been given to replay some of the obligation she felt toward him, but now, considering it in the light in which Lady Wyndham had put it, Georgie wondered if she had done more harm than good.

And then there was another emotion, more disturbing, and

certainly less easily identified—it was the way she had felt
when Brian had looked at her so intently after kissing her
hand. It had been gratifying to be thanked in such a way,
but at the same time, it was most unsettling. Gentlemen did
not kiss ladies' hands a great deal anymore. Certainly gentlemen like the Earl of Aldringham did not kiss the hand of
a ward with whom he was on less intimate terms than his
sister, furthermore, a ward who was as likely, if not more
so, to aggravate him as much as his sister did. The unsettling
part was Georgie's own reaction. She had been acutely aware
of the warmth and strength of his hand through her gloves.
It was intimate and at the same time reassuring, the way she
distantly remembered feeling when her father had held her
hand so many years ago. Yet the moment his lips had touched
it, something had changed. They had merely brushed the back
of it, a barely discernible sensation underneath the glove,
but a warm tide had washed over her that she was incapable
of explaining.

Ever since she had first encountered Brian, Georgie had
sensed that he was a friend, that somehow she could trust
him. Even when she had been her most angry at him, she
had recognized that part of her anger had stemmed from the
fact that he was special for her, that she expected him to act
differently from other people. When he had exhibited the
same prejudices or faults as the rest of the world, she had
been doubly disappointed because she had hoped for more
from him. She had looked up to him as a child, because,
though he had the experience and sophistication of the adults
in her world, he had treated her as an equal. And after their
initial quarrel, he had continued to demonstrate a respect
for her understanding and capabilities that heretofore no one
else had shown, and she, though she would have died rather
than admit it, had continued to look to him for guidance.

Today, however, when she had looked into his eyes and
read the confusion there, she had also seen something else.
There had been a vulnerable expression in his dark eyes. It
had come and gone so quickly that she almost wondered if
it had been there at all, and when she looked again, it had
been replaced by something else, something akin to tender-

ness. In that instant it had seemed to Georgie that somehow their roles had been reversed and that she was the one offering reassurance. For a brief moment she had sensed that she was as special and wonderful for him as he had been for her so many years ago when he had shared her adventure with her. It was a new and disturbing sensation and Georgie was not at all sure what to make of it. Most likely it is nothing at all, my girl, she told herself. And, tossing her head, she assured herself that Lizzy was fully recovered and under the watchful eyes of her groom and her brother, before beckoning to Digby and riding off in the direction of Berekely Square.

16

Georgie was not the only one in the party afflicted with unsettling thoughts after the little episode in the park. Driving Lady Wyndham back to Mount Street, the earl could not keep his attention focused either on the horses or on his companion's conversation. Smile and flash her dark eyes though she would, Althea could not erase the memory of serious green eyes looking directly, questioningly into his. Sensing his abstraction, Althea moved imperceptibly closer, allowing her ample curves to press against him provocatively so that her heady perfume assailed his senses and the swell of her bosom against his arm reminded Brian that he was in the presence of a seductive and accomplished woman of the world.

The earl gradually became aware of this, but all that it achieved was to call attention to the contrast between this self-conscious beauty and someone else who, with no thought for herself, had hurled herself into headlong pursuit of a runaway horse. The widow's languorous pose contrasted sharply with Georgie's energy and vitality, while her enticing gaze, so full of promise, only served to make him smile tenderly at the sudden shyness that had assailed his ward when he had kissed her hand. Any other woman of his acquaintance would have reveled in that gesture and turned it to her advantage, but not Sprite. She had been rendered acutely uncomfortable by it, and her unease had only made her appear more adorable.

Though she would never have acknowledged it, even to herself, Althea was undergoing some rather uncomfortable moments herself. Ordinarily she would not have given a second thought to an awkward, impulsive schoolgirl like Georgie Southwold. Certainly Lady Wyndham did not consider her attractive or sophisticated enough to pose any sort of threat to a worldly beauty, but Althea was woman enough, with enough intuition to recognize that the moment she had witnessed between the earl and his ward had been one of special significance and intensity, and she was not best pleased.

Accustomed as she was to slavish devotion from her lovers, Althea Wyndham was jealous enough already of the earl's affection for his sister and brother and the time and attention he lavished on them. She was not about to brook that sort of interference from a mere chit of a girl who was not even a blood relative. The moment for pleasant dalliance was past, and it was time to become serious in the pursuit of her quarry.

Having decided that, Althea plunged immediately into the next phase of her strategy. "Do you attend Lady Pemberly's masquerade tomorrow?" she inquired. Knowing the license usually allowed at such affairs, particularly at the establishment of such a dashing matron, Lady Wyndham felt reasonably certain that neither Georgie nor Lizzy would be allowed to attend. Both Lady Debenham and Lizzy's grandmother were too concerned for the reputations of their protégées to allow them to appear at such an affair. Althea also knew that the costume she had selected for herself as Cleopatra was designed to arouse the most jaded of men.

"Masquerade?" Jerked out of his reverie, Brian could only look blank.

"Yes. It should be a delightful change from all the insipid affairs contrived so that this Season's crop of young hopefuls can be introduced to the world. Lady Pemberly herself assured me that only the most sophisticated members of the *ton* would attend," Althea replied with a sly smile.

For some inexplicable reason, the idea of such an evening spent in Althea's toils, seductive though they might be, was most unappealing to the earl and he cast about frantically for an excuse, any excuse. Unbidden, the image of his little brother rose before his eyes and he seized upon it gratefully. "I'm sorry, Althea, but I promised Percy that I would take him to Astley's. He is having a rather dull time of it here, as he would infinitely prefer to be at Aldringham, and furthermore, all the attention of the household is focused on Lizzy just at present. Of course, I should be charmed to be the escort of one destined to be the cynosure of all eyes, but I am sure you understand.''

Lady Wyndham most certainly did not understand, but she was far too clever to let her displeasure show. Nor did she admit defeat so easily. "How excessively boring. I shall miss you." She pouted prettily and then brightened as if suddenly hit by a happy thought. "Why not stop by afterward and we can enjoy a late supper together." Her tantalizing expression promised a passionate end to the evening.

"Thank you. I expect to be quite done up after entertaining an excited and inquisitive ten-year-old at such a show, but we shall see," he replied carelessly.

The beauty was forced to be content with that noncommittal response because by that time they had arrived at her door. The earl helped her down, reassured her as to the good health of her cattle and the suitability of her equipage, and sauntered off, leaving her seething with such frustration that even smashing a Sèvres figurine against the mantel did little to alleviate her ill humor.

On his part, the more he considered it, the more the earl was looking forward to the promised visit to Astley's. A connoisseur of horseflesh and always an admirer of skill and daring, whatever form it took, he would have enjoyed a performance there on his own, but the thought that he would share it with two companions as enthusiastic and lively as Percy and Georgie merely heightened his anticipation.

He was not disappointed. When the earl and his exuberant brother drove around to Berkeley Square the next evening to fetch Georgie, they discovered her to be in as eager a state of expectation as Percy, though perhaps somewhat more restrained. "I have read the advertisement in the *Times*," she confided, eyes sparkling, "and I must say, if half their claims are true, it promises to be a splendid evening."

"Of course, one should never put great store by the things one reads in the popular press," Percy began in tones so reminiscent of his grandmother that Georgie could not help directing an amused glance at his elder brother, "but I believe that in this case they are not exaggerated," he concluded solemnly.

Observing the earl's quivering lip, Georgie could not entirely choke back the spurt of laughter which, fortunately for Percy's dignity, she was able to transform into a creditable cough. His elder brother, however, was not so easily deceived, and he directed a penetrating glance into the green eyes brimming with amusement. He grinned and shrugged, reflecting as he did so how very pleasant it was to have a companion so quick to appreciate the humor in things.

"But, Percy," Georgie continued in a more serious tone, "how do you suppose they will contrive to portray 'the opening of the Flood-gate' and the 'rising of the waters'?"

"I have not the least notion, but Brian tells me they are awfully clever," the little boy replied.

By then they had arrived and were quickly ushered upstairs to their awaiting box. The rest of the evening passed in a blur of magnificent horses and superb equestrian feats. Georgie and Percy was enthralled, both hanging breathlessly over the box as each new scene surpassed the other. They gasped at the ascent of the Calmuc Cavalry and held their breaths while the prince was rescued by his horse. Watching their enthusiasm, the earl was struck by how much pleasure could be derived from observing the enjoyment of others. When, in response to his "Well, children, is it all the *Times* claimed it to be?" Georgie turned a glowing face toward him, exclaiming, "Oh, it's more than I could have dreamed it would be. Thank you ever so much for inviting me along. Did you ever see such splendid horses, or the equal to Mr. Brown's horsemanship?", he thought what a pity it was that people were so desperate to acquire town bronze that they appeared bored by everything, when such unfeigned enjoyment could bring so much joy to oneself and one's companions.

"Brian," his brother broke in, "is this as well done as you remember it? I don't see how it could possibly be any better."

"It is exactly as I remember it, if not better." Looking

down at the two faces turned eagerly toward him, he smiled fondly. "Yes, it is certainly better. I never enjoyed myself so much before." And, oddly enough, it was true. Through all of his eventful life he had encountered more excitement or more adventure in more exotic locales, but he had never experienced these to their fullest because he had never had the pleasure of sharing any of it with anybody. In point of fact, he had so often had his appreciation of things spoiled by a stupid remark here, a pointless observation there, that he had grown accustomed to avoiding companions who might ruin a special moment for him. The earl had gotten so into the way of doing things alone that he had never realized that many things in life might be more enjoyable if shared with friends who could participate fully in one's pleasure and thus enhance it.

The last time he could remember the exhilaration of such companionship had been the time when, after discovering some truly fine and unusual merchandise, he and Ned Wolvercote had successfully concluded a particularly delicate bargaining session. Brian had never felt so invigorated by life as he had then, and he had never thought to recapture that feeling. But now, in a curious way, Ned had given it back to him again in the form of his niece, and Brian was oddly grateful.

"Don't you think we could ride standing up on horses if we only had somewhere to try it?" Georgie interrupted his thoughts. "Percy seems to regard these feats as some sort of magic, but I think it just comes from practice. One can do anything one sets one's mind to if one does it often enough."

"You may very well be in the right of it, sprite, but I forbid you to try," the earl replied with a ferocious glare.

Seeing the twinkle in his eyes, Georgie contented herself with making a face at him.

Percy was mightily impressed but not a little worried by such daring. "I say, Georgie, you don't want to make Brian mad at you," he cautioned. "He can become dreadfully angry sometimes, though never if you don't deserve it."

"I know, but I can get dreadfully angry myself," she

responded airily. "At any rate, he's merely jesting, you know. If we were not in such a public place, I daresay I should have stuck my tongue out at him. After all, the only reason he is so quick in forbidding us to do things is that very likely he has done exactly these things himself and knows what to expect."

The earl chuckled. "How true. I had not known you could be so circumspect, sprite. What can have possibly come over you to make you exercise such restraint?"

Georgie twinkled up at him. "Well, I am not a complete rustic, you know. Even I have been on the town long enough to know it is not at all the thing to stick one's tongue out. I am making my come-out this Season and I do have my reputation to consider," she intoned in sepulchral accents worthy of the most redoubtable of dowagers.

The earl laughed outright. "And whence has sprung this newfound decorum? It has never weighed seriously with you before. I suspect you but lacked the courage."

"I did no such thing, and very well you know it, my lord," she retorted hotly.

Seeing that his teasing had inadvertently hit a nerve, the earl recanted. "I know, I know. Believe me, I would never seriously doubt your courage. It is just that when you begin playing at propriety, I become alarmed. If I cannot look to you for straightforward behavior, where can I turn?" He spoke in fun, but the serious light in his eyes belied his flippant tone.

For his part, Percy was amazed. He had never seen anyone except Lizzy tease his brother in such a way, and even Lizzy did not dare was much as Georgie did. Furthermore, his brother seemed to be enjoying it and was actually worried what Georgie might think of him. It had never occurred to Percy that real grown-ups—he did not number his mother among these—might worry what other grown-ups thought of them. It was a startling revelation and one which kept him relatively silent during the carriage ride home.

17

The two households in Berkeley Square and Grosvenor Square were occupied with the more quotidian aspects of life for the next few days—dealing with complaints from tenants relayed through agents on various estates, answering letters from representatives handling Ned Wolvercote's affairs in India, attending fittings at Madame Celeste's, refurbishing bonnets with new ribbons, doing lessons in Sanskrit, or otherwise—so it was some time before the earl and Georgie ran into each other. Once again the encounter was in the park, but as the earl was on his way to call upon Georgie when he came upon her and Lakshmi heading eagerly toward the beckoning expanse of green, it was not a surprising meeting.

"Hello." Brian reined Caesar, who, having enjoyed a longer ride than the other horse, objected less than Lakshmi, who tossed her head and pranced impatiently. "I was just on my way to call on you. I saw Petersham in Brooks's yesterday and suggested that he look for us in the park, as you are usually to be found here in even the most inclement of weathers. He promised to do so, but took exception to any but the finest of days. Here it is a beautiful day, and I saw him mounted on a handsome chestnut talking with Alvanley not five minutes ago."

"That is most thoughtful of you. I wonder if he will take kindly to a young woman's being interested in tea cultivation, though." Georgie's brow wrinkled anxiously.

"What, the intrepid Sprite having misgivings?" he teased. "It is too late now. There he is, attired in his customary brown and matching his mount to perfection." The earl made good his threat by nodding in greeting to Lord Petersham, who happened to glance in their direction. "Besides, he is such a devotee that, once launched on the subject of tea, he becomes oblivious of all else. Have no fear. Once he discovers your very real interest, he will talk of nothing else and quite likely you will be forced to adopt desperate measures in order to break away. Ah, Petersham, delightful to see you. Lady Georgiana, may I present Lord Petersham. This is the lady I referred to as wishing to grow tea in India.''

Lord Petersham's bland look of polite interest vanished. "I say, I think it a most intriguing notion. The more tea available to us, the better. I would be most interested in seeing how cultivation in a slightly different clime and culture affects the bouquet. Even the tiniest variations in plants and soil can produce a vastly different drink, you know. Why, I myself have tried . . .'' and with the look of the zealot in his eye, he launched into impassioned speech on the varieties he had tasted and on which were most suited to what particular mood.

Georgie sat silent, overwhelmed by the torrent that had been let loose, while her companion, observing her stunned expression, gave her a knowing wink. Able to break in at last, the earl admonished, "Lady Georgiana feels that, with the British more firmly established in India than China, this ought to ensure a more abundant supply and better quality than ever before.''

"Better quality would certainly be of interest, but abundant supply . . .'' Lord Petersham paused. "I cannot speak to the advantageousness of that. Greater abundance might cheapen the quality of the product, and one would certainly not want that. One would have to do one's best to maintain the strictest control, the Indians not being as cultured as the Chinese, I believe.''

"On the contrary—'' Georgie was about to burst in, in defense of her adoptive homeland, but was stopped by the warning pressure of her guardian's hand on hers as he brought Caesar alongside Lakshmi.

"Perhaps you would be good enough to introduce Geor . . . that is, Lady Georgiana to your merchant,'' the earl suggested casually.

"Most certainly, happy to, he's a good fellow,'' Lord Petersham lisped. The light of fanaticism had faded from his eyes and he smiled amiably at Georgie. "A capital notion you have. I shall make inquiries and see what I can discover." With an airy wave he was off, tilting awkwardly in the saddle as he gave himself up to serious consideration of Georgie's scheme.

Seeing Georgie's perplexity at such an abrupt departure, Brian strove to reassure her. "An eccentric fellow is Lord Petersham, but kindhearted. You will hear from him again. Often he falls into a fit of abstraction and people are not at all certain he is attending, but he will go off by himself, ruminate, and reappear with something entirely to the point. But come, Lakshmi is in need of exercise, and so are you."

The rest of the ride passed very pleasantly, so pleasantly, in fact, that Georgie forgot that this was the evening of Lady Amersham's ball. So involved was she in her discussion of Indian mythology and the stories her ayah used to tell, all prompted by the earl's suggestion that she write some of them down and submit them for publication, that she nearly forgot the time altogether and was horrified to discover how much the sun had moved. With a conscience-stricken "Oh, good heavens, Aunt Aurelia, I must go," she broke off in the middle of a sentence, gathered up the reins, and prepared to depart.

The earl was not one inclined to overrate his claims as far as personal charm was concerned; quite the contrary, he ordinarily condemned out of hand any female who evinced a particular interest in his company as being a fortune hunter or on the catch for a title. But he felt not a little put out at the ease with which his companion was able to put all thoughts of him aside, and his response to Georgie's "Shall you and Lizzy be at Lady Amersham's tonight?" was a cold "If Lizzy wishes it, undoubtedly."

The instant he uttered the words, Brian realized that he sounded churlish. Catching sight of the bewildered look in her eyes at his rebuff, he felt doubly so. After all, she was only asking a perfectly natural question, and his response had been not only unfriendly but also unwarranted. The earl rode off, a scowl on his face, thoroughly annoyed at himself, first for caring so much that she was so casual in quitting him, and second for allowing his pique to get the better of him. Here he was, the Earl of Aldringham, supposedly as famed for his address with the fair sex as he was for his numerous conquests. Such address should not desert him in the face of a mere schoolgirl, and his ward at that.

By the time he reached Grosvenor Square, he was in a very black humor indeed, so much so that he failed to acknowledge Simpson's greeting, an oversight so unusual that the butler commented on it to the housekeeper, Mrs. Turville. "I would not have minded if he had snapped my head off, but he did not even see me and continued up the stairs with a face like thunder. Only a woman can make a man so distracted, mark my words, Mrs. Turville."

"I hope you're in the right of it, Mr. Simpson. And I most sincerely hope it is not that Lady Wyndham. I've heard tell there's many a gentleman as admires her, but she's not the one for his lordship."

Ordinarily the dignified butler would have scorned to gossip with anyone, but this was a matter too near and dear to his heart and the welfare of his household to be ignored. "Oh, Mrs. Turville, and how is that?" he wondered.

"Well, she may be as beautiful as can stare, but it takes more than that to make a woman, and she has precious little else. Why, just look at her. Any woman who looks like that must spend most of her waking hours on her toilette. And when she isn't thinking about that, she is concentrating on ways to enslave the master. Opinions on her carriage and horses, indeed," the housekeeper snorted. "She just wishes to keep him dancing attendance on her so the rest of the world can see that he is in her pocket. Besides, a woman like that knows her power only works as long as a man is there to look to her. After that she is easily forgotten. What the master needs is someone as can match his spirit, someone who shares his interests. That kind of peson doesn't need to be constantly around for him to think of her. Lady Wyndham may be the kind of woman men like to court, but they wouldn't be comfortable marrying them, I'll be bound."

The butler was much struck. "Upon my word, I do believe you have a point there, Mrs. Turville. You are wise beyond your years."

"Oh, go on with you before you turn my head, Mr.

Simpson," she laughed, shaking her head and setting the gray curls dancing under her cap.

By the time evening had rolled around, the earl was restored to good humor. Several bouts at Gentleman Jackson's had vented his spleen and made him pleasurably tired and relaxed, while supper in the company of his sister, who was bubbling over in anticipation of the ball, actually made him look forward to escorting her and his grandmother.

18

"I am far too old and you're far too sophisticated to be attending these affairs, Brian," that lady muttered, leaning on his arm as she made her way slowly up Lady Amersham's magnificent marble staircase.

"Nonsense, Grandmother, you love it. And, furthermore, we know you do." He smiled at her as her eyes raked the assemblage in search of eligible partners for her granddaughter, who, flushed with excitement, was hanging on the earl's other arm.

"Do look, Grandmama, is that not Willie Fordyce returned from India? My goodness, how he has grown," Lizzy exclaimed as she stared at a tall bronzed young man whose family estates adjoined Aldringham and who had figured largely in her childhood as an effeminate youth much given to ill health and peevish complaints.

"Don't gawk so, Lizzy, it's vulgar," the dowager rapped, turning to affix the object of her scrutiny with her own eagle eye.

All further comment was suspended as they reached the top of the stairs and their beaming hostess, whose smile, if possible, grew broader at the sight of such distinguished and eligible guests. And then they were past her effusive greeting and into the crush of the ballroom itself.

"Lord, what a squeeze," the earl complained as he surveyed the vast array of jewels and feathers, flirting fans, raised quizzing glasses, flushed faces, and a sea of beautiful gowns from his advantageous height. "Can it truly be worth the risk of life and limb?"

"Brian," his sister remonstrated, "you know it is one of the events of the Season. One must attend. Though"—she wrinkled her nose with distaste—"it does look uncomfortable."

"Discomfort is of no account if one is to take the *ton* by storm," the dowager admonished. "Come, children, let us do just that." And gathering her grandson's arm in an even firmer grip, she pushed doggedly on until she had reached a pillar where she could hold court protected somewhat from the throng around them. Her grandson immediately went in search of a chair while her granddaughter gazed rapturously at the ever-changing scene in front of her.

"Oh, look, there are Georgie and Lady Debenham!" Lizzy beckoned to her friends, who managed to squeeze their way through the crowd to the small area the dowager had claimed as her own. Barely acknowledging Georgie's aunt, Lizzy launched in enthusiastically, her eyes shining, "Hello, Georgie. Did you ever see so many people? Isn't it beautiful?"

"What?" Georgie looked around in some surprise. She had gotten so into the way of dreading such affairs as an unpleasant but necessary chore that she had never really stopped to pay attention. Now, as she inhaled the scent of hothouse flowers, listened to the music which wafted on the breeze from the French windows, and allowed herself to be dazzled by the light reflected off splendid jewels and glimmering silks and satins, she was forced to agree with her friend. "I suppose so," she began cautiously. "I hadn't considered it, but—"

"Don't be such a slowtop, Georgie," Lizzy, exasperated, scolded her. "Whether or not you like this sort of thing, it is fun to get dressed up and look at what everyone else is wearing. Did you ever see anything so ridiculous as the turban Lady Chilworthy is wearing? And just look at the diamonds on Lady Jersey. Are they not magnificent?"

Unable to resist such infectious enthusiasm, Georgie looked around her with a new appreciation, so far forgetting herself and the role she felt compelled to play that she actually began to take pleasure in it all.

"Enjoying yourself, sprite?" a deep voice inquired at her elbow.

She whirled around to find the earl smiling down at her. "Well, not . . . well, actually, I am," she conceded with some surprise.

His earlier vexation at her easy dismissal of him entirely forgotten as he surveyed her expressive face, Brian was unprepared for the happiness he felt at seeing her. It was a strange mixture of emotions, both comfort and anticipation, as he realized how relaxed he felt conversing with her, knowing that he could choose any topic and she would not only follow his lead but also have something to the point to contribute. He looked forward to hearing her comments and opinions on anything and everything, for whatever she spoke on, Georgie brought freshness, wit, and a new way of seeing things that never failed to intrigue him. "They seem to be forming for a country dance. Are you up to the rigors of executing figures on a crowded floor?" he invited.

Georgie nodded and they made their way to the set closest to them. The floor was so full of couples that they had little chance for conversation, and by the time the music ended they were both flushed with the exertion and the heat from the brilliant chandeliers and the other dancers.

"I am more done in by that than any early-morning gallop," the earl remarked, clearing a path back to the dowager's side as best he could. "Let me return you to the safety of Grandmother's pillar and I shall see what I can do about procuring some refreshment."

"Thank you," Georgie gasped, pushing the damp curls back from her forehead.

They had almost reached the relative calm of the pillar when a gay voice interrupted, "Why, Lord Brandon, how delightful to see you! I vow it has been an age."

The earl turned to find Letitia Carrington, clad in a gown that left little to the imagination, advancing purposefully toward them. "Letitia, you here?" he inquired bluntly, not bothering to disguise his surprise at finding her in such a select gathering.

Refusing to take offense, the redhead laughed gaily. "I am visiting an old school friend, Lady Dabney, who absolutely insisted that I accompany them," she responded, indicating a colorless couple behind her with no distinguishing characteristics except the wife's nervous worried look and the husband's nonexistent chin.

Bullied them, more like, the earl thought to himself as he

assessed them with one swift penetrating glance. "Just so.
If you'll pardon me, I must return Lady Georgiana to her
aunt. She is feeling rather faint—the heat, you know," he
excused himself, taking Georgie's arm in a firm grip before
she could protest.

They had barely passed out of earshot before Georgie
turned on him indignantly. "I am feeling no such thing! I
am not such a poor creature—why, I . . ."

"Have never felt faint in your life," he completed her
sentence for her. "I know, but much as you scorn such
weakness, sometimes it can be a very useful way to feel."
The earl silenced her with a meaningful look and, depositing
her next to Lizzy, went in search of the promised
refreshment.

"Why doesn't that woman leave him alone?" his sister
complained *sotto voce,* a look of disapproval marring her
unusual sunny countenance.

Georgie glanced discreetly over her shoulder. To Lizzy's
disgust she came to Letitia's defense. Taking in the redhead's
alabaster skin, flaming hair, vivacious expression, and
voluptuous figure, she remarked casually, "Why, I thought
she was rather pretty."

"That's as may be, but I think she acts like a perfect harpy
where Brian is concerned," her companion muttered darkly
before turning to her grandmother to ask the identity of a
tall dark-haired man in uniform.

At that moment the music stopped and the tinkling tones
of the colonel's lady wafted clearly over the general hum
of conversation. "Oh, undoubtedly that is who it is. I did
not think that the Earl of Aldringham's taste ran to young
women, particularly if they are lacking in dash, so it must
be his ward. Poor Lord Brandon. It must be very difficult
to bear for such a leader of fashion to be responsible for such
a perfect quiz."

Georgie felt as though she'd been tipped a leveler. So taken
aback was she that it never occurred to her that the originator
of the remark meant for it to be overheard, nor did she see
the triumphant look the redhead cast in her direction. She
felt herself go cold all over and suddenly found it difficult

to catch her breath. She wanted desperately to run and hide, but at the same time she wanted to face everyone down and prove that, if she were to choose to waste her time as a slave to fashion, she could outshine anyone. Clenching and unclenching her hands, she was fighting to maintain a bland unconcerned expression on her face when the earl appeared bearing glasses of lemonade.

"I daresay this is the greatest service any man could render to ladies fair," he complained as he handed glasses to the little coterie by the pillar. "You have no idea the risk to life and limb I incurred on your behalves, and I give you fair warning I expect profuse expressions of gratitude from all of you." Brian addressed all the ladies, but his concern was all for Georgie. He, too, had overheard Letitia's infelicitous remark and, wiser in the ways of the *ton* than his ward, immediately recognized the true audience for whom it was intended. He smiled grimly at the thought of Letitia's dismay were she to discover that it had also reached the ears of one for whom it was very definitely *not* intended, and produced an effect quite the opposite from the one she had imagined.

Glancing down at his ward, the earl reflected how refreshing it was to know a woman whose existence did not revolve around the *ton*, who did not weigh every action in terms of its possible social consequences, and who could be relied upon to speak and act just as she saw fit, according to her own interests and principles. It certainly made for more diverting companionship, uncomfortable though that might be at times. The more he considered it, the more Brian realized that no matter how attracted he was initially by a woman, it was usually no time at all before boredom began to set in, rendering her less alluring in proportion to the predictability of her thoughts.

As he passed in mental review all the women he had known in his life, he discovered that with the exception of his grandmother and his sister, no one except Georgie Southwold had stimulated his interest or kept him amused for any length of time. The earl smiled cynically to himself when he considered how often he had put up with idiocy in a woman that he would never have tolerated in a man simply because she could stir his senses. Brian, my lad, you've been a fool, he thought, shaking his head. And you have never realized it until now, when some chit who barely knows you points it out in the most inadvertent yet conclusive manner.

Meanwhile, the unwitting precipitator of these revelations was indulging in some serious reflections herself, and they were not at all pleasant. Georgie, who would have scorned to become a fashion plate for her own sake, was now seriously considering becoming one for the sake of others. As she looked at Lizzy, ravishing in an exquisitely draped gown of white muslin whose corsage was ornamented with lozenges of net and pearls, the skirt festooned with roses, or at the dowager, handsomely attired in French gray silk ornamented with blond lace, she began to feel, if not a complete antidote, at least somewhat dowdy. Even though Lizzy wore the obligatory white muslin of a young miss in her first Season, she had somehow contrived to choose a gown that was distinctive, while her grandmother, equally constrained by what society considered suitable for dowagers, also managed to appear the height of elegance.

Georgie's eyes strayed across the room to where the earl, flirting with Lady Jersey, was drawing admiring glances from a number of women of all ages. His air of fashion, the beautifully cut coat molded to perfection over his broad shoulders, the exquisitely tied cravat that emphasized the square jaw and strong tanned features set him apart from most men in the ballroom, many of whom were far better acquainted with their tailors and far more slaves to their valets than the Earl of Aldringham.

Georgie sighed when she thought of the contrast she must present, both to the ladies in his family and to the women she had seen him with. The Brandons had not only welcomed her, they had warmly included her in all their activities. It was the least she could do not to detract from their consequence. Squaring her shoulders, she set about immediately to remedy the situation. "Lizzy," she began.

That lively damsel, gazing fixedly at the other end of the ballroom, did not appear the least bit aware of her companion.

"Lizzy," Georgie tried again.

Lizzy jumped and looked conscious. "I beg your pardon, I was not attending. But, oh, Georgie, does not Ferdie Ponsonby look dashing in his regimentals?"

Georgie dismissed the dark-haired young man with the merest glance. "I suppose so, but I was wondering, do you think—?"

"You *suppose* so? Georgie, you hardly took a second look. I think he is excessively handsome," Lizzy sighed.

"I daresay he is, but do you think—?"

"You daresay! Georgie, he casts all the other young men here quite in the shade. Have you not even noticed?" The other girl was incredulous.

"Well, no, I am not generally interested in such things," Georgie apologized.

"You *are* a sad case." Lizzy shook her head, regarding her friend with amused puzzlement. "If you don't care to dance or flirt with handsome young men, why do you go to balls?"

"Because my Uncle Ned wished me to," was the prompt reply.

"But, Georgie," Lizzy wailed, "balls are fun! The music is so pretty, one can't help wishing to dance, and the clothes are so lovely and the men look so much more dashing in evening dress. If you are not careful, you'll wind up on the shelf."

"And what, pray tell, is wrong with that? I daresay I should like it. Then I should be past praying for and I could do precisely as I pleased," Georgie retorted.

This was so horrifying a thought that for once Lizzy was struck quite dumb, but, seeing her elder brother emerge from the crowd, she quickly appealed to him. "Brian, Georgie says she would not mind being on the shelf. Isn't that too dreadful?"

Her brother grinned. "I am not the least surprised. Georgie's mind is on higher things. She has little patience with such frippery." The smile faded as, looking intently at his ward, he added softly, "But it would be the greatest pity imaginable, and such a waste."

Georgie did not know where to look. The serious tone and the fixity of his gaze were unlike the earl, and it made her uncomfortable, though she would have been hard put to say exactly why.

It was some time before she was able to broach to Lizzy the subject preoccupying her mind, but several country dances later, she was able to wrest a promise from Lizzy to accompany her on a shopping expedition to Bond Street. That young lady was a trifle surprised at the request, as Georgie was known to complain about the little amount of time she was already forced to spend with dressmakers, but, never loath to become involved in the search for fashionable costume, be it hers or someone else's, Lizzy accepted the invitation with alacrity and it was fixed that Georgie would call for her the next day.

19

Though delighted to accompany Georgie to that mecca of fashionable ladies, Lizzy could not refrain from remarking that it was a queer start on the part of her friend. "For I thought you disliked such things excessively," she commented as she rolled down Brook Street.

"I do," was the succinct reply. "I, for one, do not believe that clothes make the man, but as the rest of the *ton* apparently does, I refuse to have my character maligned simply because my toilette is not as carefully attended to as the state of my soul."

Her friend stared. This was a new Georgie indeed! What could have occurred to bring about such a change? Not having had the dubious privilege of overhearing Letitia Carrington's remark herself, Lizzy cudgeled her brains trying to recall the scenes of the previous evening, but try as she would, she could not remember that Georgie had suffered any set-downs or been partnered by anyone who seemed to have captured her friend's fancy. Failing that, she was condemned to wait with as much patience as she could muster, always a trial to the impetuous Lizzy, for further developments that would shed some light on the situation.

Madame Celeste was delighted to see them, and while she expected little custom from Georgie, her aunt and her immediate companion could always be counted upon for large orders. Thus she was most surprised to discover that Lady Georgiana was the principal customer that day and that nothing less than a complete transformation was desired. "Mmmm." Madame herself took the situation in hand as she walked round and round Georgie, her expressive Gallic features furrowed by an expression of intense concentration. "Mademoiselle's toilette is, of course, *très elegante,* but

Mademoiselle desires to be a little more *éclatante, non*?''
She was silent a moment, thinking; then her features
brightened. *"Oui, c'est ça! On a besoin de plus de joie de
vivre."* With that, she clapped her hands and sent minions
scurrying in all directions, retrieving bolts of cloth, laces,
and trimmings of every description, and for the next several
hours Georgie stood as immobile as a statue while Madame
and her seamstresses pulled, prodded, draped, and pinned.

At last Madame stood back, well pleased with her work,
but a frown still hovered on her countenance. "Aha! *La
coiffure, c'est trop sévère,"* she exclaimed.

Intensely alarmed, Georgie covered her golden tresses with
protective hands, but Madame was certain of her unerring
instinct for elegance and in the long run she had her way.
The hairdresser was called in and he snipped and pulled,
twisting Georgie's head one way and then the other until she
felt the veriest puppet in the hands of an artist.

At last it was done and she was allowed to view her reflection in the looking glass in a corner of the elegant establishment. She was forced to admit that Madame knew her
business. The reflection that stared back was Georgie
Southwold and yet it was not Georgie. The finely shaped
head, relieved of its heavy tresses, had a more flirtatious tilt
to it. Her delicately molded features, surrounded by feathery
curls, looked piquant rather than defiant. The new jonquil
walking dress, cut tight to the shape, more fully revealed
the elegant figure underneath, while the color called attention
to the green of her eyes and the creaminess of her
complexion. Its high collar and the capuchin bonnet framed
her lovely face to perfection and drew all eyes to its best
features, the classic nose and perfectly sculptured lips.

"Oh, Georgie, you do look fine as fivepence," Lizzy
exclaimed delightedly. "I knew you would once you had rid
yourself of those dowdy dresses you insist upon wearing.
We must drive round the park to observe the effect."

With that, they thanked Madame profusely, ordered the
footman to gather the assorted bandboxes, and climbed into
the carriage. Madame, a smile of satisfaction lighting up her
shrewd Gallic features, watched them roll off down Bond

Street. "She is not certain she wants to be a woman yet, that one," she remarked to her assistant, who nodded eagerly. "But when she finds the right man, she will be ten times the woman that most of these simpering ladies are." Sighing audibly, she went back inside to tackle the problem of creating a ball gown that would not make Lady Blandford look like a pudding bag tied in the middle.

It was a perfect day, fresh and sunny, with a few clouds scattered here and there to call attention to the intense blue of the sky, and there were numbers of people taking the air in the park. It would have been an exaggeration to say that everyone stopped, stunned by Georgie's transformation, but there were enough of them who gazed appreciatively at the remarkably pretty picture made by the two elegantly attired young ladies, one dark and one fair, to assure Georgie that the change was noticeable. Heretofore she had not given the slightest thought to her effect on people, or stopped to wonder whether or not they found her attractive. Such things had been of the supremist indifference to her. Now, somewhat to her dismay, she found herself enjoying the glances of admiration and approval cast in her direction.

Her confidence and sense of well-being were further encouraged when they encountered Cedric, magnificent to behold in a curricle with yellow wheels. "Hello, Georgie, Lizzy," he greeted them with insouciance. Then, scrutinizing his cousin more closely, he pulled his horses to a dead halt. "That's a very dashing rig you are wearing." He ran a knowing eye over her bonnet, new coiffure, and walking dress. "Madame Celeste and Monsieur Henri, I should think," he hazarded.

"What a complete hand you are, Ceddie," Lizzy laughed, while Georgie looked at her cousin in some surprise. Despite Lady Debenham's claims as to his discriminating knowledge of fashion, she was impressed with his unerring skill in identifying the source of her transformation. Perhaps she had been naive in underestimating the sway the Bond Street modistes held over the *ton*.

"Not at all," Cedric replied with becoming modesty. "Only Madame could have selected a style that was so much

Georgie's own. Delighted to see you taking your true place in the *ton,* Coz. It is always the greatest shame not to take advantage of naturally elegant features when one has 'em.'' With an airy wave of his hand he was off, leaving Georgie to stare after him.

"He is in the right of it, you know," Lizzy remarked thoughtfully. "Your old wardrobe made you look severe and you're far too pretty, and too nice besides, to scare everyone off with such a forbidding air.''

"Perhaps I wished to." Georgie could not keep a tiny note of defiance from her voice. She was not entirely sure that she was pleased with the change. She was honest enough to admit that she enjoyed the appreciative looks directed her way, but she was not at all certain that she wanted the attention. Just because she had decided she no longer wished to look a complete antidote did not mean that she had cast aside her dislike for the vapid interests of the fashionable world, nor did she wish to be classified with the rest of the *ton.* Previously her lack of concern for the refinements of dress had proclaimed her disinterest and set her apart. With this change, however, she had lost that distinction and she was uneasy that in doing so she had somehow lost some of her independence as well.

Lady Debenham, though not ordinarily a perceptive individual, was sympathetic enough to detect some of her niece's unease and refrained from making any extravagant remarks, confining herself to one small comment. "You look vastly elegant, my dear, but come, you must help me with this letter from Chalmers and the accounts he has sent me. I cannot make head nor tail of them. Figures always did put me in such a muddle.''

Georgie took the crumpled papers and sank onto the settee, glad of the chance to distract herself with something useful. Any other time she would have been amused by her aunt's request. Though she might throw up her hands in horror at her niece's familiarity with trade and her propensity for keeping up with the newspapers, Lady Debenham had begun to have a healthy respect for her capabilities. It had first dawned on her that Georgie was a very useful person to have around when her niece had come upon her hopelessly mired in tradesmen's bills at a dire moment when Chalmers had been off somewhere in the country. Seemingly with no effort at all, Georgie had made mice feet of the impossibly tangled figures and unraveled several difficult problems, explaining them in such a way that they seemed perfectly clear to her befuddled aunt. Since then she had gradually come to rely on Georgie for dealing with that unfortunate and intrusive part of life called accounts, and no longer dreaded the missives from Chalmers or the tradesmen who received her custom.

On her part, Georgie was more than happy to do this. Afraid that because she was not taking the *ton* by storm, she was offering little to her aunt in recompense for being foisted upon her, she seized this as an opportunity to repay her in some small measure at least for her kindness in taking her in. Besides, she liked being useful and the earl's managing of her own finances, with the exception of her allowance, left her with very little to do in an area that had once occupied a great deal of her time and interest.

At the thought of this allowance, Georgie scowled. The earl had very kindly and promptly set up a generous allowance so that she was never forced to apply to him for money, but the rest of her finances were very firmly in his hands. Once, during a ride in the park when she had broached the subject of investing in the consols, he had responded, "What would a green girl like you know about the consols?" in such an amused tone that she had been too angry to trust herself with a reply and had simply urged Lakshmi forward to the more pleasurable companionship of the earl's younger brother.

Though the earl, realizing that he had truly offended her, had offered something of an apology later, which had mollified her somewhat, he nevertheless continued to retain fiscal control. While Georgie remained no more pleased with the situation than she had been at the outset, she was forced to acknowledge in all fairness that to the best of his ability, Lord Brandon was fulfilling the obligations which he had been placed under by Uncle Ned, obligations that had not been of his seeking and were certainly as irksome to him as they were to her.

With the earl still on her mind, Georgie's imagination leapt ahead to the coming evening and Lady Williston's ridotto. Despising herself for the very thought, she wondered if he would be as aware of her attempts to be more *à la mode,* as Cedric and her aunt had been. And if he were to notice, which surely someone as alert and perspicacious as he would, would he make any comment? Georgie, my girl, if you don't stop such missish nonsense at once you will soon be no better than all the other eager young things who live for nothing but the admiration they strive so desperately to win. If you don't have care, you will turn into a slave of fashion. And with this salutary admonition she returned to the accounts with such a vengeance that they were cleared up in very short order.

The object of her unwilling reflections was at that moment sauntering down St. James Street on his way to Brooks's. The earl had awakened that morning to a stifling sense of boredom, which had threatened to overwhelm him. Though a bout at Gentleman Jackson's had given him physical energy, it had done nothing to dispel his mental lethargy, which he hoped would be at least somewhat alleviated by deep play and a good bottle of port. Face it, Brandon, he sighed, the lack of challenge is rotting your brain, and you're losing your touch, what with all this respectability and inactivity.

The mood had come upon him the previous evening at Althea's after the opera. She had been looking magnificent as usual and had been as seductive as ever, but it had all been so predictable. At one particularly passionate moment he had found himself wishing that she would stop nibbling his ear and running her hands tantalizingly over his body and just talk to him. It had taken considerable concentration on his part to return her caresses, and all the while he was calling himself a fool for finding an evening with the most alluring woman in all of London dull.

In fact she had talked, but that was part of the problem. Lady Wyndham's conversation was always charming, but

never enlightening, and he had heard it all so many times
before from so many other inviting lips. His companion,
sensing his abstraction, had redoubled her efforts, and then,
when he had failed to respond with his usual skill and fervor,
pouted prettily. "You are not attending, my lord."

"I am sorry, Althea. I . . . You are the most charming
woman in the world, but my wits seem to be wandering this
evening," he apologized. "I am no fit companion for you
tonight. I shall call on you tomorrow." With that, he had
gathered his cloak and headed for the door, leaving the beauty
staring.

No man had ever left her before. Her eyes became
suspicious slits as she tried to guess which woman would
have the audacity and the skill to compete with her. The
smashing of another Sèvres figurine did little to relieve her
frustration, and she went to bed in a thoroughly nasty humor.

"Brandon . . ." A military-looking man rose from the faro
table to greet the earl with the enthusiasm of one who
recognizes a fellow sufferer caught in the unadventurous
routine of fashionable existence.

"Hello, Bertie. What, have you gone and sold out?"

Bertie looked dismal. "The pater is in a bad way and I
am the only one. I am like to go out of my mind, this life
is so dashed flat."

Knowing Bertie Etheridge and his propensity for getting
into "a spot of trouble now and then" as he phrased it, Brian
could well believe this was true. "Cheer up, man, you're
about to see someone take his chances with the faro bank.
But you're in the right of it, life is dull when all you have
to risk is your blunt."

By this time a crowd had gathered, for the earl was known
to play for high stakes and to offer stiff competition. The
earl sat down and the dealer began to draw the cards. Even
to those accustomed to seeing their cronies wager a fortune
on the turn of a card, the sums he was risking seemed
enormous. Sitting practically immobile, with barely a flicker
of interest in his eyes, Brian declared his bets. There were
some he lost, but the pile of winnings grew steadily, and the
more they grew, the more impassive he became and the

greater the sums he hazarded. Finally, shoving all that he had accumulated to the middle of the table, he rose. "You're right, Bertie. Life in London is deucedly flat," he remarked with a mirthless smile, and strode out of the club, leaving yet more people to stare after him.

"Plaguey fellow, Brandon. He's got the most beautiful woman in London as his mistress, is rich as Croesus, and he still ain't satisfied," one of them complained before turning his attention back to the cards. The others nodded in silent agreement.

Meanwhile, the subject of their speculation was riding briskly toward the park in the hopes that the fresh air and the feel of good horseflesh underneath him would restore some of his vitality. He was grateful that a letter had arrived that morning from his bailiff, making it necessary to go down to Aldringham for several days. At least there, while he would not find much in the way of adventure, he would have something besides endless social encounters to occupy his time and challenge his mind. But first there was Lady Williston's ridotto that evening, and he had promised Lizzy that he would escort her. He sighed, reined in Caesar, and urged him in the direction of Grosvenor Square.

20

The ballroom was already crowded at Lady Williston's elegant town house when Georgie and her aunt arrived. "Ah, Aurelia, delightful to see you." The diminutive hostess broke away from an overpowering dowager in a purple turban to welcome them. "You are looking prodigious elegant, as always. And this must be your niece."

Georgie found herself subjected to the scrutiny of two bright eyes which, though curious, were not unfriendly and seemed to be pleased with what they saw. "Charming. You are to be congratulated, Aurelia. Not that you would be related to a great lout of a girl, but some young people's looks these days are so unfortunate." Lady Williston turned to Georgie. "Dreadful, the way we all look at each Season's crop of young misses as though they were prime bits of blood at Tattersall's, but when one gets to be my age, it is one of the few sources of amusement, I assure you. Besides, the only thing that distinguishes one Season from another is the new faces. You needn't worry, though, with your classic features and the sense of style you share with your aunt, you should catch on immediately. And, if I am not mistaken, my young nephew is looking this way with some interest." She beckoned to a tall youth who had been gazing at them intently from some distance away.

"Philip, you remember my dear friend Lady Debenham? May I present you to her niece Lady Georgiana Southwold. Now, don't blush, my boy. We town tabbies are the very devil with our interfering ways, but if it weren't for people like us, shy young men like you would never find a partner. Now, take Georgie off for this next country dance while I catch up on the latest from Aurelia, there's a good boy." Observing her nephew's embarrassed hesitation, she turned again to Georgie. "I say, you don't bite, do you, Georgie?"

Barely able to repress a chuckle at her redoubtable hostess's forthright manner, Georgie assured her that she did not.

"There, what did I tell you? She's an unexceptionable young lady. Be off with you. I daresay if you begin by complaining to each other about matchmaking aunts, you'll soon be dealing famously with each other in no time."

Philip did not look to be completely reassured by this, but some of the alarm in his expression had subsided.

Georgie took pity on him. "I always used to wish to be a man because they are allowed to do ever so many things that girls are not, but I quite see how difficult it can be. Why, I should never have the courage to ask someone to dance."

Her prospective partner cast her a grateful look. "It's these great balls I dislike, with everyone looking at you. Why, on the hunting field or anywhere else I can hold my own with anyone and I don't feel the least bit awkward talking to women, but in the ballroom they are all tricked out in finery and they just look and act differently. They inspect you as though your cravat were all a mess or your coat didn't fit, and then they simper."

"I am sure they simper because they are excessively uncomfortable themselves and equally unsure of how they appear. I know I am," she added candidly.

"You? But you are so beautiful," he blurted.

Georgie looked up in astonishment. "What?"

"I wanted to talk to you because you seemed different— nicer than all the rest, but you are so pretty that I was afraid you would be like them after all."

Georgie laughed. "Thank you. I assure you I don't feel the least bit pretty." She was silent a moment before confiding, "It's the clothes, I expect. I put myself in the hands of my aunt's modiste." And she certainly did look particularly lovely in a dress of Urling's net over a white satin slip, the corsage molded tight to her figure and trimmed with pearls. Her curls, which clustered around her face, were also threaded with pearls whose gleam served to heighten the golden glints in her hair. Certainly others seemed to be of the opinion expressed by Philip, for numerous eyes followed their progress on the floor, and when they had finished, his friends, seeing how much he appeared to be enjoying himself, crowded round to be introduced and beg dances of their own.

Being in such demand was a novelty for Georgie, and though she did not set much store by popularity in the *ton*, she could not help enjoying the attention she was receiving. Her eyes sparkled, and her expression, which too often tended toward one of serious reflection for most people's comfort, was laughing and vivacious.

By the time the earl and his party arrived, she was the center of a lively and admiring group that immediately caught the eye of those entering the ballroom. Always alive to the charms of beautiful women, the earl took in the slim form in shimmering white whose golden curls gleamed in the candlelight. Just then she and a partner broke away from the group and he was able to catch a better glimpse of the woman who had been captivating the attention of so many young bucks. It was a shock when he suddenly realized that the alluring figure moving so gracefully on the dance floor was Georgie.

For a moment he was absolutely still, mesmerized by a welter of confused impressions and thoughts. Foremost was surprise at himself for not having recognized before what a lovely young woman she truly was. To him she had always been Sprite, with her own special and charming mixture of innocence and independence. She was older, to be sure, than the child who had enchanted him in the ancient banyan tree, but while he realized that she had grown up and acquired the experience and wisdom of an adult, he had continued to relate to her as he would to a girl, to his sister perhaps. Now he was faced with her as someone who captured his interest and stirred his senses in quite another way, and he was uncertain as to how he felt about this new Sprite, this one whose delicate form seemed to mold itself to her partner's—surely he was holding her much more closely than was necessary—this new Sprite, whose finely shaped head on its delicate neck was tilted up at the young man guiding her around the floor, the beautifully shaped lips parted, her eyes bright with interest.

All of a sudden Brian was seized with the strangest desire to wrest her from her partner and pull her to him, claiming, "She's mine. I discovered the spirit that lies beneath the outward shell that attracts the rest of the world. I know and appreciate the intelligence behind that lovely face." And then he wanted to sweep her through the half-open French doors onto the balcony, crush her in his arms, and cover her with kisses from her soft inviting lips to the hollow at the base of her throat. The vision lasted only an instant, but it was enough to overwhelm him with unexpected and unsought emotions. Suddenly he wanted nothing more than to be with her and take care of her—the person who a short time ago had been another responsibility threatening his independence. And he, admirer of so many beautiful women, accustomed to moving quickly from one to the next to protect his cherished freedom, was consumed with jealousy at the sight of her in someone else's arms.

He shook his head and took a deep breath, trying to reestablish his customary aloof detachment. Never one to labor under any illusions about himself or anyone else, the earl sought to view the situation objectively and, after a moment's struggle, was able to see the humor in it. Here he was, a man of the world, as much at the mercy of his passions as any callow youth, and all on account of a scrubby schoolgirl who wasn't even his particular style of woman.

"Doesn't Georgie look elegant? Madame Celeste certainly outshone herself this time," a voice at his elbow intruded into the turmoil of his thoughts.

If he had been less at the mercy of his own emotions, Brian would have recognized the knowing look in his sister's eye, but as it was, he was too bemused even to hear the smugness in her voice or notice the satisfaction in her smile as she stared across the room at Georgie, besieged by hopeful partners at the dance's end.

While no one else would have read the slightest thing into the earl's perusal of the assemblage upon entering the ballroom, the sharp eyes of his two companions had missed nothing. Each, with a hand through his arm, had been aware of the precise moment Brian had seen Georgie, for he had halted dead in his tracks. It had not taken Lizzy or the dowager more than an instant to follow the direction of his gaze or hazard a fairly accurate guess as to the nature of his thoughts, and each was drawing a great deal of enjoyment from his momentary stupefaction.

Now we shall see how much Letitia Carrington can command his attention, Lizzy remarked to herself with a gratification not untinged with malice. While at the same time her grandmother was thinking: That ought to make Althea Wyndham look to her laurels.

And the earl, prompted by Lizzy's remark, was undergoing another revelation. What a nodcock I am, he exclaimed to himself. Of course she looks different. She has done herself in the latest fashion. He smiled. And done it with elegance and style too. It must have been Letitia's remark, because no one could have cajoled Sprite into becoming a fashion plate. Such a dramatic change could only have come about if she were challenged to it somehow. That train of thought led to the inevitable conclusion that what she would not have done for herself, Georgie must have done, consciously or unconsciously, for him.

Brian was unprepared for the rush of tenderness that overwhelmed him at such an idea. All of his life he had somehow been doing things for other people—tumbling into scrapes while he did it, to be sure—but for the most part it had been because he had been defending the rights of those weaker than himself or he had been resisting blind, unfeeling authority on principle. Now someone had done something with him in mind and he was inexpressibly touched. He wanted to rush right over to Georgie to let her know how much her gesture meant to him, to tell her that he had always thought her beautiful, and to thank her for caring so much about his reputation in a society whose opinion she did not give a rap for. But before he could, Lizzy was begging him to dance with her and he was forced to watch his ward being led onto the floor by another from the seemingly inexhaustible supply of partners surrounding her.

At long last the earl was able to make his way to her side, only to discover that the new Georgie up close was even more disturbing than the new Georgie at a distance. Surely the décolletage which allowed such a distracting amount of beautifully sculptured shoulder and bosom to show was too daring for a girl in her first Season. And the enchanting, teasing smile she gave him that revealed just a hint of a dimple next to the lips that invited kisses was more provocative than was proper in one just out of the schoolroom. Georgie was right: you *are* in danger of being as straitlaced as the rest of the *ton,* an unpleasantly perceptive voice inside his head commented. Brian's face, already serious, grew grimmer at the thought.

Remarking the unwontedly dour expression and unsure how to read it, Georgie looked up curiously at him. "My lord?" she began cautiously.

"I came . . ." What precisely had he come for? He wasn't certain. All he knew was that he wanted to be close to her.

Georgie's eyes began to dance. Though not well versed in the ways of the world, she had felt Brian's eyes on her from across the ballroom and had done her best to ignore them. But furtively glancing over the shoulders of various partners whenever she was able to get him in her field of vision, she had caught him staring at her more than once. Now, observing him carefully, she read the confusion in his eyes, heard the uncertainty in his voice, and with a feminine intuition she would never have admitted to possessing, she knew that it was a direct result of her visit to Madame Celeste. Good! She smiled triumphantly to herself. Let him be confused. It would do him good. He was too accustomed to dominating every situation.

"I came, I wished . . ." Damn, he cursed himself, I'm as tongue-tied as a schoolboy. Courage, Brian, she's like any of the scores of women you have been able to charm. But that was just it, she wasn't. She was more innocent and vulnerable in her inexperience, while at the same time far more intelligent, observant, and sensitive than any other woman he had known, and he was at a loss. Buck up, man! He made one last desperate attempt to overcome his

ridiculous hesitancy. After all, it's only Sprite you're
addressing. "At the moment you seem to be without a
partner. May I offer my services for the waltz?" How
ridiculously stiff it sounded, but at least he had gotten it out.

Another smile, even more enchanting than the last,
appeared. "I should love to. Thank you."

She truly sounded as though she meant it, he thought in
some surprise. "Come, then." He led her onto the floor,
thinking as he put his arm around her waist that he had
himself well in hand now, but he was wrong. The nearness
of her, the scent of rosewater in her hair, the music, the
graceful way she followed his every movement, were intoxicating and he felt as though he were under some spell in
which he was unable to think or speak.

"Do my ears deceive me, or is the Earl of Aldringham
entirely without conversation?" a teasing voice interrupted.

He looked down into the big green eyes, and without
thinking, he blurted the first thing that came into his mind.
"No, I was just thinking how very beautiful you are."

A decided twinkle appeared in their emerald depths.
"Spanish coin, my lord. You forget that I am not like your
other ladies. I do not require daily doses of flattery for my
vanity."

"I am not offering you Spanish coin. And I know you're
not like my 'other ladies.' They know how to accept a
compliment gracefully." He paused. "And what, by the way,
precisely do you mean by 'other ladies'?"

"You know, Mrs. Carrington, Lady Wyndham, and I
expect there are others whose names I don't know."

The earl didn't know whether to be pleased that she had
observed his activities so closely or dismayed by her refusal
to recognize the delicacy of the subject. After some moments
he decided he was amused. "Not only do properly behaved
young women know how to accept compliments, they know
enough not to comment on their partners' 'other interests,'
if they are aware of them at all."

"Oh, pooh." Georgie dismissed properly behaved young
women with a disgusted frown. "Everyone knows you are
irresistible to women and that you are being pursued by any

number of them. As your ward, I made it my business to discover just which ones they were. I have a reputation to maintain, and it would never do to have a guardian who wasn't being sought after by diamonds of the first water. And I must say, both of them are excessively pretty,'' Georgie remarked with her usual candor. But there was the tiniest note of wistfulness in her voice that the earl, perceptive as he was, noticed immediately, and he was touched.

''Don't refine upon it too much, sprite. It is merely the fashion to admire me at the moment. I am a novelty and I come with the allure of travel to foreign parts as well as a title and a respectable income. Besides, none of these 'other ladies' is even aware that Sanskrit exists, much less wishes to know about it or learn it.''

Georgie glanced at him curiously. He was reassuring her, but why? It was not as though she cared in the least about his amatory interests, though it was true, she admitted to herself, that seeing women as beautiful and sophisticated as Lady Wyndham or as dashing as Letitia Carrington made her feel like a scrubby schoolgirl. She half-suspected him of teasing her, but his expression was serious. In fact, there was a warmth in the brown eyes looking into hers and an intimacy and kindness in the smile that were almost like a caress. It made her feel very special and cared for, and she could not help smiling back and whispering, ''Thank you.''

They would have stood there for some time, enjoying the moment of closeness and silent communication, but Lizzy, her cheeks pink from exertion on the dance floor, appeared with a tall, rather gawky youth in tow. ''Hello, Georgie, Brian, you must meet Sir Hugo Fortescue. When I mentioned to him that you both had lived in India, he begged to meet you, as he is most interested in India himself.''

Sir Hugo turned to Georgie. ''Lady Elizabeth tells me that you have only just arrived here and that you spent your entire youth in India with your uncle, who made his fortune there. I should so like to hear about it, their customs, the trade, anything.''

He looked so earnest in his interest—rather like a puppy—that Georgie could not help smiling and responding.

Watching her answer his eager questions, the earl was occupied with more cynical thoughts. "It appears that young Fortescue is far more intrigued by Georgie than by India," he remarked sardonically to his sister. "Did you say he was one of the Kent branch of Fortescues?"

Lizzy looked up, puzzled. "Why, yes. He knows Grandmama."

"And Grandmama introduced him to you?" he asked incredulously.

"Well, no, not exactly." Lizzy faltered. "She was talking to Lady Bradenham when he came up and introduced himself and said he would like to meet you because of your experience in India. And naturally, having heard that Georgie was your ward, he wished to meet her too."

"Ah." The earl nodded, a speculative frown on his face, as though this confirmed something for him.

"Whatever are you—?" his sister began curiously, but a sudden lull in the conversation next to them put a stop to her question and she was forced to content herself with the thought that she could worm the truth of her brother's odd behavior from him on their way home in the carriage. However, in the whirl of partners and flirtatious conversations, she soon forgot the strange cold way he had treated Sir Hugo. The next day, the earl was off to Aldringham to attend to the problems his bailiff had written him about, and in Brian's absence she put the scene from her mind so that it was forgotten entirely.

21

This was not the case with her brother, who, driving his curricle along country roads bursting with the beginning blossoms of spring, was entirely oblivious of the beauty around him. That fellow, he fumed to himself, with his fresh-faced look and eager, innocent ways, will stop at nothing to entrap some heiress. But why must he choose Sprite when it's Lombard Street to a China Orange that Lord Wentworth's whey-faced daughter would have him in a minute and she must command five thousand more a year? But he knew why Sir Hugo would choose Georgie. Any man would have, fortune hunter or no, he thought ruefully. For the rest of the evening at Lady Williston's he had had ample opportunity to take stock of the effect of Madame Celeste's artistry. To be sure, the mere donning of a new gown and the wearing of a new coiffure did not change Georgie from an independent young woman inclined to be a disdainful observer of the follies of the *ton* into an incomparable, but it had made her see herself in another light, which was enough to attract the attention of others and give her enough self-confidence to reveal the playful witty side of her character ordinarily reserved for her intimates, and only those intimates intelligent enough to appreciate her.

He had watched as partners, originally attracted by the slim graceful figure and enchanting smile, thronged around her. He had seen them relax and laugh, looking at her more appreciatively as they danced, and he had been aware of how their eyes followed her as another young buck led her to the floor. Yes, he understood very well why Sir Hugo would choose Sprite. Why, at this very moment he himself was remembering the way the candlelight shone on her curls, the twinkle that lurked in her green eyes as she looked up at him, the delicate smoothness of her skin that smelled so delicious. His thoughts lingered over the way she felt in his arms, soft, supple, and full of vitality, responding instantly to his touch.

Brian sighed. Here he was acting like any other callow youth, dwelling fondly on every one of her features. Why, even in his salad days he had not been so besotted. Besotted. The earl stopped short. Was he besotted, and over a mere chit of a girl who hadn't the least notion of feminine wiles, who would scorn to use any of the ploys that others had employed to attract him in the past? No, he wasn't besotted, he decided. He didn't burn with a desire to possess her. His blood didn't race at the thought of her. It was more tenderness he felt toward her than pure physical attraction. He pictured her as she must be this morning sitting among the newspapers, perusing a review, her brow furrowed in concentration as he had seen it when she was studying the book of Sanskrit he had shown her or when she was mulling over something he had said. No, he wasn't besotted, but he missed her already.

As the week wore on, the earl found himself missing Georgie more and more. Their friendship, once the initial awkwardness of the situation had worn off, had been so natural and so comfortable that he had not given it a second thought. In fact, he had hardly noticed it, but now that he was without her companionship, he felt the lack of it sorely. With the exception of Ned Wolvercote, Brian had never had a close friend and, until now, he had been content to have it that way. He had preferred the liberty of his solitary state to the constraints one naturally felt when part of a group, and to him, the freedom to go off anywhere, indulge in any sort of adventure without worrying about or consulting anyone else, had been more important than company. But now, having shared things with someone like Georgie, who went about life the same way he did, he discovered that there was an emptiness to being alone, rather than the peace, independence, and absence of complication he had enjoyed before. He found himself wondering how Georgie would deal with this tenant's complaint or that one's question on livestock, and as he galloped across the fresh-smelling fields or among hedgerows beginning to blossom, he thought often of how much she would relish the freedom to give Lakshmi her head and how much he would enjoy watching them.

While the earl was buried in the quiet of the country, prey to such unsettling self-examination and reflections, Georgie, now fully launched into the exigencies of existence as a sought-after young lady, barely had a moment to herself to reflect on any topic more serious than the choice of a bonnet or where to put the latest floral offering that had been left with Wilson. If she had stopped to consider it, she would have been amazed that she could have been the least diverted by the constant round of parties and the attention of eager young bucks. As it was, she discovered that with her newfound confidence conferred by a stylish appearance, and the appreciation it attracted, she was less defensive in her attitude toward the *ton* in general. She was more able to relax and be amused rather than irritated by its vagaries and excesses, and she actually began to enjoy herself. All this was helped, of course, by her budding friendship with Sir Hugo Fortescue.

His self-effacing manner contrasted strongly with that of so many other tulips of the *ton* who seemed to feel it incumbent upon them to make every young lady in her first Season feel the merest rustic, and his genuine interest in the customs of the country where she had spent her happiest years quickly won her trust. When he had confided to Georgie during a morning call that his interest in India, and more particularly in commerce in India, was based on a very real concern for repairing the family fortunes, she could only honor him for his forthrightness. There was something most appealing in the frank way he spoke. ''In truth, Lady Georgiana, I'd as lief remain in England with my dear mother, but to be perfectly honest, we haven't a feather to fly with and no expectations. If I do not make a fortune, how can I hope to win a wife? I am the last of our line, and if I don't have an heir, a most ancient and respected name will die out. Of course, one should never admit to such things, and in the general way of it, I shouldn't, but Lady Elizabeth tells me that you are extremely knowledgeable and somehow

I feel so comfortable with you, as though I had known you all my life. You are not like the other young ladies, who set such great store by fashion and fortune that one feels they are not the least bit interested in one as a person.''

"Why, thank you.'' Georgie could not help the blush of pleasure that rose to her cheeks as she read the admiration in his eyes. To own the truth, she was not accustomed to having such an effect on people and would have felt more uncomfortable than she did except for his deprecating posture and respectful tone.

"Lady Elizabeth also tells me that you hope to return to India someday and continue in your uncle's footsteps. He must have been remarkable to have raised single-handedly such a courageous and enterprising young woman.''

With such an interested and sympathetic audience, it was not long before Georgie was sharing scenes from the past and revealing her hopes for the future. She was shy at first. Remembering the initially discouraging reception when she had broached her plans to the earl and her aunt, she was most hesitant to confide them to someone she had been acquainted with for such a short period of time, but Sir Hugo was so enthusiastic and entered into them so wholeheartedly that she soon lost her initial reserve and responded without constraint to questions that were both pertinent and intelligent.

In fact, Georgie soon found herself quite looking forward to their encounters. With the earl in the country and Lizzy dividing her time between amusing her grandmother and responding to the attention of the many beaux attracted by her sparkling smile and playful manner, Georgie, despite the flattering number of morning callers, had been feeling rather lonely for someone to talk to.

Her constant intercourse with the inhabitants of Brandon House had spoiled her for interesting conversation, and the daily perusal of formerly engrossing journals was but a poor substitute. Thus it was an extraordinarily simple thing for Sir Hugo to establish a friendship and install himself as a favored visitor in Berkeley Square. Impressed by his ancient lineage and flattered by his manner—a judicious mixture of the gallant and the respectful—and his unfailing deference to her superior knowledge and taste on all topics remotely connected to the *ton,* Lady Debenham encouraged his presence in her drawing room and was delighted to accept his frequent escort to the theater and several musical evenings.

Sir Hugo was an easy, agreeable companion who could contribute to almost any topic of discussion. If he lacked the wit and the restless intelligence of the earl, he was certainly a more peaceful though less challenging conversationalist, and after constantly having to defend her positions and her ideas to her guardian, Georgie found his unquestioning admiration for her opinions soothing.

Though the earl was not as often in Georgie's thoughts as she was in his, she did miss their rides in the park. Being an indifferent horseman and lacking the wherewithal to keep a stable, Sir Hugo was unable to accompany her, so she and Lakshmi were forced to go with only a groom for companionship. While Georgie reveled in the physical exhilaration of the exercise and the chance to drink in the fresh air and the scent of newly blossomed flowers and trees, and dearly as she loved Lakshmi, she longed for the companionship of their rides. There had been many times when they had fallen quiet after some long involved discussion and had ridden along in friendly silence, at ease enough with each other to be alone with their own thoughts.

It was on one of these solitary morning rides that she saw a small sturdy figure mounted on a pony which was being urged to rear on its hind legs in a manner very similar to some of the performers at Astley's. "Georgie!" Percy's shout of delight made her name echo across the deserted park as he urged Prince to a gallop.

"Why, hello, Percy. How are you? You seem to be making a deal of progress with Prince. I daresay you'll be standing on his back and riding around the paddock at Aldringham in no time, if you haven't tried already."

"Well, I would do, if I had anyone to help me." His childish face was serious. "I tell you, it's deadly dull at home. Brian is down at Aldringham doing some fusty business, so he couldn't take me, and all Lizzy cares about is parties," he complained. Suddenly he brightened. "I say, why don't you come home with me? We could practice cricket and I could show you my tin soldiers and you could tell me stories about India and we'll be merry as grigs in no time. After all," he concluded, "you must find life sadly flat without Brian too."

And she did, Georgie reflected. Being an independent and resourceful person, she had always managed to keep herself occupied and interested throughout her life, wherever she was, but having grown accustomed to the earl's vital presence and the aura of energy he brought with him everywhere he went, she realized that without him she did find life more quiet than was to her liking. "Why, thank you, Percy, I should love to, but I could not intrude on the household like that without an invitation."

"I'm inviting you, aren't I, Fenton?" Percy appealed to his groom.

"That you are, Master Percy." Fenton's wizened face broke into a grin.

The little boy's face took on a pleading look. "Please say you will, Georgie. Please. I'm ever so bored."

Georgie laughed. She could not remember when her presence had been so important to anyone's amusement. Besides, she found it difficult to resist the entreaty in his brown eyes, so very like his brother's. "Very well, then, but we mustn't bother anyone else at Brandon House."

"Oh, no," he assured her solemnly. "I always try to be ever so quiet because of Mama's nerves. I'm glad you don't have nerves. They make people ever so cross."

"No, Percy, I am afraid I don't have a nerve in my body. Nothing gives me the vapors, though I daresay there are many that think I would be the better for an attack of them now and then."

"Grandmama doesn't have nerves either. She doesn't believe in them. Next to Brian, Grandmama is my favorite. She's a great gun, like you, but she is so old she gets tired. Come on. I want to show you my new cricket bat." And with that he dug his heels into Prince's flanks and trotted off in the direction of Grosvenor Square.

Having instructed Digby to inform her aunt of her whereabouts and to come collect her in two hours' time, Georgie followed suit. She did suffer a few qualms over her sudden and unannounced appearance at Brandon House, but she soon put those to rest, reassuring herself that she was only going to visit Percy and would not intrude on the others. Though she was loath to admit such a weakness, she too was the tiniest bit bored, and there was something about Percy's enthusiastic presence that, because it reminded her of his brother, made her more acutely aware of the earl's absence, but at the same time made her miss him less.

22

Far from being discommoded by Georgie's unexpected materialization at Grosvenor Square, the inhabitants of Brandon House were delighted to see her when Percy, in hopes of discovering some sort of refreshment, led her into the drawing room.

"Georgie! How famous to see you. You must tell me what you think of this for Grandmama. She says she's too old to wear such frippery," Lizzy exclaimed, making a frantic grab for the copy of *La Belle Assemblée* that slid off her lap as she jumped up to greet the visitor. "But where is Sir Hugo? I saw you with him at Drury Lane last evening. I vow he never seems to leave your side," she remarked slyly.

Looking extremely conscious, Georgie was about to launch into a disclaimer that it was no such thing when the dowager broke in acidly, "Elizabeth, can't you see that Georgie is wearing a riding habit? You know one would never find Sir Hugo within ten leagues of a horse if he could help it. He has the worst seat in the county! He's the most cow-handed . . . Well, I always did say you could never count on a man that a horse wouldn't follow. Georgiana, delightful to see you, my dear. Do sit down and tell me that you don't agree with my foolish granddaughter here, who insists that I should try to ape some fashion plate." The dowager patted the chair next to her invitingly.

"I must apologize to both of you, but I did come at Percy's special request and I believe he has a variety of activities planned for my amusement," Georgie excused herself, winking at Percy, who now stood in the door expectantly, his cricket bat and ball in hand.

"Here it is, Georgie. Brian gave it to me. Isn't it a bang-up bat?" he asked as he led her toward the walled garden behind the house.

"Now, that's what I like," the dowager declared, "a gel with spirit and a proper sense of what's important. My other grandson would do well to seek out her company as much as his brother does." She peered out the window to the green patch where Georgie and Percy had just emerged and were deep in discussion of the layout of the pitch, so she did not see her granddaughter's quickly suppressed smile of triumph.

"Just so, Grandmama," she responded smugly. Goodness, it was taking everyone an inordinate amount of time to recognize what Lizzy had perceived from the moment Georgie had stormed out of the library after her first encounter with her guardian: Lady Georgian Southwold and the Earl of Aldringham were a perfect match for one another.

Insouciant though she might seem, Lady Elizabeth Brandon was nobody's fool, and she had been quick to take action once she saw how it should be. Both Georgie and her brother were extraordinarily perceptive as far as the rest of the world was concerned, and energetic in pursuing their interests, but they had both failed to notice what was clearly obvious to anyone who knew them and, furthermore, they seemed likely to continue in their blindness unless someone took their lives in hand. Lizzy had decided that it was up to her to be that particular someone.

She had not been privileged to overhear the remark that had prompted Georgie's sudden interest in fashion, but once privy to its consequences, she had thrown herself with enthusiasm into the project. She had also observed with interest her elder brother's reaction to the results of Georgie's trip to Bond Street and had immediately reinforced his sudden recognition of his ward as an attractive woman by thrusting competition for her regard under his nose.

Lizzy had been guilty of a slight prevarication when Brian had questioned her as to her grandmother's introduction of Sir Hugo, but assuaged any pangs of remorse by assuring herself that deception in the promotion of a good cause was not such a very bad thing after all. In fact, her grandmother had most pointedly *not* introduced Sir Hugo to her, her very words being, "He may be a neighbor and he may be of a good family, but his only purpose in seeking out any young woman is to secure himself a fortune, and he shall not have the opportunity to turn the head of any granddaughter of mine while I am alive to prevent it.''

Lizzy had pricked up her ears at this. Here was the perfect opportunity to pique her brother's jealousy and to arouse his protective instincts as well, and as soon as the dowager's back was turned, she had contrived to introduce not only herself but also the obvious attractions of Georgie's person and fortune to Sir Hugo. It had been well worth the risk she had run of incurring Grandmama's displeasure at such blatant disobedience. Brian had looked like a thundercloud the rest of the evening, and his eyes, which previously had only occasionally strayed to whatever part of the room Lady Georgiana Southwold graced, now never left it.

Lizzy had since learned from her maid that Sir Hugo had been a frequent caller in Berkeley Square, and had herself witnessed his presence at the theater and various other social functions honored by the attendance of two of the Season's most promising young ladies. All in all, Lizzy was well pleased with her stratagem. She did not for the slightest moment consider her friend to be in danger of falling victim to Sir Hugo's charms. On the contrary, the contrast he afforded to her brother might make that absent gentleman more sorely missed, especially if Sir Hugo were as indifferent a rider as her grandmother claimed. Lizzy, who had not been aware of this particular failing, had been extraordinarily pleased to hear of it. All she knew was that next to her brother's vital presence, Sir Hugo's agreeable manners would eventually appear ingratiating and his eager interest become fawning, which would no doubt pall on Georgie's independent spirit. Besides, any woman who had eyes in her head would prefer her brother's powerful physique and commanding features to a countenance which, though pleasant enough, tended toward the insipid. Now, if only the earl would return to town and render the contrast between the two even more striking, all would be well.

Lizzy was not destined to have to wait very long before this occurred. Always one to conclude his business with dispatch, the earl, who found his mind straying more and more frequently back to London in general and to one of its inhabitants in particular, managed to cut short his visit to the country and return in time for Lady Stoneham's rout.

In fact, he was in such haste to return that rather than put off his trip to the metropolis till the next day, he arrived home just after his grandmother and his sister had driven off. Stopping off long enough only to discover their direction, ascertain that it was a large and brilliant-enough affair to attract Lady Georgiana Southwold as well, and to change his clothes, Brian soon followed his relatives to the brightly lit mansion in Hanover Square.

The square was packed with carriages and the linkboys had all they could do to avert disaster. Inside the enormous ballroom the situation was no better. It appeared that the entire Upper Ten Thousand had responded to my lady's gilt-edged invitations, yet despite the crush, the earl singled out Georgie in an instant. It was as though he instinctively felt her presence and knew precisely where to look for her. As always, she stood slightly apart from the rest of the crowd in an alcove that created a space where she and her companions could catch their breaths and enjoy rational conversation. The light from a sconce overhead cast a golden glow around her, making her seem like some vibrant young goddess just descended from Olympian heights to survey the foolishness of the fashionable mortals below.

At that moment she was conversing animatedly with her aunt and a gentleman whose back was to the room, but whose attentive posture was a clear indication of his rapt interest in and attraction to the speaker. As Brian took in the expressive features, the sparkling eyes, an occasional toss of the head, the raising of a beautifully arched brow, and the quirking of delicately sculptured lips, he reflected on how Georgie managed to imbue every activity with her own special vitality. Even her conversations were charged with energy. As he watched, her companion laughed and then extended his arm to lead her to the dance floor.

The earl's brow darkened as he saw that the eager swain was none other than Sir Hugo Fortescue. That puppy! The earl felt the anger rise up in him. With hundreds—well, no, perhaps lesser numbers—of young ladies of good fortune hoping to snare an ancient title, why must he monopolize the one person who did not set much store by those things? Sir Hugo's arm encircled Georgie's waist as the waltz began. She looked up at him, smiled, and nodded at something he'd said. The scene released such violent emotions in one particular onlooker that he was taken completely by surprise. Brian was overwhelmed by the most primitive desire to stalk up to Sir Hugo, rip Georgie out of his arms, and take her back to Aldringham, where she would talk only to him, smile only for him. At the same time, he felt a yearning that was more like an aching tenderness, since looking at them reminded him of the way she had felt in his arms during a waltz—soft, graceful, and responsive to his every move.

What was wrong with him? He was not by nature a selfish or jealous person. Yet here he was, feeling hot and cold, tense and angry at the sight of a woman—no, a girl—who was, after all, only his ward, dancing with an unexceptionable young man. The earl tried to tell himself that his reaction was a natural one for a guardian concerned about protecting the fortune entrusted to his care, but somehow he had the sneaking suspicion that this was not precisely true, and he was not prepared to acknowledge any other possibility. A pretty sort of guardian I should be if I weren't upset by this turn of events, he reassured himself, and he resolved to put Georgie on her guard when the opportunity arose.

Calming himself with that salutary thought and congratulating himself on his maturity, the earl promptly made his way to the spot where Georgie and her partner would return directly the waltz was ended. He barely had a civil word for Lady Debenham, whom, accustomed to his skillful and flattering repartee, would have been miffed if she had not seen the intensity in the gaze directed at her niece and Sir Hugo. A thought which had occasionally crossed the lady's mind, inveterate observer of society that she was, now became a certainty, and she sighed with satisfaction, entirely forgetting how alarmed she would have been only a short time earlier by such a state of affairs. But what woman could resist the idea of a rake reformed by the love of an innocent girl?

If he had not been too much in the grip of seething and conflicting emotions to notice, the earl would have been warned by the special smile of welcome that lit up his ward's face when she recognized his tall figure standing next to her aunt. Entirely forgetting her partner, she hurried over to Brian, exclaiming, "Oh, famous, you're back! Percy must be delighted at your return. He showed me the bat you bought him. I must say it's ever so nice. He even let me use it, but I am no replacement for you and I was beginning to fear he would go into a decline or fall into a dreadful scrape if you didn't return soon."

The earl, wrapped up in his own confused thoughts—happiness at seeing her again, irritation at the encroaching insect by her side, fury at his own anger, and frustration over the effect she was having on him—barely heard her. "What? Oh, yes . . . the bat. I thought it was time he had a proper one."

The silence that ensued was deafening. Sir Hugo, never one to display much backbone, fled before the earl's forbidding stare. Made of much sterner stuff, Georgie stood her ground, regarding her guardian with some curiosity. What could have happened to put him in such a temper? Since his grandmother had arrived in Grosvenor Square, his mother had confined her endless complaints and discussions of her nerves to her bosom companions, and, as far as Georgie knew, Lizzy had been unusually demure, behaving just as a young lady in her first Season ought. Even she herself had done nothing to cause comment. She wrinkled her brow as she cast back over the past several days, trying to fathom the cause for the alarming severity of the gaze bent on her.

"You want to watch out for Fortescue, you know," Brian growled.

"What? Hugo?" Georgie looked up in astonishment.

"Oh, so it's 'Hugo' now, is it? You have progressed mightily since I last saw you."

Misliking the tone of his voice, she eyed him warily, chin up. "He is a perfectly unexceptionable young man. As I recall, it was your sister that first made him known to me."

Entirely forgetting that he had earlier applied those very same words to the young man in question, the earl replied curtly, "Well, he ain't a fit person for you to know."

Georgie's eyes flashed dangerously. "And why is that, may I ask? And who, pray tell, are you to dictate my society to me?"

Brian's jaw clenched. He could see he was going about this all wrong. After all, he would resent such interference on anyone's part, but her defense of the wretch merely aggravated him and goaded him on. "What right have I? I'll tell you, my girl, what right I have. Everyone knows he's on the catch for an heiress, and anyone but the greenest of greenhorns would know that he's only after your fortune."

If Georgie's eyes had flashed before, they were shooting green sparks now, but, her back rigid, her hands clenched at her sides, she was just able to control her voice as she replied with deadly calm, "Well, I, at least, have a fortune to give him."

A red mist rose before Brian's eyes. He wanted to shake her until she recognized the truth, that Sir Hugo didn't care a rap for her, that she belonged to him, Brian Brandon. Too furious to realize the import of these revelations, he raged at her, "What, that puppy? Why, he's half the man you are! He has no more sense than a baby. If you marry him, you'll end up taking care of him for the rest of your life."

Georgie, who had no more intention of marrying Sir Hugo Fortescue than she did of flying, drew a deep breath. "At least if I marry him I shan't be treated as a child or an idiot. He may not be your idea of a husband, whatever that may be, but he's a gentleman at any rate, and I had a great deal rather have a gentleman than a bully," she hissed. She would have liked to stalk off, but having no doors to slam and unable to quit the ballroom without causing comment, she abruptly turned her back on her fuming companion and began to devote assiduous attention to her aunt, who had been eavesdropping with barely concealed satisfaction.

So it was left to the earl to depart as best he might in the face of such a rebuff. You idiot, Brandon, he muttered to himself. For a man of the world, you are singularly inept. Now that you've made a complete cake of yourself, done all the damage you meant to avoid, utterly destroyed her confidence in you, the best thing to do is to take yourself off as quickly and quietly as possible. Smiling grimly at his own folly, he left as swiftly as he had come.

Brian's precipitate exit and entrance to Brandon House did not pass unnoticed, however, and Simpson, after he had delivered the two bottles of port his master had requested, held forth to his colleagues belowstairs. "Drowning his sorrows, he is. I haven't seen him do that since he came back from India. Used to do it all the time as a lad, lose his temper or fall into a scrape and then be in a black mood over it for days, but he hasn't done that since he came back. It must be a woman behind it. Didn't even see me when I came in, and him always with a nod and a smile and a kind word for everybody. He's in a bad way, he is. Only a woman could make a man look like that."

The others nodded solemnly as they resolved to treat their master with kid gloves in the ensuing days.

23

Though she did not have recourse to the bottle and though she was forced to remain smiling, gay, and responsive to the company in Lady Stoneham's ballroom, Georgie was no less upset by their contretemps than her guardian. Returning to Berkeley Square after what seemed forever, she sought the privacy and comfort of her bed as eagerly as he pursued the anesthetic effects of quantities of port. But the welcome oblivion of sleep refused to come despite the hot milk she had, in an uncharacteristic moment of weakness, asked Alice to bring to her, and she tossed and turned in a desperate attempt to find a position comfortable enough to relax muscles weary from dancing and the effort to appear as though she were enjoying herself. Her head ached fiercely and, try as she would, she could not erase the memory of the scornful curl of the earl's lips and the scathing tone in which he had ridiculed her friendship with Sir Hugo. But that was all it was, she thought to herself indignantly. She had not the least notion of marrying him or anyone else. But the idea that the earl should presume to judge her conduct infuriated her. That his comments were very probably true only served to anger her the more. If Georgie wanted to throw her life away on someone like Sir Hugo, why shouldn't she?

By now she was so agitated she threw off the bedclothes and began to pace the room. High-handed, interfering, autocratic—she ran out of words to describe the extent of his lordship's tyranny. The more she paced, the more Georgie realized that what upset her the most was Brian's critical and condescending attitude toward her. That he should think her such a ninnyhammer that she could not recognize and defend herself against the likes of Sir Hugo made her positively furious—no, not furious, but hurt. That was it. His contemptuous air had hurt her sorely—hurt her pride and something more, call it trust or friendship.

Of late, Georgie had found herself relaxing in the earl's company and enjoying it above everyone else's simply because, after their initial dispute, he had recognized her intelligence, acknowledged her good judgment, and encouraged them both. Now, in one disastrous moment he had destroyed all that, as well as the feelings of respect and fellowship that had existed between them. There was something so disheartening about this state of affairs that Georgie threw herself on her bed and began to sob into her pillow. And I don't cry, she told herself angrily, but she continued to weep until exhausted. At last, feeling lonelier than she had since her parents died, she fell into an uneasy slumber.

The morning did not bring refreshment—she awoke feeling as miserably bereft as ever—but it did bring determination. I will show him, she resolved, jumping out of bed, her head held high. I shall encourage Sir Hugo in his scheme to go to India to make his fortune, and then we shall see who is a puppy!

That decided, she threw on her wrapper, took the morning chocolate that Alice had brought her over to her escritoire, and began to compile a list of Uncle Ned's acquaintances who might be of some assistance in furthering Sir Hugo's aspirations. So involved was she in these plans that she was hardly aware of the time and was most astonished to see how late it was when Alice reminded her of her appointment with Madame Celeste.

All during the fitting Georgie was silent as Madame pulled and prodded, draped and exclaimed. She scarcely noticed the exquisite creation being fashioned around her, so intent was she on carrying out her stratagem. She could hardly call on Sir Hugo to inform him of her efforts on his behalf. Georgie truly did not wish to raise expectations that she had no intention of fulfilling, but she did wish to be seen in his company, if not by the *ton* at large, at least by one person who needed to be taught that he was not omnipotent and that he did not have the license to interfere in other people's lives.

At last she concluded that a drive through the park at the fashionable hour was sure to discover her hopeful suitor, who would be more than happy to be taken up in Lady Debenham's elegant carriage. As Brian, already feeling too confined by his enforced fashionable existence, never missed an opportunity to exercise himself and Caesar, he would in all likelihood be witness to this gracious invitation. "That should do nicely," she remarked with some satisfaction.

"Mademoiselle thinks so? I do not agree. It is too weak a color and makes mademoiselle's curls appear brassy," the dressmaker replied as she removed the wreath of pale pink roses she had placed in Georgie's hair.

Georgie came to with a start. "Oh, no, Madame, I apologize. My wits were wandering. I was referring to something else. I should never dare to question your exquisite taste. But I must be on my way. I promised Aunt Aurelia I would return in time to drive in the park."

Madame smiled. Lady Georgiana had been more docile today than usual. Undoubtedly some young gentleman was the cause of the faintly abstracted look on the normally animated face. The dressmaker smiled indulgently. She only hoped that the young man was worth it. This young lady was an original. It would take an unusual man to appreciate and nurture that independent spirit, which also hinted at a passionate nature just beneath the surface. Such men were few and far between, and Madame worried lest this vibrant girl settle for something less simply because society demanded it of her. Madame could not say precisely why, but she had a soft spot for this customer, who ordinarily took a lively interest in everyone and everything around her. It was refreshing to be near someone so aware, so eager to learn about every aspect of life that she encountered, regardless of whether or not it was considered to be the proper concern of someone in her station.

The fineness of the weather had encouraged even the most delicate members of the *ton* to seek the fresh air, and the park was thronged with splendid horseflesh and equipages of every description. Despite the press of carriages, Georgie immediately distinguished the earl's tall form as, keeping a weather eye on his sister's mount, he guided Caesar easily through the crush. What was it about the man, that he dominated every scene, whether it be a dusty parade ground, a crowded ballroom, or a sea of horses and carriages? Annoyed as she was with him, Georgie had to admit to herself that it was more than the splendid physique, the erect posture, or the handsome profile. The Earl of Aldringham was a man at ease with himself in any situation. He had no need of, and even less use for, the approbation of society, and it was this supreme indifference for its opinion, coupled with confidence in his own powers, that gave him an air of assurance so lacking in most of the members of the *ton*.

By contrast, it took some time before she located Sir Hugo sauntering along, smiling affably at everyone, stopping constantly to bow to Miss So-and-So or doff his curly beaver to Lady-Such-a-One.

The Earl of Aldringham was not the only one to stand out in the multitude. From the moment he had entered the park, Brian had been acutely aware of a certain barouche and one of its occupants. He was aware the instant it stopped to allow Sir Hugo to climb in. His jaw tightened and his hands clenched the reins so tightly that Caesar, accustomed to the best of treatment, objected mightily, tossing his head and sidling. "Impudent jackanapes," the earl growled under his breath.

"Why, Brian, whatever is amiss?" his sister inquired with an innocent air, for all the world as though she had not been observing the train of events with a great deal of satisfaction.

"That fellow has the infernal gall to pursue Georgie, and why she puts up with him is more than I can tell. He is only out for her fortune and—"

"And like the greaty booby you are, you told her so," Lizzy continued.

"Of course I did. I should be remiss in my duties if I did not," he replied, irritated at having to defend himself.

"Really, Brian, Georgie is quite old enough to take care of herself. She has enough fortune for two. Sir Hugo is a pretty-behaved young man from an old and distinguished family. I do not see the objection."

"The objection is that he is not the man for her," her brother explained in the tones of utmost patience ordinarily reserved for infants or the mentally infirm.

"I fail to see why not. He is kind, considerate, he respects her, and if she were to marry him, one of the irksome charges you complain of would be off your hands."

"Hah! He's no match for her. She would wind him around her thumb within a week and be bored to tears in a fortnight."

His sister wrinkled her brow thoughtfully. "You may be in the right of it, but surely that is her choice. After all, you discharged your obligation by warning her he was after her inheritance, in all likelihood setting up her back by doing so."

"If she has no more sense than to fall for the first young buck—" he began angrily.

"Pooh, Georgie is no fool. Why, the notion of marriage doesn't appeal to her above half." Lizzy glanced over to the trio in the barouche, engaged in animated conversation. "But you know that she doesn't take kindly to people telling her what to do, any more than you do."

Annoyed though he was, her brother was forced to acknowledge the justice of this remark. He again cast an eye at the barouche long enough to observe that the discussion was now all between Lady Debenham and Sir Hugo, while Georgie, appearing heartily bored, was sizing up the mounts of the passing riders. As he gazed, the earl saw her peep cautiously at him, and then, seeing that he was looking in her direction, she put up her chin and, smiling brilliantly, leaned foward to address Sir Hugo.

Brian grinned in spite of himself. The little devil! The entire scene was being enacted for his benefit. Georgie would no more promenade tamely in a barouche if she could help it than she would simper, giggle, and indulge in all the other behaviors she so deplored in those eager to win the *ton*'s approbation, but she was determined to show him that if not immediately mistress of her fortune, she was mistress of her own fate and did not appreciate being told how to go about it.

Suddenly it semed to the earl as though the sun had broken through the clouds, and he realized that it was a very fine day after all. It was not that Georgie cared so much for Sir

Hugo as it was that she was proving something to him, Brian Brandon, Earl of Aldringham. Then she did care for his opinion after all. The reins whose tension had made poor Caesar to uncomfortable suddenly fell slack as the enormity of this revelation struck his rider. Since when had he cared so very much what she thought of him? How long had he been doing things in the hopes of pleasing her? The more he considered it, the more Brian realized that for quite some time concern for Georgie's happiness had always been there in the back of his mind, and that so many things he did were done solely to bring a glow of happiness to her face. Somehow he had begun to feel that he was the only one who could inspire that special smile and the sparkle in the green eyes when he was amused or challenged, or the intent look that appeared in their emerald depths when she considered a knotty question. The possibility that someone else might be able to do the same thing for her had shaken him to the core of his being. The earl wanted to be everything to her, as she was rapidly coming to mean everything to him. Not entirely convinced that this was so, he found the state of affairs extremely unnerving.

Accustomed to relying solely on himself for his stimulation and amusement, Brian was dismayed to discover how important a slim, vital, green-eyed being had become to his happiness, and he resolved to put a stop to such a dangerous dependency as quickly as possible.

With this in mind, directly he returned to Grosvenor Square, he sent a note to Althea, inviting her to accompany him to the opera that evening. That lady was delighted. Never one to sit quietly at home, she had kept herself creditably amused in the earl's absence by dint of prodigious flirting at the routs and balls she attended, but her heart had not been in it. The heady sense of conquest she usually felt at the admiration reflected in men's eyes was gone. Gone too was the pleasurable anticipation of dressing to tantalize and distract. Now there was only one pair of eyes she cared about capturing, only one slow smile of appreciation she wanted to inspire. Without the earl as an audience, it was all so much empty habit and Althea had began to feel so very bored by it all that she had even considered staying at home.

Fortunately, before things could reach such a desperate state, the invitation had arrived. The mere sight of the forceful masculine scrawl had sent her pulses racing and made her breathing irregular. All languorous indifference disappeared as she leapt up from the couch where she had been lounging and sent maids scurrying to prepare a bath, arrange her boudoir, procure fresh flowers, candles, wines, and delicacies to entice the most jaded palate for the intimate supper she planned afterward.

As luck would have it, a sumptuous new gown had just arrived from Madame Celeste, and Althea sighed with satisfaction as she admired its effect in the pier glass. Cut very low across the bosom, with a short waist that showed off her generous curves, the ponceau satin, though a color much favored for promenade dresses, was a trifle daring in an evening gown. She didn't care. The rich poppy red emphasized glossy black curls and made the dark eyes pools of mystery and desire, besides which, it was bound to make anything else appear insipid next to it. The beauty was competitive, if nothing else, and being the cynosure of all eyes while casting others in the shade constituted one of her chief amusements.

The effect was not lost on her escort. "You look dazzling tonight, Althea." The earl smiled appreciatively at the full red lips and the creamy expanse of bosom above the tight corsage. He inhaled the heady perfume. She was a sight to stir the senses of any man, and her entrance into the box did just that, but the earl soon grew tired of the envious glances of his peers and the seductive sighs of his companion. He would have liked to concentrate on the music and the singing, but when one escorted Althea Wyndham, there was only one spectacle one was allowed to appreciate. Try as he would, the image of an enraptured face hanging over the edge of the box rose unbidden in his mind as he thought of the last time he had attended the opera.

The intimate dinner was no better. The seductively lit boudoir, the satin furnishings, the exquisite dishes with wines chosen as carefully as every gesture of his hostess were all so predictable, so calculated with one effect in mind—passion and its satiation—that he found his attention wandering. He longed to hear what Sprite would have to say to the entire scene. No doubt she would give a delightful gurgle of laughter at the contrived nature of it all and dismiss it as absurd. And it was absurd. He grinned to himself as he thought of how he would describe it to her. He felt like some rare and elusive sort of prey that was being carefully and expertly stalked.

"You are not attending, Brian," a husky voice breathed in his ear.

Visions of dancing green eyes and a piquant face surrounded by golden curls vanished. "I beg your pardon, Althea. What did you say?"

"I was asking if you planned to attend the Countess of Roystoke's ridotto. It is certain to be vastly amusing. The entertainments at her villa always are."

"I hadn't thought of it," he replied, wondering frantically if it were the sort of event his sister and Georgie were likely to attend, and if they were, why his escort had not been requested. "Quite a large affair, I collect?"

"Oh, yes. Anyone who is anyone is invited, and no one would dare refuse, even if they wished to."

"Then I expect I shall," was the offhand reply.

But the lady was not to be put off. Laying a hand on one muscular arm and leaning over so that the generous curves pressed tantalizingly against him, she tilted her face up to look deep into his eyes. "I count upon your escort to protect a poor defenseless widow across the heath."

He gave a bark of laughter. "You have never been defenseless in your life, Althea, nor have I ever seen you without some champion to vanquish all threats to your person."

She pouted prettily, running a dainty tongue over full red lips. "You may be in the right of it, but no one has ever been like you. The others are all very well in their way, but they are no more capable of dealing with the dangerous side of life than I am. You, on the other hand, are so strong and bold, you let nothing stop you."

Brian recoiled from the hunger he read in her eyes and the need he heard in her voice. "You flatter me." He laughed uneasily, wishing there were some way out of it, but there was none. "And I shall do my poor best to see that you arrive without a hair out of place and that you return in the same condition."

"Well, now, I would not want such an outing to be that tame," she breathed, nibbling his ear and smiling coquettishly at him in the glass that reflected their every move. "Would you?" She turned his chin toward her, raising her lips invitingly and shrugging beautiful white shoulders to reveal the charms so scantily concealed by her décolletage.

He bent his head to touch her lips. What could he do but respond to such a clear command? His thoughts, however, were miles away on another woman as he cast about for ways to reestablish his footing with his ward. He knew better than to resist, having experienced more often than he cared to the wrath of a woman scorned, but it was a perfunctory kiss, as was the lovemaking that followed. When he departed soon after, both he and the lady in question knew that his attention had not been completely hers.

But it will be, my lord, it will be, the beauty vowed to her reflection, which looked back through narrowed eyes.

24

Never one to resist a challenge, especially when it was a mere scrub of a schoolgirl who had thrown down the gauntlet, the earl was up betimes the next morning, hoping to catch his ward as she rode in the park. He did not have to wait long, for he had just had time to survey the few riders abroad at that hour when she came trotting by, her carriage erect, hands on the reins just so, eyes fixed directly ahead, seemingly with no thoughts on her mind beyond her mount. But he could tell from the elevation of her chin that Georgie had caught a glimpse of him. He grinned as he maneuvered Caesar directly into Lakshmi's path. "Good morning, sprite."

"Good morning, my lord," was the frosty reply.

"I had not thought to find you out so early, but I am delighted that the opportunity has arisen to speak with you privately."

He received a withering look. "More censorious comments on my behavior?"

He smiled broadly. "No, quite the contrary. I came to offer you my apologies." There, that startled her out of her aloof posture.

Georgie reined in Lakshmi, who had been maintaining half a head on Caesar. "Apologies?" Try as she would, she could not keep the curiosity out of her voice.

"Yes. I realize that while your fortune is my concern, your life is not. If it is anybody's affair, it is Lady Debenham's, and it is the highest piece of impertinence for me to offer any suggestions as to how to conduct it. Just as long as you use your inheritance to ensure your own continued comfort, I have nothing to say in the matter."

"Oh." Georgie felt oddly deflated. She had been furious at his interference, but now that he was withdrawing it, she felt strangely hurt by his apparent lack of interest. Did he no longer care for her welfare? It was a lowering thought, but she rallied enough to reply, "That is sporting of you. Thank you."

Her confusion was not lost on her guardian, who, accurately interpreting the variety of conflicting emotions that flitted across her expressive features, was highly gratified by the unenthusiastic response. He smiled down at her, his eyes full of a tenderness that Georgie would have found infinitely reassuring if all her attention had not been fixed on the reins that she toyed with self-consciously. The earl held out his hand. "Apologies accepted and forgotten? We are friends again?"

She glanced up shyly, then put her hand in his. "Friends."

"Good. That's settled. Now, though we cannot gallop *ventre à terre* through the park, I can at least encourage you to a faster pace," he teased, urging Caesar into a canter.

Lakshmi pricked up her ears and followed suit, and they were off, reveling in the freshness of the dew and the morning sunlight, the fineness of the day, the motion of the horses, and the opportunity to share it with someone else who was equally appreciative of it all.

Their horses slowed down and Brian was able to ask Georgie if she had read either *A Key to the Chronology of the Hindus* or *A Voyage to India,* so recently mentioned in the *Edinburgh Review.* "No, indeed, I have not, though I have been most anxious to procure copies. Have you?"

He acknowledged that, having been away, and with his mind much preoccupied with matters on various estates, he had relied upon her to procure them and give him her opinion of them, "as you are never without an opinion on anything, and I pity the poor author subjected to your critical faculties in an area that is familiar to you."

"I?" she gasped. "Why, I didn't think I was one of those knowing, pushy females."

"No, no," he laughed, "merely very sure of your own capacities." He saw that she was truly distressed by this view of herself, and he reached over to pat her gloved hand. "Don't fly up in the boughs. You are one of the rare people in this world who think about everything, and thus you know your own mind—a refreshing state of affairs, I assure you. You can have no idea how tiresome it is to be dancing with someone who never ventures a remark on anything until she has thoroughly ascertained what my views are likely to be. It would be far more enlightening to be talking to myself, because I should at least answer myself with some wit and intelligence, even though I didn't offer any new perspective. You, on the other hand, keep me tolerably amused and definitely humble, because you are as likely to disagree with me as not and you marshal your arguments with maddening attention to logic. But, speaking of vapid partners, do you attend the Countess of Roystoke's ridotto this evening?''

Georgie assured him that she did and that, furthermore, Cedric, in a burst of generosity, had offered to escort Lizzy as well as the ladies from Berkeley Square, so as to relieve the dowager of some of the exhaustion of the Season. ''But personally, I think it is more for the sake of Lizzy's favor than for your grandmother's health that he invited her.''

''Do you, now?'' The earl looked thoughtful.

''Oh, most certainly, but poor Ceddie is sadly mistaken if he has his sights set on Lizzy. He is a dear, but she is far too lively for him,'' she concluded candidly.

''Perhaps I shall help Cedric's suit by playing the ogre of a brother and forbidding him to her. That should send her flying into his arms,'' he teased.

Georgie had the grace to blush. ''Oh, no, Lizzy is not so contrary as all that. Only a true hoyden would be so bold.''

''Touché, sprite. You may have adopted the outward trappings of the Season's toast, but underneath you have the same spirit that won my heart twelve years ago.''

''And I do not know whether to feel flattered or rebuked, but I must go or Aunt will think something dreadful has occurred.'' With a little wave of her hand and a touch of her heels to Lakshmi's flank, she was off across the park.

Georgie's aunt, who had been deep in discussion with the dressmaker, was not so likely to have missed her as her niece would have had it appear, but the conversation had taken an awkward turn and, shy and unsure of herself, she had reacted by running away.

The sight of her guardian at Lady Stoneham's rout had thrown her considerably because it was not until she had caught sight of the earl's commanding figure that Georgie became aware of how very much she had missed him. This discovery had been upsetting enough, but when, instead of being glad to see her, he had behaved in such a perfectly gothic manner, as though she were some silly wet goose infatuated with nothing more than a charming manner, she had felt more hurt and rejected than she had allowed herself to realize until today, when she had been so overjoyed at their reconciliation. What was wrong with her? She was ordinarily the most rational creature in the world, yet here she was reacting like any fluttering schoolroom miss. Nothing had changed. He had not acknowledged that her judgment of Sir Hugo was correct and his was wrong. No, he had merely apologized for taking an overly protective interest in her. But had she pressed home the true issue, which was the accuracy of her judgment? No. She had allowed herself to be mollified by his wish to reestablish an easy intercourse between them.

And then, instead of being angered by these evasive tactics, she had been distressed lest they were indicative of a lessening of interest on his part, when all along what she had been trying to establish was her own independence from him. Lastly, to be so highly flattered merely because he had remembered her fondly all those years that she had been wondering what had ever become of her Naughty Soldier was ridiculous in the extreme. Yet she had been pleased beyond measure by his reference to their first encounter. You must be all about in the head, my girl, she admonished herself severely. A man like that says such things to every lady he knows. That's why they made such cakes of themselves over him. *You* are *not* going to make a cake of yourself over him, are you? The more she examined this, the less she was sure of it, because she knew that somewhere in her heart of hearts she was hoping that the earl did think of her as being different from everyone else and that he did consider their friendship to be as unique and special as she did.

Georgie sighed. It was all very confusing and uncomfortable, to be sure, but at the same time she couldn't help the warm feeling of happiness that would rise up in her all because he had wanted to become friends again and seemed to have sought her out expressly for that purpose. Nor could she keep herself from repeating under her breath "the same spirit that won my heart twelve years ago" and recalling the intimacy of his smile and the warmth of his brown eyes as he had said it.

Georgie had been so wrapped up in her own thoughts that she had given Lakshmi her head and was therefore somewhat startled to hear the groom addressing her. "Be you wantin' me to help you down, Miss Georgie?"

"No, thank you, Digby." She slid down and handed him the reins, shaking her head as she did so. Enough woolgathering, Georgie Southwold, time to put your mind to good use, she scolded herself as she headed upstairs to change out of her habit and clear her head with the edifying "Safe Method for Rendering Income Arising from Personal Property Available to the Poor Laws," just the sort of salutary activity that would recall her to reality from her daydreams, which, pleasant though they were, were the merest fancy.

25

The evening promised to be a fine one. The skies were clear and studded with stars, while the full moon lighted the road to the Countess of Roystoke's villa almost as brilliantly as if it were daylight. The air was mild, with soft breezes stirring. Rather than minding the distance of the drive, most of the guests enjoyed the opportunity to escape the city and admire the countryside bathed in moonlight.

Lizzy was enchanted with the entire prospect, and she and Ceddie kept up a steady chatter the entire journey. Lady Debenham interspersed a comment or two here and there, while Georgie was content to sit silent with her thoughts as she admired the passing scene.

Following the dictates of Georgie's aunt, they arrived fashionably late and had to make their way through a press of carriages in the courtyard of the countess's magnificent villa. As they moved slowly toward the door, Georgie thought she caught a glimpse of the earl's tall figure descending from one of the elegant equipages, but ascribed it to an overactive imagination that had of late been uncomfortably preoccupied with one particular person. Their coach drew abreast of the now empty carriage as they jockeyed for a place at the foot of the broad staircase leading to the magnificent marble entrance hall. Trying not to appear too obvious, Georgie peered inside, but its occupants had long since gone and the coachman was descending from the box to help the groom attend the horses. "Now, you mind what Lady Wyndham said," he admonished the young man, who was casting an anxious eye over a piece of harness that looked worn.

"Aye, John. Oi've me instructions. Saw into that there spoke so it breaks, but mind that it's not so weak it breaks too soon. Don't you fret. I know 'er ladyship's got a temper. What's worritin' me is how are we going to lose our way without 'is lordship knowing? There ain't many in the world as can pull the wool over the Earl of Aldringham's eyes, and that's fer sartin.''

"Never you mind, lad," the coachman replied. " 'Er lady-ship 'as her ways, and there ain't been a gentleman yet as can resist 'em. Rest assured, if she wants to distract 'is lordship, she will. There's not a man alive as is a match for Lady Wyndham when she wants something." He nodded sagely.

Georgie, who had been idly observing the scene, sat up with a jolt. It *had* been the earl she had seen, and in Lady Wyndham's carriage! A gentle tapping on her foot made her look up to see Lizzy's brown eyes fixed significantly upon her. Then a footman was opening the door and they were being escorted up the steps to the brilliantly lit hall, where the crush of people soon closed round them.

Lady Debenham and her niece moved forward as their names were announced, and they were greeted by their hostess, alight with diamonds and wearing an enormous turban. As they moved into the ballroom, Georgie was almost blinded by the light from thousands of candles and the scent from quantities of flowers arranged in banks around the room. Her mind reeled. Accustomed as she had grown to London entertainments, she was staggered by the magnificence of the scene before her. "Psst." She turned toward the sound, but saw only a marble column. "Psst, Georgie. Over here." Georgie caught a glimpse of Lizzy's anxious face as it disappeared behind the column. Cautiously she slipped from Lady Debenham's side to join her friend.

"Whatever are we going to do?" Lizzy demanded in an agonized whisper.

"Do?"

"That . . . that . . ." Lizzy's voice failed her. "That *creature* is going to trap Brian in a compromising situation and then he will be forced to marry her. We must do something!"

Georgie thought a moment. "Perhaps he wishes to marry

her," she suggested. "She is very pretty, after all," she continued, the memory of her own fury at someone's interference in her life still fresh in her mind.

"What, Althea? She'll be hag-ridden in no time. Besides, she doesn't care about Brian, not really. Why, it's Lombard Street to a China orange she won't even let Percy and me live with him. She'll want him to dance attendance on her, and he won't have a moment for Percy or me or Grandmama."

"Oh." Georgie considered this dreadful state of affairs. "When you put it like that . . ."

Lizzy's eyes glowed. "I knew you would understand! Now, we must act quickly."

"And what do you propose to do, short of riding to his rescue," her friend wondered.

"The very thing! I *knew* you'd think of something!" Lizzy clapped her hands. "But here is Ceddie, and I promised him the first dance. You must tell me the plan later." And she waltzed off, leaving Georgie casting about frantically for a plan to rescue her guardian.

By the time Lizzy and her partner had returned, she had worked it out very creditably. She waited until Ceddie and her aunt had become embroiled in a discussion of the likelihood of Amanda Ormesby-Smythe's ever catching a husband and then pulled Lizzy aside. "We must both be on the watch to see when they appear to be leaving, and then one of us will develop a most excruciating headache. The difficulty will be to make sure that our carriage and Lady Wyndham's arrive at the door to fetch us far enough apart so that they don't notice, but close enough together so that we can follow them. Perhaps I had best take the precaution of alerting Speen and Digby. If anyone asks, I have torn the flounce on my dress and have gone to repair it." With these parting words she disappeared into the crowd and went in search of Lady Debenham's coachman and groom.

"Very well, Miss Georgie," the coachman agreed when, at long last, he was located. He scratched his head. "You know what you're about, I'll warrant, but I ain't all that sure we can keep it from his lordship that he's being followed, him being one who's awake on all suits and not likely to be fooled.''

"I am sure you and Digby will manage excellently, Speen. You're both clever fellows. And remember that Lady Wyndham will be doing her utmost to distract his lordship,'' she reassured him.

"Aye, aye, Miss Georgie. We'll keep a weather eye on her carriage,'' Speen replied. One thing that could be said for Miss Georgie was that life had picked up considerable since she had arrived. It was an odd request, to be sure, but however unusual Miss Georgie was, she was not one given to queer starts and harebrained schemes. There's a good reason behind it all, I don't misdoubt, he muttered to himself as he went to find Digby, who was hobnobbing with a raucous group of grooms from the other carriages.

Georgie hurried back into the ballroom, anxious lest her absence had been remarked on, but her aunt and Ceddie were still deep in conversation and Lizzy was listening intently.

Sir Hugo came to claim a waltz and spoke to her so earnestly concerning his plans for India, thanked her so gratefully for the books she had recommended, that she apologized in her heart for ever believing for a moment the animadversions her guardian had cast upon his character. "I confess that I find the idea of trade rather fascinating— far more purposeful than the aimless existence we all now lead. I quite understand how frivolous this endless round of the *ton* must seem to one who has led so much more adventurous and useful a life,'' he confided to her, quite winning her approval in the process.

"Yes,'' she sighed, "I truly would prefer to wake up each day wondering how my tea plants are doing than what morning dress to select and which invitation to what ball I shall accept. Trying to prove to the East India Company the soundness of my scheme seems a far worthier outlet for my energies than trying to convince the patronesses of Almack's of my social acceptability.''

He pressed her hand, declaring warmly, "I would that every woman could be like you. You are an inspiration to us all.''

Georgie flushed with pleasure. The compliment was designed to appeal to her, while unmistakable admiration in his eyes would have made the pulses of even the most experienced and coldest of flirts race. Despite herself, she could not help feeling highly gratified by the constant and devoted attention of such an estimable young man. Had she but known it, Georgie would have been astonished to learn that she was also capturing the close attention of two other people in the room.

Unwilling escort that he was, the earl was being extremely circumspect about his true interest in the countess's rout, and by a great effort of will only occasionally allowed his eyes to stray to that corner of the room where the candlelight glinted on golden curls. However, he had not been able to conceal his concern completely when Georgie had disappeared, and, jealous of his regard as she was, Althea had immediately identified the cause of his abstracted air and the replies delivered at random. Soon she too was watching Georgie's every movement, almost as closely as she was observing her partner's reactions. Detecting a certain rigidity in her escort's powerful frame, and the set of his jaw when he saw Sir Hugo approach his ward, Althea saw all that she needed to confirm her suspicions as to the cooling of his interest in her. Deeming it high time to intervene, she laid an attractively plump hand on the earl's arm. Her eyes glowing suggestively, she murmured, "I am finding this increasingly dull, my love, are you not? I propose we leave this crush for the more enlivening air of London."

Engrossed in his scrutiny of Georgie's *tête-à-tête* with Sir Hugo, Brian did not immediately reply. The beauty frowned and repeated herself, telling herself that it was high time she took action. No man, Earl of Aldringham though he might be, forced Lady Althea Wyndham to beg for his attention. "I do wish to go *now,* Brian," she reiterated more forcefully as she gently propelled him toward the door.

The earl gave himself up to the inevitable, all the while calculating precisely how long it would take him to deposit the lady in Mount Street, repair to Grosvenor Square, have Caesar saddled up, and return to the countess's. With allowance for some demur from Althea, made up for by the capability of those staffing the Brandon House stables and Caesar's prowess, he figured that he might return in time to claim the last waltz with Georgie, who would not object to evening clothes that had been ridden in. So he acquiesced gracefully to her ladyship's wishes and they made their way toward the deserted entrance hall.

"Psst, Georgie! They're leaving." Lizzy's sharp eyes had observed Althea's initial gesture and foreseen the pair's imminent departure.

"Very well, then. Do you contract a violent headache," Georgie whispered back.

"I've never had a headache in my life," her friend protested.

"Nor have I, but of the two of us, you are more likely to be overset by the excitement than I."

A faint moan was the only response as Lizzy pressed her hand to a painfully contracted brow and slumped against a convenient pillar.

"Lizzy! You look dreadfully unwell." Georgie rushed to her rescue, but not before she had assured herself that Cedric would reach the young lady's side before she did. "Aunt, we must take her outside for fresh air."

"Mama . . . " Lizzy, who had also never in her life looked to her mother for assistance, managed to squeeze one delicate tear from a pansy-brown eye.

"Of course, dear." Lady Debenham was all solicitude. "Ceddie, do you call the carriage. Georgie and I will help Elizabeth. Are you able to walk, child?" In her concern, the lady failed to catch the triumphant look exchanged between her charge for the evening and her niece as Ceddie hurried off.

In no time at all, they were ensconced in Lady Debenham's carriage, rolling out between the magnificent gates with Speen on the box, his eyes glued to the receding wheels of the vehicle in front of him.

26

As the carriages bowled along the moonlit road, Althea, moving as close to the earl as possible without sitting in his lap, traced the line of his jaw with a delicate fingertip. "There," she breathed into his ear, "isn't this a great deal better than a stuffy old ballroom?" She sighed and inhaled deeply so as to make her décolletage rise and fall enticingly. "I am positively revived by the fresh air."

"And here I thought it was boredom you suffered and that an insufficient number of admirers drove you from the countess's soiree," he responded blandly. The earl was indeed put out by Althea's queer start. He would have much preferred keeping his eye on his ward, but as his escorting of the luscious widow precluded any chance to dance or speak with Georgie, he had consented to leave only so that he might relieve himself of his attractive burden. He was doing his best to keep his annoyance in check, but, to his mind, indulging her whims did not extend to conversation or responding to amorous advances. He positioned himself as close as possible to the window and stared out fixedly.

Althea was becoming uneasy. This state of affairs would never do, as they were fast approaching the fork where a wrong turn would take them away from London and toward deeper countryside populated by scattered villages and a few hostelries, which she had taken care to have her groom check out. Had she but known it, she needn't have worried, because the earl saw not the ribbon of road or the occasional cottage bathed in moonlight, but a slender figure dressed in white with a vivacious face and shining curls.

Having ascertained that the approaching crossroads was near at hand, the beauty reached up and pulled Brian's face toward her. "Why so distant, milord? We must do our best to while away the tedium of the journey." She drew his head down and pressed her lips against his. Somehow she had contrived to twist her body around practically facing his so that the next bump they hit, he was forced to grab her to keep her from falling. As he did this, Althea flung her arms around his neck, clutching him ever closer.

I must be in more desperate straits than I realized, Brian reflected to himself as he sat unmoved by the delicious expanse of bosom revealed to his gaze and feeling stifled rather than intoxicated by the heady perfume enveloping him. But Althea's ardor had been effective in one respect: he had quite failed to notice the turning which headed them in the wrong direction.

Unconscious of this though the earl might have been, others were well aware of the mistake. "Lor' lumme, that hain't the way to London," Speen exclaimed on the box, while inside the coach, Georgie and Lizzy, each seated next to a window, exchanged significant looks.

For Lady Wyndham's coachman, the difficult part lay ahead, for he was to drive as carefully as possible until he had seen a respectable-enough inn and then contrive to hit a bump large enough to smash the already weakened wheel. He drove on in the moonlight some time before he spied the lights of a village and was able to assure himself that the Royal Crown looked to be some place equipped to deal with the Quality. It was not large, but it was the best-maintained of those that Lady Wyndham's servants had visited. Now a departing customer stood in the open doorway bidding his host good night long enough for him to reassure himself of the respectability of both the taproom and the proprietor. Passing it, he picked up speed until he spied the perfect place—a curve with deep ruts hardened by the recent sunny weather. He whipped up the horses and took it at a slapping pace. The carriage swung precariously around the curve. There was a resounding crack and it bounced to a halt.

Fortunately for the safety of the two occupants, the coachman had begun to check the horses even as they rounded the curve, so that the two passengers were only thrown into a closer embrace by the mishap. Althea gasped and clung to the earl, moaning, "Save me, Brian, save me," while her companion, already ascertaining that they had survived a none-too-dangerous accident, was fuming at the delay and eager to get down to assess the situation.

"Calm yourself, Althea." He patted her and set her in the uppermost corner of the carriage before he leapt down.

"Wheel's broke, my lord," the coachman explained as he slid down from the box.

"So I see." The earl bent over the wheel, hoping against hope that it was a minor break that he could somehow repair. What he saw caused his brows to draw together alarmingly. His face darkened and his jaw clenched. The scheming jade! The Earl of Aldringham was not fool enough to be caught in the parson's mousetrap, and any lady who thought so was fair and far off. Despite the dirt the groom had rubbed into the fresh cuts in the wood, he saw immediately that the wheel had been tampered with.

The coachman quailed before the fury in the earl's face. 'E knows, he thought despairingly. 'Er ladyship's goose is cooked and she'll be in a rare temper for weeks. With an effort he maintained a wooden countenance. "I spied an inn not a mile back, my lord. Perhaps I could ride for help," he volunteered in a mollifying tone.

"Thank you, no. The lady and I will take the horses. I shall escort her to the inn and return with a horse for you. Then I shall ride to London for my own carriage, once I have discovered the direction to London from this dismal place," the earl responded grimly.

"Oh, no, Brian," the lady wailed in dismay, sticking her head out the door. "Don't leave me! There's no telling what could happen in a deserted place like this."

"Althea, I feel certain that within a moment of laying eyes on you, mine host will become your devoted champion. In addition, you will have your own two stout men to afford you more protection than I could," he replied unsympathetically.

Tears welled in her eyes. "Brian, please don't leave me here," she begged piteously.

"I shan't. I shall take you to the inn. Now, allow me to

help you descend while the horses are being unharnessed.''
He held out a hand—knowing full well that Althea was
counting on his catching her in his arms—and there was
nothing for her to do but accept it and climb down as
gracefully as she could.

"Ah, here are the horses." The earl turned to thank the
groom and take the reins, effectively thwarthing the beauty's
second attempt to fling herself upon him.

"But, Brian, I cannot ride in this gown and alone," she
protested as he helped her mount.

"Believe me, Althea, though it may be less romantic, it
is far more comfortable and a good deal safer than riding
pillion with me," was the acid reply.

"Oh, Brian, I . . ." the lady began, preparing to break
into fresh floods of tears, when the sound of an approaching
vehicle caused them all to look back in the direction they
had just come.

Lady Debenham's elegant carriage swept into view and
slowed to a halt as its driver took in the scene. A blond head
leaned out. "Have you had an accident? May we be of any
assistance?"

Immediately grasping the implications of this timely
rescue, the earl grinned to himself in the darkness. Sprite,
he chuckled to himself. "Why, thank you. Your arrival is
most opportune." He stressed the final word, but it was lost
on both the ladies to whom it was directed. Althea was too
seething with frustration to care and Georgie too intent on
finding room in the carriage and smiling conspiratorially at
Lizzy to notice. "Come, Althea, let me assist you. How
fortunate we are to have been overtaken at the *precise*
moment of our difficulty."Again the ironic undertone was
wasted on everyone.

Gritting her teeth, Althea climbed into the carriage, where
she listened with ill-concealed annoyance to the expressions
of sympathy on all sides, exclamations on the fortuitous
nature of the encounter, and tales of other coaching disasters,
while the earl leaned back against the squabs surveying his
companions with a sardonic eye.

They displayed varying degrees of consciousness. Lady

Debenham and Ceddie, after commiserating, promptly resumed their dissection of the evening, while Lizzy, appearing to be wrapped up in their conversation, could not forbear directing occasional speaking glances at Georgie or curious ones at Althea. Georgie, having offered all that was polite on the subject, retreated into silence, but with an air of satisfaction that was all out of proportion to that which one would naturally feel upon rendering assistance to a fellow creature in distress.

Brian, considering the situation for a time, was unsure of the precise nature of his own feelings on the episode. On the one hand, he was glad to have been spared an awkward situation. Though he never would have fallen victim to Althea's plot, his escape from it would have been considerably less pleasant had not his sister and Georgie shown up. On the other hand, after the tedium of his recent existence, he had just begun to enjoy being in yet another scrape. It made him feel absurdly young again. But he preferred to conduct his own affairs without assistance or interference from anyone. In addition, he felt some chagrin that he had been extricated from his difficulties by a mere chit of a girl, an unusual one to be sure, but still a girl. At one and the same time, he was touched by Georgie's concern for him and her immediate assumption that the compromising situation he had been put in was one that he wished to avoid. After all, Althea was a beautiful, wealthy, independent, wordly woman—a man would have to be touched in the upper story not to want to marry her—but Georgie had understood that, whether or not he wanted to marry her, he wanted to be free to do it on his own terms.

He sighed. He must be all about in the head, but he did wish to run his own life and he did not want to be leg-shackled to anyone, no matter how alluring, without having some say in the matter. He was more than happy to help Althea descend when they reached Mount Street after dropping off Ceddie, who further annoyed the simmering lady by remarking how fortunate it was she had not been forced to ride in such a flimsy gown. The earl could not force himself to utter more than a curt "Good evening," as he escorted Althea up the steps. The frustration and hunger he read in her eyes made him more glad than ever for Georgie and Lizzy's successful stratagems, and by the time they reached Grosvenor Square he was feeling quite charitable enough toward his sister and his ward that he pressed Georgie's hand and murmured, "Thank you, sprite," before helping Lizzy alight.

Brian carried the picture of the adorable confusion on Georgie's face with him as he allowed his valet to help him out of his clothes, and then he sat for some time staring unseeing into the fire, glass of brandy in hand while a piquant face with a half-defiant, half-apologetic smile on its soft lips and reflected in the green eyes rose before him. He smiled tenderly. What an odd and lovable creature she was—more resourceful and independent than most men, as blue as the bluest of bluestockings, as irrepressible and innocent as a child by turns. One could never be sure at any given instant which one of those she would be, but whichever one it was, he never failed to enjoy himself, to be amused and challenged by it, and he always looked forward to their next encounter. No matter how ordinary an event, Georgie seemed to charge it with her own special brand of vitality, always bringing interest to the dullest of moments or encounters. For his part, the earl could not wait to discover what the next one would be, but this time he hoped that he would be the rescuer instead of the rescued.

27

Life flowed smoothly after the Countess of Roystoke's ridotto, and it seemed destined to continue that way, with rides in the park, a ball here, a musicale there, until both the earl and his ward were feeling restless in the extreme. Georgie returned to her program of devouring everything she could lay her hands on concerning the cultivation and commerce of tea and, fearing interference in her plans for the East India Company, discussed that monolithic empire at length with her guardian. "For you know, I sometimes fear they have grown so large that they stifle trade rather than encourage it," she ventured during an early-morning ride.

"Ever the rebel, are you not?" he teased.

Georgie came to a halt, a worried frown puckering her brow. "I do not intend to be, but all too often I find myself pursuing a course only to discover that I have set up people's backs or am making them uncomfortable."

Brian smiled. "How well I know the feeling myself. That is because you are a true individual and an independent thinker. Fortunately, you are wealthy enough and beautiful enough that you will, at worst, merely be labeled eccentric by people who would otherwise refuse to have anything to do with you," he replied gently.

"Beautiful, I?" she gasped.

His brown eyes twinkled down at her. "Yes, you. You need not be so surprised. Perhaps you are not quite in the common way, but that sort of beauty can be very dull. Your nose may not be retroussé, but it has character, as does that defiant chin of yours. As to the eyes, they reveal a lively spirit and an intelligent mind. Yes, you are beautiful in so many ways, whereas most women are in only one. You . . ."

He broke off, gazing down at her as the impact of these words sank into both of them.

As for Georgie, she sat mesmerized, afraid to look at him, but unable to look away, wishing to say something light that would alleviate the intensity of the moment, yet hoping it would go on forever. Fortunately, providence, in the form of Percy, intervened.

Having discovered that his elder brother had gone out riding, he had begged Fenton to take him to the park until that minion, accustomed as he was to years of pleading from Percy's older siblings, was unable to resist the appeal in the little boy's eyes. "Brian! Georgie!" Percy exclaimed joyfully as he trotted up. "Famous! Georgie, we're going to watch a balloon ascension tomorrow." He was bursting with enthusiasm.

"How exciting that will be. I have never seen one, but I have heard the most interesting sto—"

"Brian, may we take her with us, may we, may we?" Percy begged.

"But of course, that is, if she is free to join us," his brother replied, smiling indulgently.

"Oh, I would like it excessively," Georgie began, "but only if you truly wish me to come with you. After all, you were rather coerced into inviting me."

"If you come, it will be like a party," Percy seconded his brother's invitation.

"There, it is all set, then. But you, my lad, have lessons to do, and I"—the earl paused, looking significantly into the disappointed face turned up to his—"have the equally dull and unpleasant task of going over the estate accounts with Smedley and, let me assure you, I had liefer be doing my Latin. Bid you adieu, Georgie, but perhaps I shall see you this evening at Lady Astley's?"

Georgie nodded, appalled at herself because she now was looking forward to an event which had previously seemed a very dull prospect.

"Georgie is a great gun, ain't she, Brian? I wish she were my sister," Percy volunteered as the two trotted off in the direction of Grosvenor Square.

The earl was amused. "You have a perfectly good sister, my lad."

"I know," the boy sighed, "Lizzy is nice, but she likes to do . . . to do . . . lady things. Georgie is up for any sort of a lark."

His brother was silent, struck by the felicity of this remark. The idea of Georgie at Brandon House or Aldringham was a singularly appealing one, and the more he thought about it, the more he realized how enjoyable life would be if that were the state of things.

Brian was still thinking this as he entered Lady Astley's crowded ballroom that evening and, without even consciously seeking her out, immediately discovered Georgie and her aunt off in a corner with Cedric. As the evening wore on, he was constantly aware of her presence, whether she was gliding gracefully around the floor with some young buck or chatting with her aunt and her cousin. In fact, his observation was so intense that he didn't ask a single partner to stand up with him, replied to his grandmother and sister in monosyllables, and gave Letitia Carrington a cut direct when she approached him all delighted flirtatiousness at discovering him free of partners. Never one to bear a grudge, especially against such a handsome and desirable man, she raised her eyebrows, shrugged her shoulders, and departed in search of fairer game, while Lizzy and the dowager, highly intrigued by the earl's air of preoccupation, exchanged amused glances.

He would have been content to remain this way the entire evening, broad shoulders propped up against a pillar, admiring Georgie's energy and vivacity, fondly recalling all their times together, even their quarrels, and envisioning a future where she would always be with him, challenging him, discussing with him, learning new things and exploring new places with him, when he saw Sir Hugo materialize by her side. He scowled but restrained himself as the young man led her to the floor for the quadrille. Though fuming inwardly, Brian managed to keep his countenance as they executed their figures. However, when at the end of the dance Sir Hugo led her, not back to Lady Debenham, but out through the French doors onto a balcony, the earl could no longer hold himself in check and made his way as best he could across the crowded room to the spot where they had disappeared.

While she had not kept the constant watch on the earl that he had on her, Georgie had been instantly aware of the moment his imposing presence had appeared in the ballroom and, try as she would to ignore him, she could not keep her eyes from straying over to the pillar that supported her guardian. She endured partners and dull conversations with more than her usual patience in the hopes that the earl would rescue her, but he would remain glued to his post, the provoking creature! Finally, in a fit of pique, she had smiled at Sir Hugo across the throng and was just feminine enough to feel highly gratified by the alacrity with which he rushed to her side.

Consummate social being that he was, Sir Hugo was a graceful dancer and Georgie enjoyed performing the quadrille with someone so adroit. It was soothing to go through the various steps in time to the music, and calming to her spirits, which had been unpleasantly disordered since the earl had appeared. Much as she hated to acknowledge it, his presence, for her at least, had charged the ballroom with an excitement it had not previously possessed, and she felt a restless eagerness in herself that she was at a loss to explain. Thus when Sir Hugo had proposed to sit the next dance out on the balcony, where they could revive themselves with a breath of fresh air, she had followed him in the hopes that it would restore some degree of equanimity.

Much to Georgie's dismay, the moment they escaped the bright lights of the ballroom, her partner threw himself at her feet and launched into a passionate declaration. "Georgiana, may I call you that? I do not wish to alarm you with my precipitateness, but you must allow me to tell you how fervently I admire you."

Georgie, speechless for a moment at the unexpected turn of events, recovered from her shock long enough to stammer, "Why th . . . thank you, Sir Hugo," as she frantically sought to free her hand from his tenacious grip.

"I perceive that you are unaware of the depths of my feelings. Georgiana, I beg you to do me the honor of becoming my wife."

If Georgie had been taken aback before, she was stunned now. "I . . . The thought had not occurred to me." She gulped, regained her composure and perspective, and continued, "Thank you, Sir Hugo, I am indeed flattered, but I have no wish to be married."

Her suitor began to grow desperate as visions of a comfortable life with a wealthy wife began to be replaced by the all-too-real prospects of quitting the country for the wilds of India. He rose to his feet, only to fling his arms around her in a frenzied embrace designed to convince her of the extent of his passion, but he only succeeded in rendering her more acutely uncomfortable. "You shall marry me. You must. I love you," he insisted.

Retaining what little dignity she could, Georgie objected, "But you hardly know me, nor I you. How could you possibly—?"

Her partner stopped these very sensible objections with a series of frantic wet kisses which rendered their recipient decidedly queasy. Ill as she felt, Georgie struggled to free herself, but succeeded in making him all the more insistent. Courage, now, Georgie, she comforted herself. You have never yet been conquered by a situation. She was beginning to wonder despairingly if this were to be the first time when she felt herself violently released from Sir Hugo's suffocating grasp as a furious voice demanded, "What the devil are you at, forcing your attentions on a lady?" and the earl's angry face came into view as he hauled her importunate suitor off by his collar.

"I was, I . . . you have no right . . ." the miserable young man stuttered.

"On the contrary, I have every right—as a civilized human being, as a gentleman, and as a guardian." The earl's voice dripped with contempt.

"You are a fine one to talk, what with your reputation," Sir Hugo whined, slinking slowly in the direction of the ballroom.

Oddly enough, the earl seemed amused rather than annoyed by this slur on his character. "That's as may be, but I only engage myself with willing partners, and this lady looks decidedly unwilling."

"You . . . you, blackguard, you . . ." The young man's courage increased with his distance from the earl.

More concerned with his ward's patent distress, her rescuer responded mildly, "Oh, be off with you, Fortescue. Haven't you caused enough trouble?" Brian reached for one of Georgie's hands. "Sprite?" he whispered softly. There was no response as she struggled to swallow her tears and catch her breath. "My poor girl," he sighed, pulling her gently into his arms.

Georgie, who by a tremendous act of will had almost succeeded in recovering her self-possession, was completely unnerved by his tenderness and burst into tears. "There, there, sprite." He stroked her hair and patted her shoulder gently. "Hush, my girl. Everything is all right."

She leaned her head against his chest, giving herself up to the reassurance of his touch and the comfort of his arms. Not since she was a little girl sobbing out the hurt of a scraped knee to her mother had she felt so comforted and protected. At last she relaxed and the tears subsided. For some time she let herself be held, reveling in the warmth and security of the feeling, but then honesty compelled her to pull away. Looking up at her guardian through tear-drenched lashes, she spoke unsteadily. "You were right and I was wrong. I thought he just wanted to be friends, but he was out after my fortune. I didn't matter . . ." Her voice broke pathetically.

The earl's heart ached for the misery he saw in her face, and he pulled her close to him again. "He's nothing but a paltry fellow, sweetheart, soon to be forgotten. He's not worth a moment's concern or a single one of your tears. Here . . ." He pulled out a handkerchief and wiped the streaks off her face. Cupping her chin in his hand, he commanded, "Now, smile for me. There's my brave sprite."

It was a watery and wavering smile, but the spark had come back into her eyes and the defeated look had gone. "There's my courageous girl." Without thinking, he bent to kiss the lips smiling up at him, and was instantly drowned in a sea of emotion that was as intense as it was unexpected. He felt her body tremble. A sigh escaped her and she melted into his embrace. Her lips were soft and yielding. For one who always did her best to appear strong and independent, she felt so fragile and delicate in his embrace that he feared he might hurt her. Gently he moved his mouth on hers, almost afraid to breathe at the unbearable sweetness of the moment. Then her lips responded gently, shyly, and a wave of desire swept over him. He gathered her closer, feeling the slender body molded to his, chest to chest, thigh to thigh. Her breathing quickened, her head tilted back, and her lips parted. He devoured them hungrily, willing her to return his passion, to let him know that she wanted him as much as he wanted her.

"Sprite," he murmured as his lips slid from her mouth and down the slender column of her neck. He could feel the throbbing pulse in her throat as she stood there, overwhelmed by the intensity of the moment. A long shuddering sigh escaped her and he looked into her green eyes, now dark with passion, the lids half-closed. Gazing down at her, the earl experienced a sudden shock of realization as though someone had tossed a bucket of cold water over him. This irresistible vibrant creature in his arms was Sprite, the little girl who had charmed him so many years ago, the independent spirit who had scorned his guardianship, the person he wanted most to shield from the unpleasantness of life, to protect from people like Sir Hugo, and here he was doing precisely what he wished to spare her. Cad, he berated himself. How could he have let his emotions, his desires, run away with him so!

With a supreme effort Brian relaxed his embrace, took one of her hands gently in his, and, raising it to his lips, apologized in a stricken voice. "Forgive me. I don't know what came over me. Believe me, I never meant to hurt you. I never would hurt you. I promise you I shall never do it again. Forgive me." And with that he was gone, disappearing through the French doors, leaving Georgie alone on the balcony struggling with thoughts and feelings she had never before experienced, never known existed.

28

For the longest time Georgie could do nothing except lean
against the balcony railing gazing after him in bewilderment
and running a finger over her lips, where the earl had so
recently evoked such an overwhelming response. She had
always known that love existed for other people. She had
seen how her mother glowed whenever Mad Jack was
around. She had watched her father's eyes seek out her
mother every time he entered a room, how they rested
tenderly on her. Often as a child she had intercepted secret
looks between them and been ever so slightly jealous of their
intimacy. But she herself had never expected, nor wanted,
to feel that way. She had scorned the girls she knew who
constantly sighed over a handsome face, who allowed their
entire existences to be ruled by a smile or a frown from a
certain direction, and she had resolved never to be so
dependent on another person for happiness.

Georgie had become even firmer in this resolve since her
arrival in London, when she had had ample opportunity to
observe how such things affected women, socially as well
as emotionally. She had become more convinced than ever
of the importance of maintaining her independence and
avoiding such crippling entanglements. And now, all with
one kiss, she saw that all her good intentions, all the sound
advice she had given herself, and all her resolution were for
naught.

She sighed wearily. It was a most dispiriting discovery.
Not only that, but she was suffering all of this over someone
who did not even want her, who had apologized for awaken-
ing all these wonderful and frightening sensations in her. And
the sensations were wonderful and frightening. She had never

felt so alive or experienced such heady excitement, nor had she ever felt so vulnerable and helpless. What was worse was that she wanted those feelings to go on and on. Even more impossible was that she wanted to make the earl feel the same way. Don't be a nodcock, she chided herself bitterly, he has had scores of women in his life and it would take someone far more alluring and sophisticated than you to elevate his pulses even the tiniest bit.

Had she but known it, Brian's pulses were racing so much and his thoughts and feelings in such disarray that he had slipped unnoticed from the ballroom, out the front door, and was now pacing the square in front of Lady Astley's magnificent edifice. It's only Georgie, after all. There's not the least reason to act the besotted lover over a mere schoolgirl, and one who would scorn such feelings as the merest romantic nonsense at that. He strode around the square several times, gulping in the fresh air, then, believing he had himself well in hand, returned to the ballroom, only to discover that while the walk might have stretched his legs, it had not restored his equanimity.

When Georgie finally reappeared through the doors looking pale and subdued, his heart hammered so loudly he was convinced his sister and grandmother must surely hear it. The traces of distress, though hidden from the casual observer, were still there for him to see, and he wanted nothing so much as to rush over, take her in his arms, kiss her . . . and upset her all over again, Brian, you idiot. This time his sigh was audible enough to attract the attention of his companions, who, glancing up at the same time, ascertained the object of his scrutiny and smiled privately, each highly gratified by the sight of his tense and troubled expession.

Georgie, who had remained on the balcony for what seemed hours, finally gave up all hope of achieving a calmer state of nerves, and when the earl saw her return, it was only to seek out her aunt to say that she had the headache and wished to go home to Berkeley Square. One look at her niece and Lady Debenham was all concern. The child truly did look pale and listless enough to worry anyone, but when this was contrasted with Georgie's usual energetic mien, it was cause for alarm.

"Yes, dear child, we shall quit Lady Astley's instantly." She began making for the door.

"Oh, no, Aunt, I am quite well enough to go myself, truly. And I wouldn't for the world have you leave in the middle of the ball," Georgie protested, desperate to be alone.

At first Lady Debenham wouldn't hear of such a thing, but Georgie was so insistent and appeared to be growing so much more agitated by the minute that she finally relented. Besides, she still had not had the opportunity to ask her especial friend Amanda Delamere if she didn't think Lady Waltham's décolletage looked perfectly ridiculous on someone who more nearly resembled a plucked chicken than anything else.

With the greatest relief, Georgie allowed Ceddie to fetch her wrap and hand her into the carriage, where she laid her throbbing head back against the squabs with a sigh of exhaustion. Her throat ached with unshed tears and her chest hurt from suppressed sobs. Really, she couldn't understand how she could be so foolish and agitated, but she wanted nothing more than to climb into bed and indulge in a good cry.

Though not as visibly distraught as his ward, the earl was only barely able to evince the slightest interest in his surroundings, and hurried his grandmother and sister off at the earliest opportunity without having stood up for a single dance. Indeed, when a hopeful young lady had smiled at him, she had received a frown so thunderous that then and there she had decided that a huge fortune and elevated rank were no compensation for the punishment of enduring such ill humor.

Barely bidding his grandmother and sister good night, Brian hurried to his room, ordered a bottle of brandy, dismissed his valet, and after quickly dumping several glasses of the fiery liquid down his throat, sat staring into the fire waiting for it to take effect. However, he must have become more hardheaded in his old age or he was more upset than he could ever remember having been, because no matter how many glasses he consumed, he could not erase the vision of Georgie, her head thrown back, lips parted with the faint light from the ballroom making her skin glow and her curls shimmer. Nor could he forget how perfect she felt in his arms, how natural.

He had never before, even in the days of calf love, been so overwhelmed by tenderness and desire, and he wanted the euphoria of it to last forever. He smiled cynically to himself as he recalled the women who had thrown themselves at his head, and now he wanted to spend the rest of his life with one who not only had no use for a husband but also saw him at best as a rake and at worst as a figure of unwanted authority.

Husband! He sat up in astonishment. Yes, by God, for the first time in his life he wanted nothing more than to take care of someone, to share her life, and to produce independent-minded brats who would be as stubborn and enchanting as she. But what was he going to do to convince Georgie of the absolute rightness of this vision? With any other woman he would have known how to proceed, using constant attention, admiration, and a steady stream of extravagant gifts. With Georgie, all this would elicit would be an incredulous stare or derisive laughter. She would be insulted by such ploys.

Brian dropped his head into his hands with a groan, remaining there for some time before tossing off a final glass of brandy. Now, Brandon, he admonished himself, nothing ever stopped you from getting what you wanted in the past. Why should it stop you now, when you want this more than anything you have ever wanted in your life? Get some rest and you'll be more the thing in the morning. And with these sage words of advice he tumbled fully clothed into bed and oblivion.

The other participate in the recent dramatic encounter was not so fortunate. Having undressed and drunk the hot milk which Alice had pressed upon her, Georgie lay down uneasily, anticipating a restless night. She was entirely correct in her fears, for she did nothing but toss and turn, and whatever direction she turned, wherever she faced, she saw before her the earl's dark eyes regarding her with an intensity that seemed to pierce right through her. She still savored the warmth and strength of his hands on her shoulders and their gentle caress as they slid to her waist to pull her toward him. Again and again she felt the response of her own body to the insistence of his lips, and the firmness of his arms and chest as he held her close. She wanted nothing more than to remain there always, protected, cherished, and desired.

She tried to thump her pillow into a more comfortable position, but as she laid her head back down upon it, all she could think of was how comforting it had been to lay it on Brian's shoulder. How kind and gentle he had been. He had recognized her distress and sympathized with it immediately, when truly she had brought the situation upon herself, bacon-brain that she had been. Furthermore, it had been something he had warned her against, but he had made no mention of that at all, only striving to soothe her as best he could. And he had. It was her own silly fault that she was so upset now. The earl had been all that was solicitous; it was she who was behaving like some lovesick romantic young miss. Love, Georgie sighed deeply. That was what was wrong with her. No wonder it was the subject of so much poetry, art, and music. She had never before experienced such a welter of emotions, such a longing to be with someone even if he did not want her the way she wanted him.

She thought of the many kindnesses the earl had shown her, the respect he accorded her ideas, the way he teased her, the rides and conversations they had shared, and a great sob of despair rose up in her. She knew she was strong. Uncle Ned had made her self-reliant and independent, but he had not made her strong enough to endure the agony of constantly seeing someone who did not want her the same way she wanted him. Georgie was part ashamed, part intrigued, and part proud of the physical longing she felt for the earl. At last, so many things that had mystified her before had become clear to her, and though she suffered intensely over this discovery, she felt more alive and aware because of it.

That's as may be, my girl, but you cannot stay here. Seeing

him would be torture, and you do not wish to run the risk of making him uncomfortable. There is only one place you belong, the only place you have ever belonged, on your own, back in India. The sooner you get there, the better it will be for everyone.

Resolved on this course of action, she regained enough peace of mind to fall into uneasy slumber for what little remained of the night.

29

Georgie was up betimes the next morning, in a fever of excitement to be gone. The first step was to establish what ships were due to sail for Calcutta within the next few days, and she waited impatiently for Alice to bring the morning paper with her chocolate.

Having ascertained that the departure of one of the East India Company's ships, the *Lady Kenneway*, bound for Madras and Calcutta, was imminent, Georgie immediately sprang into action. The first concern, of course, was money. She had fixed upon selling her mother's jewels, a decision which had caused a pang of regret, for Lady Southwold's jewels, particularly the magnificent emeralds and a rope of baroque pearls, were some of the only reminders Georgie possessed of her mother. Courage, Georgie, she said briskly to herself as she took a final look at them gleaming in their velvet box. No plan was ever accomplished without some sacrifice.

She had resolved to take these to Rundell and Bridge's, but the problem was Alice. How was she to accomplish her business without arousing the little maid's suspicions? Her mind worked busily as she was helped into a lavender walking dress made of the new zephyrine silk. It was extraordinarily becoming, but Georgie's mind was too distracted with the problem at hand to take the slightest notice. She finally hit upon the solution of sending Alice in the carriage to Hatchard's when they reached the jewelers', but even this part of her plan was fraught with difficulties. "Why, Miss Georgie, I can take your jewels to be cleaned. You needn't waste your time," the maid objected.

Trying her best to conceal her annoyance, Georgie thanked her. "It is most kind of you, but several of the stones appear to be loose, and as I am the one most aware of which ones they are, it would be more expedient if I were to speak to the jeweler myself. I also have some loose stones from Uncle Ned I would like to see about having made up into something, and I need to confer with him about that.'' Then, seizing Alice's cue, she continued, ''But I should be ever so grateful if you could execute a small commission while I am doing this.''

Happy to be of assistance, Alice agreed with alacrity, thus disposing of one problem. To Georgie's relief, the jewelers' establishment was empty when they arrived, and as soon as a clerk had been informed of the nature of the young lady's business, he ushered her into a private chamber so there was no one to observe the transaction whose curiosity might have been aroused.

Mr. Philip Rundell himself waited on Lady Georgiana. Being a man of infinite discretion and well accustomed to helping his fair customers out of difficulties, he agreed to take the jewels for a price that was more than fair. Nor did he blink when his client expressed her immediate need for the money. A boy was dispatched to procure the balance of the payment that was not in the safe, and in no time at all Georgie was handed a bulging packet, as though the proprietor bought a fortune in jewels from titled young ladies every day. Then she was ushered graciously to the door.

Her heart beating furiously, Georgie equally calmly thanked him for his kindness, climbed into the carriage in which Alice sat patiently waiting, little dreaming that the man who had been the soul of tactful understanding was even now penning a note to her guardian delicately suggesting that he might be of some assistance to him in the matter of his ward.

Now all that remained to be done was to fill a few bandboxes with the essentials from the clothes she had brought from India and somehow convey them to the docks without giving any cause for comment. A less redoubtable young lady might have lost her nerve at this juncture, but to someone as resourceful as Georgie, the challenge served merely to inspire her and to take her mind off other things, such has how comforting a pair of strong arms could feel around one and how painful was the ache whenever she remembered the touch of a certain pair of lips and the warmth in a certain pair of dark eyes. Shaking the vision of the moonlit balcony from her head, she sighed and applied her ingenuity to the problem at hand. In no time it had come to her. She had no sooner invented a former nurse of her mother's, now fallen on hard times, than she had gathered together several boxes of clothes to be sent to 147 Leadenhall Street, which, coincidentally, happened to be the direction of Mr. Horsley, who handled passage arrangements for the *Lady Kenneway*.

That accomplished, there was nothing to do but await the next morning with as much patience as she could muster. They were engaged to attend Lady Tilney's musicale, but the possibility of encountering the earl, or worse yet, attending an evening not enlivened by his presence, was more than Georgie could bear, so she pleaded a headache. Lady Debenham's offers to remain at home were so steadily and firmly refused that she finally went alone after assuring herself that every arrangement had been made for her niece's comfort, and Georgie settled down to enjoy the rare quiet of an evening at home.

At any other time she would have reveled in the opportunity to sit peacefully in front of the fire reading whatever she wished without fear of interruption or comment, but tonight her powers of concentration were nonexistent. Her mind wandered, she paced the room restlessly, wondering what the earl was doing. Resolutely she pushed all thoughts of him from her mind and then wondered again. After enjoying his company, the thrust and parry of their conversations, the range of knowledge he exhibited, and the breadth of the experiences which he shared with her, Georgie was finding her own company, hitherto entirely sufficient for her amusement, very dull indeed.

At last she could bear it no longer and went to bed in the hopes that sleep would bring some respite, but no sooner had she laid her head on the pillow than she recalled laying it on a broad shoulder, and all the disturbing thoughts came rushing back again. Climbing out of bed, she padded over to the escritoire to pen a farewell note. This exercise took a good deal of skill because, while wishing on the one hand to offer enough by way of explanation of her future plans to reassure her aunt of her safety, she did not want to reveal so much as to allow them to be thwarted. Several crossed-out sheets later, she was satisfied enough with the results to try to sleep one more time. This time, with the finished letter giving her a sense of accomplishment and representing, as it did, a break with the existence she had recently been pursuing, she was able to look upon the future, if not with any expectation of happiness, at least with enough equanimity so as to be able to fall asleep.

Georgie would have been astounded to know that the inspirer of all the thoughts and activities of her day was spending a remarkably similar evening. Wishing only to hold Georgie in his arms, to kiss her and tell her he loved her, and knowing that such a delightful way of passing the time was impossible, the earl was pacing his library as Georgie was wearing out the patterns in her drawing-room carpet. Making love to an unwilling woman was a situation he had never before encountered. Now the woman was as unconscious as she was likely to be unwilling. Never having bothered to flirt, Georgie was unaware of and unlikely to recognize the signs of love and passion in herself or anyone else. In his heart, Brian felt they were there. He prayed that they were there. Or had he been deluding himself? Did he think that he'd felt a tremor of response in her only because he wished so desperately that it existed? He tossed off a glass of brandy. There was nothing to do to put an end to this agony of suspense except to put it to the touch, something he resolved to do at the earliest possible moment.

At the first light of dawn Georgie was in a fever of impatience to be gone, but she was forced to wait as calmly as she could to put her plan into action until her aunt had left for a visit to Madame Celeste's.

Allowing some time to pass after she had heard the carriage wheels roll off in the direction of Bond Street, she rushed downstairs, a look of concern on her face. "Oh, Wilson, I have just remembered I promised to call on Lady Elizabeth Brandon this morning. She was most insistent that I do so, and now Aunt is gone. Could you possibly procure a hackney for me?''

Always ready to oblige the young mistress, Wilson rounded one up in no time and handed Georgie in. The jarvey, instructed to proceed to the docks after he had gone a short distance in the direction of Grosvenor Square, shook his head and took a minute to disparage the flighty ways of Quality before heading off.

Georgie leaned back, a smile of triumph on her face. She had done it! And the prospect of India lay like a glittering promise of adventure after the confined existence of the *ton*. A great sob rose up within her as she remembered one dusty day in India and a particular gentleman who had shared one of these adventures with her. And try as she would, she could not stop the tears from coursing down her cheeks.

Georgie had not been long gone before Lady Debenham returned and, proceeding to her niece's room to consult with her over the color of the ribbons she had found to go with her new walking dress, stopped dead on the threshold of the empty room. Then, perceiving the note on the escritoire, she tore it open.

Some minutes later a shriek brought Alice running to her ladyship's side with the vinaigrette. ''Fetch the Earl of Aldringham. She must be found before she is ruined,'' the unhappy lady moaned. And Alice, though unclear as to the exact details, but certain that her mistress had run away, hurried off to find a footman to take a hastily scribbled note to Brandon House.

The earl, just on the point of leaving to call on Georgie, read the note, interpreted all the implications behind the imperative summons, and dashed off toward Berkeley Square. There he found Lady Debenham alternately wringing her hands and having recourse to the vinaigrette.

''Where can she have gone? Such a sweet child, though a trifle serious to be sure. But she seemed to be coming on so well. What can have happened?'' she wailed.

At long last, with much patient questioning having elicited the information that Georgie had been present in Berkeley Square that very morning, the earl then demanded the morning paper.

"The paper? Surely you are not going to read the news now?" A note of hysteria crept into the lady's voice.

"No, ma'am. I merely intend to see whether there are any ships bound for India."

"India?" Lady Debenham's vinaigrette tumbled to the floor. "India?" She addressed the earl's retreating back as, having read the prospective departure of the *Lady Kenneway*, he raced down the stairs two at a time shouting for his horse and wishing he'd thought to look to see what time the tide was to change.

He tore through the streets like a madman, afraid to think, all his concentration on getting through the press of carriages and wagons as expeditiously as possible. At last he reached the docks and began his frantic search, stopping at every ship to read its name and inquire if anyone knew where to find the *Lady Kenneway*.

At last a grizzled sailor replied, "Would that be the one going to Madras and Calcutta, your honor? Why, she be right there." Tossing the man a sovereign, the earl tore off in the direction the old tar pointed. Not a hundred yards further he saw the graceful bow of the Indiaman. Sailors were swarming on the rigging and porters were hauling bundles of all shapes and sizes up the gangplank leading to a deck alive with activity. Reining in his horse, Brian scanned the scene with anxious eyes and a fast-beating heart. At last he saw her, a diminutive figure perched on a huge bale, surrounded by a clutter of bandboxes, her left foot swinging, her eyes fixed intently on the preparations for departure.

By the time he reached her side, the earl's hands were clammy with sweat, his heart beating so loudly surely anyone within ten feet could hear it. "Hello, sprite," he said conversationally, amazed that he was able to speak at all.

She whirled around, green eyes ablaze, her chin up, looking like nothing so much as a furious kitten. "I won't go back to Aunt Aurelia, and you can't make me. I . . ."

"I wasn't asking you to," he interrupted mildly, jumping down.

"Then why are you here?" she demanded, sliding off the bale to stand, feet planted defiantly apart, looking up at him half-angrily, half-defensively.

"I thought I might join you," he responded blandly, taking a seat on the table.

"You what?"

The earl smiled. "I can't live without you, you know," he began casually, "and since you feel it incumbent upon you to run away, why, then, so shall I." However calm his outward demeanor, Brian was inwardly so tense he could hardly breathe. Careful now, man, he counseled himself. Go slowly. Don't frighten her. But it was so damnably difficult not to laugh with relief, not to crush her to him and say, "You're mine, you're mine."

"But you can't. Your family . . . your responsibilities . . . Why would you . . . ?" Georgie began to tremble.

The earl sat silently, apparently relaxed, but there was an intensity in his eyes that was most unsettling.

"Hang my responsibilities," he replied airily, rising to stand next to her. He cupped her chin in his hands. "Because I love you. Because I think—no, I hope—you love me," he answered softly.

Tears welled up in her eyes. "But, you can't love me."

"Why not?"

"B-because there are so many other beautiful women who know what to do to amuse you, who know all about . . . about . . . that sort of thing."

He smiled tenderly. "Those others may be beautiful, but they are not you. For me, you are the perfect woman—intelligent, independent, resourceful, and so very lovely." His hand caressed her cheek. "And I suspect you will discover that you know all about 'that sort of thing.' All it takes to be very good at 'that sort of thing' is love."

"It does?" The green eyes were enormous.

She looked so small and lost he wanted to crush her to him, to give her some of his strength and certainty, but not yet. "Why are you running away?" he asked gently.

She was silent, staring down at her slippers.

"Sprite?"

One slipper began to describe circles in the dust, "Well, you see . . . I . . . I decided I didn't belong here."

"You belong here as well as anyone else does—more so.

But you don't care whether you belong or not, not really."
He tilted her chin up, forcing her to meet his gaze.

"P-please," she begged. "Don't ask me. I just had to get away."

"What are you running away from, love," he whispered so gently she could barely hear.

She was silent, her head bowed. The tears began to run silently down her cheeks.

His heart ached for her, but he had to be sure. "Were you running away because of me?"

Georgie gulped and nodded.

"Were you running away because I kissed you?"

There was an audible sniffle. "No . . . because you stopped," she gasped, crying even harder now.

"My darling girl!" At last he pulled her close. "I stopped because I was so terribly afraid."

That caught her attention. "Afraid?" She looked up in astonishment.

"Sweetheart, don't you think I was as afraid of love as you? Don't you think I was as uncertain about how you felt about me?"

"But I love you."

"Thank you for saying it," he responded drily. "I have never in my life had a more difficult time asking anybody about anything."

"Well, you're the rake and libertine, you are supposed to know what to do in these situations . . ." she began angrily.

"I do." He snatched her to him and kissed her hungrily, her lips, her cheeks, her eyes, her throat. "I love you, I love you, I love you," he shouted breathlessly. "There, now do you believe me?"

She nodded.

"Good! Then marry me."

"Marry you?" she asked stupidly.

"Really, sprite, you've never been obtuse before. Don't start now," he snorted with disgust. "Yes, marry me. You're the best friend I've ever had. I want to spend the rest of my life with you."

"But . . ."

"No 'buts.' I know you would rather have a brother than a husband. But look at it this way: if you marry me, you get a husband and a brother . . . and a sister, grandmother, mother, all the dogs and horses you could want"—he pulled her close and looked deep into her eyes—"and someone who adores you. Say yes, sweetheart."

She looked up shyly and was overwhelmed by the love and trust she saw in his face. "Very well, then, yes."

The sailors observing the entire scene from the rigging with great interest cheered as Lord Brian Brandon, Earl of Aldringham, enveloped his ward in a crushing embrace.